# DOCTOR SYNTAX

# DOCTOR SYNTAX

## by Michael Petracca

JOSHUA ODELL EDITIONS  CAPRA PRESS  1991

Published by Joshua Odell Editions, Capra Press.
Box 2158, Santa Barbara, California 93105


Typography: Cragmont publications

**Library of Congress Cataloging-in-Publication Data**

Petracca, Michael, 1947-
    Doctor Syntax / by Michael Petracca.
       p.   cm.
    Includes index.
    ISBN 1877741-03-5  : $9.95
    I. Title.
PS3566.E779D63  1991
813'.54--dc20
                           91-4639
                             CIP

First Edition

10 9 8 7 6 5 4 3 2 1

Printed in the United States of America

For my parents who would have kvelled
if not plotzed outright:
*abbracciandovi con tutto il mio cuore.*

Grateful acknowledgment is made to the people who lent editorial support and/or encouragement to this project: Linda Allen, Christopher Buckley, Mark Comstock, Mark Ferrer, Dr. Deborah Hein, Valerie Hobbs, Chris Ingram, Jan Ingram, John Landsberg, Francess Lantz, Otto "Baba" Laula, Mike and Annie Lorimer, Penelope Maddy, Steve Marx, Lee Morgan, Joshua Odell, Peg O'Donnell, Frances Petracca, Gary Soto, Judith Spencer, Craig Spirka, Albert Sweet, Betsy Uhrig, Marianne Walker, Noel Young, Donald Pearce, Stephen Williamson.

# PART ONE

♣ ♦ ♠ ♥

## MY OWN PLACE

## ♣ ONE ♣

A slow death by nagging: My mother would kill me if she knew I was dogging *Doctor Syntax*.

In the Nails family, long champions of doomed liberal causes, investigation means sticking your nose into other people's constitutionally guarded business, and that's a public shame as damning as canvassing door-to-door for Ford's reelection. The only other family member who does anything even remotely resembling detective work is my cousin Brad the insurance man, and Ma speaks of him always with contempt, as, ". . . that Bradford hocked me two hours about adding a trailer to my policy, he's already got a fortune out of me, isn't it enough he's always snooping around poor unfortunates, accident victims no less, trying to save his company a few pennies, he ought to get a real job . . ."

Ma is proud of my job. My still-unfinished dissertation on authorial self-awareness in George Eliot's novels doesn't bother her. Just the fact that I have a master's and a part-time lectureship at UCLA gives Ma license to call me "Professor" to her card club, and that makes her happy enough to complain with mitigated frequency that I'm twenty-eight, divorced, and living with her again.

But while my academic life gives Ma pleasure, it gives me none and is in fact a source of aggravation I can measure precisely by the frequency of the bladder spasms I get when I'm torturing a passage of Eliot into supporting my thesis or having to listen to some complacent tenured pedant like old RearWind Wessex discuss the Homeric allusions in Spenser's *Faerie Queene*. School, literary criticism—deconstructobation, as my ex-roommate Thrasher calls it—doesn't gratify me . . . one reason, I suppose, why I got involved solving this crime in the first place. It's more fun than studying.

But if George Eliot teaches us anything, it's that "there is always a deeper cause for human behavior than the one we just posited."[1] When I was eight, I wanted a bicycle, not an outrageous request from the son of an almost-wealthy commercial launderer. Philip Meer next door had had one for three years, and only once did he brodie into the middle of rush-hour traffic, causing front-end and frame damage to a Buick Skylark. Philip's parents believed that pain builds character, and toward this end they gave him every opportunity to mangle his body, in Pop Warner's tackle football, on Boy Scout overnighters into the Santa Monica mountains, and on his Schwinn, among cars. The Meers valued pain as an instructional aid; my father, by contrast, believed his own Brooklyn childhood had given him enough hard knocks for several succeeding generations, and so he wanted to spare me even the slightest hurt. Ma, meanwhile, knew that all L.A. drivers had but one goal: to run innocents off the road, causing them to dash their heads against the curb and therefore to spend the rest of their lives as drooling invalids dependent on their moth-

---

[1] George Eliot never said this. I invented it. But it sounds like the kind of penetrating insight for which George is famous. I'm sure I can pass it off somewhere in my thesis, verifying its authenticity with a bogus footnote.

ers. By the time I got a bike at thirteen, so convinced was I that I was going to kill myself in traffic that I spent months turning timid circles and figure eights in our cul-de-sac before I ever ventured out onto city streets.

This is just an off-the-top example of how my parents' smothering protectiveness turned me into a wimp. Ironically, this pathological timidity of mine turns out to be the root of my attraction to danger—recklessness, some would call it; "idiotic foolishness" by Ma's standards—because as much as I was (and still am) abnormally scared and reserved, I have become to that same degree a risk-taker.

Liz[2] once theorized that something snapped in me seven years ago, at my father's deathbed. He was comatose, but I imagined he might be able to hear me, so I talked anyway. I talked about the kid practicing his skateboard moves in the parking garage across the street from Pop's private room; I talked about Ma, who was holding up remarkably well considering her usual hysteria about such relative trivialities as dustbunnies and scuffmarks, and who, exhausted by the too-real rigors of the deathwatch, was presently crashed in the unoccupied room adjacent to Pop's; I talked about the odd tensile stillness of the ocean's surface under the kelp beds despite a stiffly squalling downshore wind, an effect I had marked on my drive to the hospital that morning; and I talked about the even odder gift the night nursing staff had left my father: They had inflated a surgical glove into an udder-shaped balloon and knotted it off, had written, "Have a Nice day From Your friends on 4-West," in magic marker across the glove's edematous-looking skin, and had suspended this grotesque artifact from my father's bedside lamp, presumably with genuine bonhomie and no conscious intention to lampoon his own moribund bloat. I

2 My sometime analyst, Elizabeth Browner, Ph.D., refuses to let her patients call her Dr. Browner, joking, "If I wanted to be called Doctor, my couch would have stirrups."

talked about these and other things in equally slack association, and as I talked an unexpected feeling surfaced and mingled with my love for this man of stubbly cheek and jaundiced flesh, this passionately opinionated salesman-philosopher who had once stormed out of a restaurant because an acquaintance disagreed with Pop's assertion that Mark Twain was the greatest writer in the history of American letters, this gentlest of gentlemen who never once upraised a hand to discipline me (although he did once dropkick me halfway across the living room when my relentless sassing took him beyond the wide bounds of his patience), who raised his voice only to make a point and then rarely in anger, who kept things light, sometimes even giddy, in the midst of Ma's cyclonic moods, and who, despite having to hold down a day delivery job to support several younger siblings, had managed to educate himself at night school, to claw his way out of Brooklyn's squalid Wallabout Basin and to establish something of an empire in the West Coast linen rental industry, a stately Mediterranean villa-style home with an olive-lined drive, a lovely wife, a neat stack of dollars, and a son who was a hell of a kid, if you could get past his backtalk and his chronic ambivalent lethargies born of too many talents.

The intrusive and unanticipated feeling that surfaced in me, along with the o'erweening love, was contempt. As my father had sheltered me, so had he protected himself. Or maybe it was the other way around. In either case, he hadn't walked a flight of stairs for twenty years, worrying that a heart weakened by infantile rheumatic fever would give out. Although he had enjoyed smoking for years, he quit, fearing cancer or stroke. He claimed that drinking depleted his body of its immunological reserves; club soda was his usual. Pop played safe, dealt honestly in linens, raised a family, never cheated (as far as I know) on his wife, and all it got him was a bed in the intensive ward at St. John's, intravenous morphine in his mercifully infrequent waking moments, a rich man's funeral in his fiftieth year.

What galled me was that I had bought his whole neurotic's bill of goods, of which every piece of inventory will sit in the psychic warehouse until I die, Liz's sunny promises of my self-actualization notwithstanding. Worse, for every one of my father's fears I invented five of my own. I brood about tumors, cringe at the sight of spiders. I dread insanity, avoid potluck dinners because the food might have psychoactive chemicals in it, which would lead to my becoming even more fearful, insanely so. I've shunned peanuts ever since a former roommate warned me that goobers sometimes grow a fungus containing one of the most potent carcinogens yet discovered; I switched to almonds and dumped the roommate. Also left over from my childhood is a chronic insomnia which, when I was younger, made it impossible for me to sleep over at Braddy's [3] and which now causes women confusion, sometimes anger (and occasionally, I suppose, relief) when I announce, after rounds of transcendent loving, that it's time for me to go home. To be sure, a burdensome pack of neuroses to carry for a lifetime, and one whose weight would certainly have crushed me even sooner than my father's destroyed him. But the cruel tedium of Pop's last days and hours enervated and scourged me, admitted me into a kind of decisive yawning anarchy out of which I emerged not necessarily transformed—that is to say, not any less fearful—but mutinous and determined not to live scared and therefore die young.

By dying my father saved me, pushed me in the direction of abandon. If once I had been timid on my ten-speed, I swung to the opposite extreme, collecting speeding tickets,

[3] A blessing, it appears in retrospect, given Braddy's former habit of crawling into my bed and yelling, "Peeny patrol!" while making bawdy stabs at my privates under the covers.

arms hairline-fractured and knees scraped raw on my semi-chopped Triumph Bonneville. If, as a child, I had a terror of the Deep End in swimming pools, I took up bodysurfing the Newport wedge, where two double-overhead swells hump up into one wall, fat as it is high, that pitches abruptly forward as it hits land, dumping me in three inches of water over concrete-hard beach and jagged granite-block jetty.

In short, I came to embrace the edge, a life constantly surging against the granitic seawall of my fear . . . which is why I sometimes find myself in big trouble, as I did when *Doctor Syntax* disappeared.

# ◆ TWO ◆

Usually I make it a policy not to think about psychology, especially my own. There's little percentage in trying to come up with explanations for self-destructive behavior so firmly rooted that there's no way (Liz again to the contrary) to change it even if I did understand. A sound rule; any rule is worth obeying that promotes mental health. But sometimes I can't help myself: When you're lying face down on a Chinese rug and a lout with a ski mask is pointing a pump-action Remington at the base of your skull, you arrive at unusual answers—such as the preceding discourse concerning the origin and nature of my quirky doubled-edged personality—for crucial questions, such as what am I doing on this floor, possibly thinking my last obsessive thoughts?

The gunmen had had practice. Or else, if this was their first time holding up innocent strangers, they had an innate aptitude for thuggery, real career potential, as you might say. With the shotgun under an arm, the short one kept guard over his three prone and trembling (if I could use my own behavior as a touchstone) charges, while the hulking one, also masked, moved with surprising nimbleness around the study, rummaging for valuables. Apparently irritated at his partner's finding nothing worth stealing, the short one began to lift our possessions roughly. He started with Ernst's digital wristwatch, at which he glanced, then complained in a voice that bore an uncanny resemblance to talk-show host Dick Cavett's—a smooth, slightly nasal patter as flat as the corn belt, with an irritating hint of snide mirth, "A Timex. A *Timex*. I hope the rest of you can come up with something better than this. The docs in the joint said disappointment makes me mean." He stuck the muzzle of the shotgun into the small of my back.

I was following my imagination through lurid yellow-tabloid stills of my lifeblood splattered across this quaint Victorian office, when Dick Cavett broke into my reverie, "And where do you hide your cash, sweetheart?" He had moved on to Lissa and was addressing her now. From my prone position I could see in my right periphery the barrel of his rifle poking her, beginning at the head and moving deliberately down her body. He was laughing quietly to himself. Each time he jabbed her with the gun, he elicited from her a squeak, the kind of sound bath toys make, which might have been comical in other circumstances but which made the situation here seem all the more un-real and therefore more nightmarish.

When he reached the area of her rump, he stopped chuckling and said, "No jewelry? Too bad. Let's see what you have in your purse." Hefting the shotgun like a tent-pole, he raised the hem of her dress with dramatic deliber-ation, so that I could see the material draped over the end of the weapon like a species of pastel-flowered ghost. Then it disappeared from view, and Lissa's thin squeaks turned to increasingly shrill cries. I couldn't see what was going on, but it was obviously starting to get brutal.

Enraged, Ernst said, "Schtup sat at fonz. Sat iss an orrr-der." Cavett ignored him, and I admit with some embarrassment that I developed a swelling that pressed into the rug, a condition that had nothing to do with sex but which arose rather from an encounter with the basest human drives gone out of control, the kind of engorgement that visits men when they're forced to witness a lynching, or are themselves strung up by a mob, and all the valves and sphincters open simultaneously at the savage inhumanity of it.

This condition didn't last long, however, because someone shrieked, "No more," and in a mindless fit of bravado charged at Cavett, to rescue Lissa from whatever unspeakable indignities were about to be performed on her. Remarkably, the someone turned out to be your narrator, who found myself stationed bristlingly, in a kind of pseudo-karate horse-rider stance, between the shotgun and the supine Lissa. Real martial artists stand this way to lower their centers of gravity, so that they might launch powerful kicks quickly from either foot. In my case, the exaggerated straddle did nothing more than offer the gunman a convenient and obvious target: the crotch of my trousers, whose resident member was still one-third swollen. This unhappy addendum he found without hesitation with a violent thrust of the thick wooden gunstock's butt-end cap. No pain. I coughed out all my air and collapsed over Lissa.

As compensation for a childless future I had at least succeeded in distracting our short assailant before he got as far as violating Lissa. It didn't seem to matter to him whose privates he savaged, as long as he savaged someone's; in this case mine were handy. Looking down on my crumpled formlessness atop Lissa, he exclaimed, "What a cute couple!" He nudged my ribcage with the steel-reinforced toe of his boot. "Hey, I think the babe's hot for some action, bigshot," he said to me in a mock-confidential tone. "Do her for me, will you? I got business."

I heard Ernst say, as menacingly as possible given his compromised, butt-skyward posture and his silly accent, "You fill regrrat sis, Dill," and in the middle of this impotent and cryptic warning I checked out.

# ♠ THREE ♠

A couple of white-smocked paramedics were kneeling and busy, one with some kind of aromatic ampule in the vicinity of my nose and the other deep inside my choners. My brown Levi cords were lying nearby, looking like the carcass of a small deer that had been savaged by coyotes. The medic nearer my face asked me how I felt and I said I didn't know. He continued his ministrations and after a while asked me again and I told him fine this time and arose by stages—side, elbow, knee, knees, chin, knee, knees, foot, feet—and walked unsteadily around the study, feeling a dull tightening in the neighborhood where my maleness used to live. Lissa put an arm around my waist to steady me, and the medic who had been puttering with my genitals like a garage mechanic tuning a carburetor said, "You took a hard blow, but nothing seems ruptured. You'll have some pain and swelling for a few days, but it should go away pretty fast. If it lasts more than a week or so, you ought to see a urologist."

As the medics left, they admitted a uniformed police officer, who addressed us generally, "Whose house is this?" Ernst introduced himself and answered his questions patiently: How did the thieves get in? Did we recognize them? Was anyone else hurt? Did they take anything of value? To the latter question Ernst volunteered, "Mein Timeggs voss schtöllen. It voss off no fallyew."

"They stole your egg-timer?"

Lissa patched the momentary breakdown in communication. "He means they got his watch. It was a Timex."

"Oh." Impatiently the cop scratched out something on the notepad, presumably the egg-timer entry, and wrote something else, presumably the Timex.

Lissa continued, "After the smaller man hit Harmon, he tore the room apart." A glance around the ravaged study confirmed this piece of testimony. "Then he threw some things into Harmon's tennis bag and they both left."

"What kind of things?"

"Just junk, mostly—a letter opener, a brass elephant . . . knickknacks. But they also got Harmon's books. He brought them here to be appraised, but we didn't have a chance to look at them. It all happened so fast." As she listed the stolen stuff, the cop made some notes in a small bluish notebook.

"How much do you think they're worth?"

Lissa said, "Who knows? Maybe not much, maybe a lot."

"How much is a lot?"

"I can't really say. We can tell pretty quickly if an article is authentic, but gauging the market takes time. You have to make inquiries. His books might be quite ordinary, but if there's some interest among collectors, a mint *Syntax* could be worth thousands of dollars."

"More prrobably they are off no more fallyew than my Timeggs, howeffer," Ernst said. I wished he hadn't. I imagined the authorities would make a more serious effort to find pricey books than worthless ones.

"So what we have here is the theft of a watch worth a few bucks and some books which we don't know their value. Any other items missing?"

"Nein," said Ernst.

"Nine what?" said the cop.

"He means 'No,'" Lissa explained.

"Oh. Well, that's about it, then. You say they were wearing gloves, so there's no point in looking for prints. We'll let you know if anything turns up."

Naively expecting promises of a swifter justice, I worked myself into a huff of moderate dimension: "'That's about it'? I just got robbed and physically assaulted, Lissa almost got raped with the barrel of a shotgun . . ."

The patrolman interrupted me as though he had heard similar irate rantings by victims of petty crime many times before, and he was sick of it. "There's really nothing I can say," he said in an astringent tone, "I'd love to camp on your doorstep tonight, but of course that's impossible."

"Of course," I had to agree.

"We'll be giving the house some extra patrol tonight. If they're stupid enough to come back, we're bound to catch them."

More rote apologies on his side, some reserved thanks on ours, and he left. I continued to pace, weighted now not only by my traumatized genitalia but also by the dispiriting impression that the police had about as much time for, or interest in, recovering our petty property or in avenging an effete intellectual's wounded testicles, as they had, say, in putting on a production of "Lady Windermere's Fan" at the drama department's Little Playhouse. If I wanted those books back, I was going to have to find them myself . . . and I did want them, I needed them. Beyond my usual bent toward danger, the acrophobe's attraction to the precipice, I had two more practical reasons for hunting down my books. If they turned out to be worth anything, I could use the proceeds from their sale to get a place of my own, out from under Ma's wide apron—as I say, any action is worth pursuing that promotes mental health. Also, on the previous night I had transformed a scrap of recycled newsprint almost alchemically into the key to my dissertation[4] and had secreted it within one of the volumes. Recovering *Doctor Syntax* was my only hope of becoming a critic, a professor, a mensch.

[4] Admittedly, as will soon be revealed, the twin muses of dope and sex aided me in this lofty enterprise.

# ♥ FOUR ♥

Enzo Impagliatore, my paternal grandfather, came to this country around the turn of the century, from a tiny farming village near Sorrento, on the Tyrrhenian coast at Italy's mid-calf. His father had been a woodworker who barely managed to keep a wife and nine children alive with a cabinet here, a fence job there, some stonemasonry on the side, the occasional shed-framing. Of those nine my Nonno left Italy with the intention of saving enough cash in an old shoe to return one day to Italy and provide for the family. He booked passage on a freighter carrying seafood on ice: *Calamari, Moscardini, Scungilli.*[5]

Upon my grandfather's arrival at Ellis island, the immigrations agent asked him the usual questions—name, occupation, childhood diseases—and my Nonno, fiercely proud of the English he had struggled to learn from a primer called *Voci Inglesi*, refused to converse in Italian. When asked for his name, my grandfather confused the English "name" for "occupation" and answered brightly, "I'm a hammerin' nails," referring to his carpentry trade.

[5] This was, incidentally, also the infield of the '51 Yankees, if memory serves, with Moscardini in the pivot.

This reply the agent, no doubt with a healthy appreciation of the absurd and not a little contempt for wetbacks just off the boat, took to be my grandfather's name: Harmon Nails.

My Nonno kept the new name, even wore it with pride, it being his first American possession. He stayed in New York, eventually built up a reasonably prosperous construction contracting firm, and had a son, Harmon "Bud" Nails, Jr., who became first a laundry delivery boy in the neighborhood of Richmond Hill, and later a well-to-do Los Angeles linen rental service mogul. In time, he passed the embarrassingly droll name down to his firstborn and only child, me, Harmon Nails III, dilettante grad student and boy sleuth.

In Neapolitan dialect there's a term that embodies all the qualities considered necessary to get by—and ahead, if the breaks fall right—in a world of cutthroat material struggle. *Scugnizzi* refers to kids of eight and ten, barefoot wharf urchins who keep themselves fed by pilfering fish, lifting tourists' cameras, a little light pandering, all the while frolicsome as otters, diving noisily off the long stone quay and roughhousing in the oily seawater, Vesuvio puffing picturesquely on the horizon. The *scugnizz'* emblematize my paternal heritage, child-men with a sometimes ruthless but always sporting opportunism. By this quality my father's family guided its own business affairs and therefore made a beautiful dollar, as my Nonno used to say.

In contrast, when my mother's father died last year, he left practically nothing to his descendants, since he owned practically nothing. My Zaydeh had had all the success he hoped for in this country, escaping the persecution his forebears had suffered through decades of pogroms in his native Ukraine, and he made a good living for himself and his bride, working his way up to a small artificial flavoring factory in Atlanta, which break-even concern supported him, my grandmother, and their kids until his retirement and my grandmother's death fifteen years ago.

That factory stands out as the highlight of my visits to Atlanta when I was little: the still, cold air, vaulted corrugated-tin ceilings, steel girders and druidic vats from which rose a thick tropical syrup-steam of strawberry, lime, banana, vanilla. To me at five, anyone who could fill the air with candy had to be God, and I adored Zaydeh. As I grew older, that feeling matured gradually (leapfrogging my bratty early teen years, of course) into a passionate admiration for his simple, honest strength. So, when I learned after his death last year that he had willed me a book called *Doctor Syntax*, I considered it no less than a treasure with which I would never consider parting.

*Doctor Syntax* turned out to be not one volume but three, which arrived one day by registered mail, and with them a short and clumsily typed letter of introduction from one Arnold Middenish, J.D., the obviously low-rent Georgia attorney who had supervised the distribution of my Zaydeh's estate. To the note was stapled a Xeroxed copy of a document in my Zaydeh's own hand, a fragment of a larger directive:

> . . . at the end of the work day I am emptying a carton. In the bottom I find three books tied together with twine. I know a little Talmud, it says Finding Is Keeping applies only when there is no hope to find the owner. I took to work the books everyday and in the Kemfer placed a notice. No-one answered therefore by law I keep the books. A collector of things who married my wife's dear friend Frieda's cousin examined the books. He said the books were worth money and he offers fifty dollars. I turn down his offer because I have already an idea to pass the books

on to my grandson who shows such promise as a man of learning. That is why to my daughter's son, Harmon Nails III, who will be an honored professor of literature one day I will this set of books called Doctor Syntax by William Combe . . .

The story, underlining as it did both my grandfather's firm righteousness and his belief in my success as an academician—a faith that was, up to this point, wholly unfounded—touched me deeply. Even though I had never heard of William Combe[6] and didn't care for the frivolous doggerel that filled the three volumes, the purely *scugnizzaiol'* notion that I could sell a family heirloom for big money never would have entered my mind, had Mr. Middenish, J.D.'s note not also suggested that the volumes were rare, that they might now be worth thousands in the collectible book market, and that I should have them appraised for taxes. Call it the practicality of my paternal heritage winning out over sentimentality, or call it a hands-down victory for sheer crass greed; whatever you call it, I began to entertain serious retail fantasies of candy-apple sport sedans, tastefully pegged and pleated ice-cream

[6] You probably never have, either, but Combe really existed. Here's what I know about him, to the best of my recollection: He was born around 1750 and lived until sometime in the nineteenth century—1833 I think it was, or maybe '23; who's counting? One encyclopedia I read about him called him a "miscellaneous writer," which in English means he was a hack, I guess. He was perpetually in debt—a gambler like me, maybe, and (unlike me) a loser—and he issued the *Doctor Syntax* and *Johnny Quae Genus* series anonymously, to avoid his creditors' attaching the proceeds. That's all I remember. You can look it up for yourself if you don't believe me or if you want to know more. There's also a book about Combe in the library, by a biographer named Hamilton or Haarwhal or something. I never took the time to read it, but you can check it out and *op cit* it to your heart's content, if research gets you off.

slacks, years of sweet leisure occupied by nothing more academically demanding than an occasional glance at the *New Yorker's* book review section by the side of the pool.

But above all these speculations, one notion outshone and dimmed their combined thin light: My Own Place.

# ♣    FIVE    ♣

It isn't easy living with Ma. I occupy the guest house, which my father for years used as an office, and although the English garden[7] between the studio and the main house affords me a certain physical autonomy, I am still, as far as Ma is concerned, under her roof—which, in her eyes, reinstates all her former maternal privileges. She can satisfy herself that I'm well fed and well rested, and she can nip at my heels like some monomaniacal sheepdog as I falteringly pursue academic excellence. But worst of all, my mother is a sexual assassin. I cannot with unmuddied conscience bring home a female friend, because there's only one access to the guest house. Bordered on one side by a thick hedge of pittisporum and pomegranate and on the other by the white stucco main house, the path to the back is usually covered with a layer of leaves that crunch underfoot like cornflakes, is always well-lit at night by two glaring,

---

[7] To be truthful, the glories of the Nails estate have declined somewhat since my father died, and what was once a verdant bower that would have inspired a sonnet or two out of Coleridge has become a largely untended, unpruned tangle of impenetrable ceanothus, avocado bushes and trumpet vines.

burglar-foiling floodlights, and leads directly past the dining room window, the kitchen window, and the master bedroom French doors. I'm loath to lead a date down that walkway, because I always imagine Ma watching at one of those windows like a prison guard in the tower; her reproving presence—real or imagined—causes in me an overpowering weakening of appendage, which always spoils my loveplay before it gets started . . . which is exactly what happened the afternoon I brought Diane Droddy home with me, the evening I put the notes in *Doctor Syntax*.

Diane Droddy and I were enrolled in a phys-ed department folk-dance class—I, because I understood the ratio of women to men in such situations to be a favorable twelve or fifteen to one, and Diane because she was a dance major and needed some elective "movement" units to graduate. If you've never folk-danced, you should. It's an invigorating and uncommonly intimate social situation in which you're forced to perform the most humiliating physical movements while gripping and being gripped by total strangers. I mean, when you're doing the Bulgarian walnut-stomping dance, and you're embracing your partner in the traditional Bulgarian grapevine-armlock, there's no way you and your partner can keep from laughing hysterically at your own awkwardness in accomplishing the unfamiliar posturings, and this lowering of inhibitions, combined with a natural, endorphin-induced euphoria that comes with vigorous exercise, breeds a glowing, breathless, *presque*-sexual kind of familiarity with your partner. So it was with Diane: After a few class sessions we found ourselves pairing up as frequently as possible and abandoning ourselves to lustful eye contact as we whipspun around the gym in some Swedish polka.

On the way to our respective locker rooms one day, I called up all my Nails suave to ask Diane, "Do you want to do something sometime?"

She hesitated. "I don't know."

"It sounds like you don't know." Liz taught me well: When you're nervous and can't think of anything to say, restate the obvious.

"It sounds like that because it's what I said." Liz didn't prepare me for Diane—a dancer and a literalist, too. I did what I have always done in unfamiliar situations, before Liz started modifying my behavior. I clammed up and waited.

It worked. Diane explained, "I think I have a boyfriend. He moved to Boston, for law school. We've been trying to keep it together, but he's been pretty distant lately."

I pressed subtly, "We don't have to call it a date. We could just go to the beach or have lunch or something. Just spend some time together and talk or something."

The idea that there could exist a male who might not pounce panting and salivating after a few minutes of preliminary chat usually seems novel and therefore irresistible to women. If the tales that battle-worn single women tell me are true, guys—even superficially civilized ones with shy smiles and empathic words—are at heart a collection of shallow, competitive, sloppy, and manipulative boors. Therefore, suggesting a tame daylit pastime I intuited to be a good opening, even if there lurked in an unevolved limbic lizardhole of my own psyche the instinct to pounce like the rest of the beasts.

In the case of Diane this reasoning proved sound. She reflected a moment, then said, "The beach sounds good. How about next Thursday? I have my last final from seven to ten. We can celebrate my graduation."

"And my whole summer of freedom."

I've also made the discovery that women feel more comfortable driving on dates, especially with men they don't know well. So it was that Diane picked me up in front of my house, where I sat, on the bottom step of the long brick walkway that passed through the rose garden, down the ivy-covered hill, to the entrance at the street.

Diane got out of her car. Pointing in the direction of the house she said, "This is such a nice place. Do you share it?"

"I live in the studio in back."

"Rent must be terrible around here. I didn't think T.A.s made that kind of money."

Wanting to avoid at all costs any admission of my continuing dependent connection with Mommie, since it might diminish Diane's impression of me as a manly, self-reliant guy, I omitted the kernel of truth. She got bran: "The rent's really not that bad. I do some work around the place. Gardening, take out the trash, you know."

Diane swallowed this roughage. She opened the passenger door for me and said, "Let's go. I want to get a parking space before it gets too crowded."

She had on a white cotton beach shift, sleeveless, with a short hemline that gave way to cappuccino-tanned and dance-sculpted legs. These she tucked back into her '67 Karmann-Ghia. Ragtop down, Beverly Hills casual chic with me in my Hawaiian print shirt, tennis visor and Fiorini shades, we drove to Will Rogers beach, just down the hill from my house at the top of Santa Monica canyon.

On the way Diane described her current effort in modern dance, a student adaptation of a nineteenth-century tragedy by an obscure Czech expressionist named Vaclav Kleptar. In the original play a young female student gets seduced by her mathematics professor, winds up pregnant, has the baby, is ostracized by the community, and flings herself despondently into the half-frozen Danube. The baby, raised by abusive foster parents, grows up to be a notorious thief. While robbing a small general store, he kills an innocent bystander, who turns out to be the very same math professor, his father. He's arrested. The prosecutor brings out the real identity of his victim at the trial.

Our thief uses his belt to hang himself in his cell.

Kleptar no doubt intended the play to be an indictment of the growing scientism of the age, the tyranny of geometry over innocent wonder, the compass over the conundrum. But Diane's colleagues wanted to avoid any such heavy-handed symbolism and instead saw the story as a simple tragic story of love and betrayal, relevant today as the original play was in Kleptar's time. It also had its racy moments. "In the central, climatic[8] piece, which we call the Podium Dance, the stage goes all black. Then a single spot falls on a teacher's podium rising up out of a trapdoor in the stage.

"You don't call that heavy-handed? Freud would cream in his jeans if he were alive and wearing jeans and watching your recital."

"I just dance, all right?"

"Sorry."

"So five of us, all in skintight body stockings and white hoods, do a kind of fertility ritual around this podium. We whip it with nylon cords, we rub ourselves up against it as it rises to full height in the center of the stage. Then the spot starts to strobe on and off, faster and faster, and then the stage goes dark again."

The image of the blatantly phallic lectern being stroked, frottaged, lashed to a tropical climate by seminude dancers in a disciplinary frenzy was too much for me. I put my visor in my lap, which it rode like an empronged quoit. Diane laughed. "I see you can relate to the scenario. As a teacher," she commented.

[8] People who say "climatic" for "climactic," or "relator" for "realtor," or "nucular" for "nuclear," reveal in themselves a singular lack of attention to the one thing in the world I really take seriously: spelling. In Diane's case, however, the eloquence of her riding hemline and sleek quadriceps made up for her faulty orthography.

"Well, uh, yes, the lectern obviously represents the whole of the teaching profession, I suppose, while the strobing light, presumably the jism of intellectual truth, illuminates but at the same time enslaves a submissive student body, trapping them like specks of dust dancing in its whiteness . . ."

"We're there."

"What?"

"At the beach."

"Ah. The beach."

Diane gunned the Ghia impatiently around the lines of cars, looking for a space, which gave me time to calm myself. A family in a station wagon eased out of a slot. Diane pulled in.

We found a space on the sand at a reasonable distance from any clots of squalling kids or leering, hawhawing teenage beer drinkers, and there we spread our blanket—actually my mother's old red-and-white-checkered cloth that used to cover the patio table when, of summers, my father would barbecue burgers and corn in tinfoil. I let the wind catch the material like a spinnaker and set it down gently. The thought of my mother annoyed me like a fat horsefly. I didn't want anything to remind me of her now, not even her tablecloth. I looked around to dispel the delusion Ma was here, smeared with sunblock and watching our every move. I didn't see her, although there was one striped umbrella tilted in such a way that I couldn't see the party behind it. I shooed away the buzzing fly.

While I was going through this familiar psychotic routine, Diane had taken off her beach dress and stretched out in a metallic blue one-piece, cut high at the hips. I joined her on the cloth. We lay quietly, making occasional jokes about students in our dance class. We ate oranges under the hot sun and then went in the water, where there wasn't much surf but the water was cool and we rode some gentle waves into the shore together, rolling and splashing as we washed up on the wet sand. We went back to the blanket and lay down on our bellies, wet and breathing hard from the exertion. Pressure from the seawater in my semicircular canals made a high-tension whine, as from a swarm of midges. Diane turned onto her side, facing me, and said, "You have the nicest ears."

I smiled and let her touch my ears, even though it was more itching than arousing. My soul cried out for a Q-tip. She said, "Has anyone ever told you you have beautiful ears?"

An ear fetishist. This was promising. "Once," I said.

"I could get jealous. Who was it?"

"I was seventeen, hitching up to Hollywood to hear some band on the Strip, the Shallow Plotz, I think. A guy in a Corvette picked me up. He said I had ears like delicate sea-shells and started playing with my left one just like you're doing. Then he reached across and grabbed my crotch."

"Not exactly what you'd call romantic, but direct. What did you do?"

"I jumped out of the car. He had slowed down for some traffic but we were still moving. I sprained my ankle. I've never hitched since."

"I guess I'll have to change my approach. I was going to reach over and grab." Instead of my crotch she grabbed my thigh playfully, her hair dripping cold salt water onto my cheek, and, aware that we were in public and couldn't make too much of an erotic spectacle of ourselves, we held ourselves to mere ardent kissing and stroking of the lesser erogenous parts: backs, arms, faces, hair.

After a while we unclinched and stretched out on our backs, and then Diane climbed playfully on top of me. She looked into my eyes and said, in a husky, parodic soap-opera tone, "Let's go back to your place. I . . . want . . . you . . . now."

# ◆ SIX ◆

I have dwelt thus far on the well-trodden ways in which my mother fits the stereotype of the clutching yenta who dotes poisonously on her kids—especially on the firstborn son—and even more poisonously if he turns out to be the only child. My new girlfriend, Marianne Evans, reminds us in her latest article on gender-role myths that stereotypes are by their insidious nature mere simpleminded exaggerations, for the sake of chat or cattiness or full-blown bigotry, of real and unique human traits. In the case of my mother, Marianne is right. Even though Ma is the full-blooded Russian Jewish daughter of an immigrant artificial flavorer, she looks less Israeli than Irish, with a blaze of tight red curls, fair skin, upturned colleen's nose. To add to the confusion, where the cartoon B'nai B'rith princess has a tooth-shattering New York *whoiiine*, my mother spent four years at the University of Georgia, which mellowed her voice down to a soft, slow, Deep-South sorority purr. Even now, long after my folks' move to the West Coast, Ma will lapse back into that biscuits-and-gravy drawl if she gets really mad. [9]

So, at least in looks and sounds, my mother flies at the vile anti-Semite's caricature of the Jewess. Going deeper, Ma despised her own *Yiddische*-mama's clutching and doting so thoroughly that she put into practice the teaching of humanistic juvenile shrinks from Spock to Piaget, many of whom believed that a kid should be left alone to make his own mistakes and grow thereby. Consequently, Fay Nails has always (since I've been around, anyway) been torn between two poles: an instinct to clutch and dote and bar me from using the swingset in the backyard for fear that I would fly off and mash my melon on an ornamental lava boulder; and a firm intellectual belief that kids have resilient little bodies and must be allowed to learn by their knots and scrapes.

This opposition within my mother has kept her in a constant state of agitation, which makes her dangerous and unpredictable. She might one minute be the most warm-hearted of friends. I might come in exhausted after a

---

[9] Like the time I walked into the bedroom where she and Pop were locked in an *après*-sex embrace, he on top asleep or at least inert, she underneath, on her belly; both smooth, sweaty, naked. Ma lashed out, "Hahmin, yew gayet otta this room rot nah, and don't yew evvvaaah come in heah agayan withaht knockin' . . ." This is not by itself a prominent event in my developmental history, but one of many like degradations that contributed to my feeling during adolescence and marriage that sex is something not to be undertaken without a heavy dose of embarrassment. Through hard work with Liz, though, I made progress toward overcoming that hangup, and, following my customary reactive pattern, I swung to the opposite extreme. I slept with anything that would have me, until I finally caught the Laotian clap from the waitress at the health-food restaurant I always used to go to. For five weeks my gonorrhea resisted courses of Dicloxicillin and Amoxicillin until some broad-spectrum sulfa derivative finally knocked it out. Five long weeks: which explains the urgency I was presently feeling in getting down with Diane.

long day of classes and flop on the couch, and she will put down her *Times* to hear me complain hysterically about higher education—more precisely, my straining like a door-to-door brushman to sell college freshmen the idea that Wordsworth's poetic focus on humble and rustic life provides a better soil in which the essential passions of the heart can attain their maturity, blabla, while my students, mostly business-econ majors and prospective missile-guidance engineers, stare out the window, chitchat idly among themselves, do physics homework on pocket calculators, chew gum, draw pictures, look in mirrors, nod out on the desk (I send them out for coffee when they start snoring). Ma can be a great listener, and she approached sainthood after the failure of my marriage. Without her uncharacteristically judgment-free ministering I would probably still be the hopeless, finger-thin, frosting-eyed game-show addict I became after Brenny left.

Yet if Ma can be a pal, she can as easily become shrewish, unreasonable, hyper-critical, suspicious, calculating, overbearing . . . all for no reason save the passage of a little time, which seems to work some kind of devilish neuroscience on her, transforming a delightful, witty, and relaxed human being into a carping bitch. Harsh words for the woman who gave one breath and blood and milk, but I don't exaggerate, and it's a stone tragedy. Because of her emotional lability, one has to protect himself by forgetting the good times and treat her as one would a Doberman with a cortical malfunction: Assume the worst, be prepared for a vicious and unprovoked attack on one's areas of greatest vulnerability. Therefore, although I had directed Diane Droddy to park on the street instead of the driveway to avoid being spotted, and although en route to the back house I had seen no sign of my mother's face pressed against any window, I couldn't help imagining her witchlike, Morgan le Fay Nails plotting some diabolical means of withering my all-too-vulnerable excalibur by re-mote control.

My small room was a mess. All the furniture—the teak dining table, the foldout polyfoam futon-couch-bed against the far wall, the antique church-pew bench by the entry, the butter block in the kitchenette—was strewn with volumes of Browning criticism,[10] coffee cups, fast-food hamburger and taco cartons, waxed wrappers and typing paper crumpled and tossed, notebooks in tipsy piles. I set about straightening up the clutter on the table.

Diane said, "Don't bother cleaning up. With three roommates, I'm used to a lot more mess than this. Besides, I have other plans for you." She dug into her bag and, producing a fat cigarette rolled in yellow wheatstraw paper, smiled over at me. "Thai stick," she said. "It's killer."

I smiled back, although in truth I'm not much of a dope-smoker. In fact, most drugs make me ill. I have a Medic-Alert tag (I never wear it, for the same reason Hell's Angels don't wear helmets), which warns any potential good samaritan that I'm allergic to almost every pharma-ceutical, legal or otherwise. Antihistamines, decongestants, amphetamines, and cocaine make my heart beat too fast, my hands and feet swell up, and my head feel like it's acquiring the shape and internal consistency of a crook-neck squash. Barbiturates, opiates and sedative-hypnotics cause me to pass out immediately and suffer two or three days afterward with motion sickness, even when I'm just sitting and watching TV. Psychedelics, not only LSD,[11] but

---

[10] I was at the point in my thesis—the first chapter, actually—where I was trying to prove that George Eliot takes herself as the first object of her scrutiny, and Browning was an especially boring example of this.

[11] Which I tried once years ago with the result that I still have cold sweats whenever I see a chicken bone at a Passover dinner. Cf. Chapter 9.

even milder hallucinogens like marijuana, force me to focus obsessively on whatever stimulus happens to present itself, including my own obsessive thoughts, on which I focus obsessively, especially on the thought that I'm focusing on my obsessive thoughts, and so on until I realize I'm trapped in a tailor's mirror of infinitely regressive reflection and I get scared that I'm going crazy and then focus obsessively on that.

For this reason, and also because it always gives me tonsillitis, I never smoke pot. However, I reasoned that being on parallel psychic planes with Diane was essential to moving in the direction of physical abandon, so I had to make an exception to my dope rule. When Diane, fixing me seductively with her eyes, snapped her disposable plastic butane lighter, took a long hit, and then passed me the joint, I inhaled deeply, too, and held my breath. The smoke was hot and seemed to defy the laws of physics by doubling in volume and temperature while in my lungs and bronchi. A violent coughing fit racked my frame like an old car dieseling on cheap gas.

Diane Droddy wasn't deterred by my tubercular routine. She led me to the bed and laid me down. Once again we faced each other and inscribed light finger-traces on each other's brows. I was feeling relaxed and was even distracted from my usually obsessive thoughts by the rush of pleasurable physical sensations: her fingers on my eyes, cheek, jawline, neck; scent of salt and coconut oil strong as we warmed, palms over bellies and backs, then thighs, both drawing air in hard gasps and moving flanks subtly against the other as we explored delicately the outer ridges of lips with tonguetips, then one limpet kiss that lasted longer than some nineteenth-century romantic soaring on laudanum could ever have dreamed, at which point I became self-aware that the Thai stick had made me lose control over the track my thoughts would take and they were moving in a decidedly literary direction; no problem, I could exist on the carnal and the theoretical, one firing the other, which put me in mind of the young Keats, who described foreplay as a winning near the goal, consummation an end that one never wants to reach, itself being a death of spirit, passion, imagination, and Keats must have known someone very like my mother, because at that moment, when two small deities poised at that height, making sounds like sacrificial cattle lowing at the skies and he slid her suit down and then his own and she laughed and called him creepy caterpillar because he was rippling up her body all the while thrusting in time to . . .

. . . then the Buzzer went off.

Unfortunately Buzzer, in this context, has nothing to do with the erogenous anatomy. It refers instead to an intercom device that my father had installed some nine years earlier. Anyone in the house could press a button connected by wire to the sounding device in the office. This would prompt my father to pick up the telephone, through which Ma could tell him dinner was ready or that he was late for his haircut. But that was then, and now the hideous protracted cawing could mean only one thing: Ma had seen us go in, had judged the amount of time it would take me to become fully aroused, and then hit the button and held it down with a vengeance born of a widow's deprivation.

Caught up as Diane and I were, our first reaction to the noise was to ignore it, although bitter experience told me that Ma wouldn't lift her finger off the button until I had satisfied her by interrupting whatever horrible perversion she imagined I was engaged in. There was no way to cut off the buzzing, either, without picking up the phone and talking to Ma, which, even when I'm completely straight, is confusing enough, but which, in my current cannabis- and hormone-addled condition, promised disaster.

The sustained whine gnawed ratlike through our ability

to pretend it wasn't happening. Finally Diane said crossly, "What's that noise!"

Too far gone to keep up the pretense, I blurted out tragically, "My *mother*! I didn't want to spoil a nice afternoon by worrying you, but she's been tailing us all day. Remember the scuba diver who crawled up out of the water? It was my *mother*! And the bag lady with the metal detector? My *mother*! And the silver El Camino I said was following us? She's everywhere, there's no getting away from her . . ." And on I ranted, driven by exasperated fury, by terror of the demonic manifest in my own sweet mama, and by a malformed last-ditch plan to render the ugly situation comical by exaggeration.

Diane wasn't amused. She sneered, "You said you rented this place. You really have a thing for your mother, don't you? Now that I think back on it, you've been talking about her all day," all the while picking up her things. Juggling sandals, shift, wicker bag in one hand, she opened the door with the other, muttered, "See you around, Harmon," without turning to look back, and pulled the door shut behind her.

Crushed, incapable of divining the thinnest tapeworm-thread of logic in the progress of the preceding events, I lifted the receiver and spoke wearily. "It's all right, Ma; she's gone."

Her voice sounded positively maritime. "Harmon," she boomed, "what took so long? I was starting to worry. Who's gone?" Her words echoplexed: "GONE, Gone, gone, gon . . ."

"Never mind. What is it, Ma?"

"What is what?"

I paused and waited for a vision of endless interrogative loops, spiraling toward a vanishing point far away, to approach and then recede, like a low-buzzing helicopter. "What do you mean, what is what?"

"I can't answer what it is until you tell me what 'it' is. Harmon, what are those gurgling sounds? Are you running a tub?"

"Right, just a little tired, you know . . ."

"Take a hot bath and a nap before dinner. I've got chops, your favorite. That's why I buzzed."

"Sounds good. Bye, Ma."

Sleep. I tried once more, hopelessly, to fix on and make sense of the chain of events that led to this almost insupportable fatigue, like the pull of a denser geology where gravity claws at the eye sockets . . . a car, a beach, a woman. George Eliot, of all people, appeared before me, her every feature etched in genial detail, her homeliness growing in complexity until my whole visual screen filled with fine cross-hatching . . . my eyes closed and I became Her . . . saw the world, perceived others as George would . . . my mother, an odd revolving-headed owl who thought her deceptions opaque while she believed mine transparent. I was synthesizing obscure and disparate bytes of memory now at incredible speed, and all at once my aimless scribbling of the last two years fell into place in an orgasm of intellect. A thesis, a central idea, the heretofore-missing core of my dissertation, took shape in my mind. Seizing the nearest paper—a scrap of newsprint torn from the previous day's sports page—I recorded like a fanatic scribe each spasm of inspiration. I wrote until I was spent. For safekeeping, I folded the paper and slipped it in the first volume of *Doctor Syntax*, which happened to be lying nearby. Modern critical brilliancies I had produced, one after the other, like a frogwife laying her eggs. From such prodigious ova would my reputation as a scholar hatch.

But then they stole *Doctor Syntax*.

# ♠ SEVEN ♠

I slept through dinner and the late news and my morning instant hot cereal. I came awake just before noon, with the radio tuned mysteriously[12] to some evangelical channel and a rapturous congregation of peckerwoods working over a number that sounded like "If You Really Love Me, Then Eat My Sheets." I am, with all due humility, a hottish lead guitarist and used to work in rhythm-and-blues bands around town before I got locked into this literary thing, so I know fourth-rate gospel when I hear it. Dismissing the white-bread chorale with a turn of the dial, I barely had time to shave and dress for my appointment with Ernst Gablonzer. I had been referred to Ernst a couple days earlier by a library science friend as a "highly regarded but eccentric" local bibliographic researcher and therefore a person likely to know the value of a complete set of *Doctor Syntax*. I had called him, explained the circumstances of my inheritance briefly to

---

[12] I usually leave it on KJZZ (Thrasher, my former roommate who likes nothing but Led Zep and other sixties proto-thrash, irreverently calls it "K-Jizz"), the hip, low-power jazz and soul station coming out of Compton.

him, and he had made the appointment for today, at one.

Ernst had an address in Echo Park, one of the oldest and quaintest parts of town, a hospitable blue-collar Latino and Asian neighborhood[13] with steep hills, narrow streets laid out at irregular angles instead of the usual tract-development grid, with dogs romping on lawns, kids running through sprinklers, and porches with hanging potted succulents, all just a pop foul from where the Dodgers play ball down in Chavez Ravine . . . which is why I'm familiar with the area. I'm a lifelong Dodger fan; my father was from Brooklyn, so I guess it's in the genes.

To get to Ernst's I took surface streets. They're faster to certain parts of the city. The disappointments and revelations of the previous evening had already retreated to that elephant graveyard where memories born of excess flock to die, and this blurring or complete erosion of detail was in part a blessing—the less I could recall of the incident with Diane, the less despondent I would be—and in part a vexation, since I could not bring to mind even one of the luminous insights I had written on the small scrap of paper. But I had the scrap tucked away safely in my *Doctor Syntax*, and I took comfort in projecting a future scene in which I would sweep the clutter off my worktable in a symbolic gesture of purgation, I would sit down with a yellow pad, and incontrovertible proof would arrange itself organically, in a manner more suggesting the layered growth of a coral reef than the Brownian erring of a crazed seastar. [14]

---

[13] Unlike my own Mandeville Heights where movie stars, real estate developers, linen rental service executives and their progeny have settled the twisting chaparral canyons from which, on high, they hold off the Third World with immaculate pansy beds and armed-response alarm systems.

[14] The allusion here is to my high-school advanced placement lit teacher, Mrs. Convoy, a superannuated Emily Dickinson type, dried up from disuse in the passion department but uncannily accurate in her personal insights [continued on next page]

Ernst Gablonzer greeted me at the door to his cottage. What tapped the eye first about Ernst was not his extreme shortness, although he was indeed extremely short. Even I, well below the surgeon-general's recommended height for adult males, had an aerial perspective of Ernst's scalp, mostly bald though covered irregularly by wisps of coarse white hair combed across the top, from ear to ear. But more striking than his baldness or his shortness was a certain force, intangible as the polarizing properties of magnets. I imagined that wherever he walked, pieces of furniture would organize themselves around him, as if awaiting emancipation from their objecthood. Ernst wore a goatee and glasses with frames of thick black plastic and opaquely smoked lenses, all of which added to the mystique. He shook my hand warmly with both of his and took my arm. Usually I'm distrustful of people who touch you before they know you, like certain therapy groupies who enwrap you in a smothering hug whenever they see you, as though you just got off the plane after a long trip, or out of the hospital after a triple bypass; but coming from Ernst, I found the gesture strangely comforting, in a fatherly sort of way.

He walked me into the study, which in truth encompassed most of the house. The living room, dining room, and even the kitchen were obviously used more as library space than as areas for entertaining, eating, or cooking. Old pine bookcases and metal library shelves filled with hardbound volumes lined the walls, yellowing manuscripts covered the oak drop-leaf dining table, paperbacks overflowed gray plastic milk crates stacked five high, each bearing a freezer-taped label. The scene reminded me of

(which is probably why she never got married in the first place). She told me, in front of the whole class while I was doing my carrot-swallowing act, "Mr. Nails, you are a neurotic starfish." She never elaborated, apparently trusting that the maturing process would clarify the metaphor for me, but I was never sure what she meant until I started writing this narrative.

those widows who breed swarms of cats for company in their apartments. Books appeared to have bred unchecked in Ernst's house and were now taking over, making themselves comfy in every corner of every room.

Behind one of the banks of plastic crates was the desk, surprisingly free of literature, just a stack of unlined paper, a typewriter even older than my pop's, a tape-recording device of some kind, and a small vase with pencils and pens in it. Behind the desk a young woman sat, absorbed in some kind of transcription work with the recorder. Bent over as she was, her face was hidden by a fall of wavy red-copper hair.

Ernst spoke in a strange, almost parodic accent, something Slavic or Germanic with a heavy overlay of Oxford: "Mr. Nels, I food like to intrrroduce you to Lisa Sturrrrm. Lisa, this is Harrrmon Nels, a grreduit schtudnt who hess brrought us some ault folumes off poooetry for appresl." Silly, as I have said: He sounded like Alistair Cooke doing a bad impression of Henry Kissinger, but who among us has flawless speech? Certainly not I. In allergy season (which in Southern California is nine months out of the year) I resemble one of those cardboard losers in Restoration farce, a puffy cove with a clownish nose and a perpetual case of the grippe or the rheum or even the choryza, and my voice is positively adenoidal. So when I tell you I responded, "Nice to meet you, Lisa Sturm" to Ernst's introduction, what actually came out was this: "Dice to beet chew, Lisa Sturb."

The woman looked up and fixed me with eyes the deep pupilless brown they used to call shoe-button when shoes had buttons. Her regard was expressive of nothing in particular yet stunning, almost overwhelming in its intensity, as if the responsibility of gathering and storing visual images fell in the category of religious duty. She said without a hint of reproval, "It's pronounced 'Lissa.' Two esses. I'm glad to meet you, too, Mr. Nails."

If Lissa knew she was beautiful—how could she not?—it didn't seem to matter to her. She wore no makeup, left her light brown brows full, and her faded print dress was shapeless. She was youngish. Women's flesh (and maybe that of males as well; I haven't paid that much attention) takes on a taut, gessoed-canvas quality at adolescence, when budding sex swells the insides but the outer covering is still too baby-new to have much give to it, so that it acquires the surface tension of a ripened honeydew, shiny and firm, and retains this for perhaps ten years, when the skin begins making barely noticeable concessions to entropy. I guessed Lissa to be at this latter stage, around my own age, twenty-five maybe. She was furthermore so fair-skinned that one could make out on her forearms the ghosts of blue vessels below.[15] At first sight one had to perceive in Lissa a certain purity, as if she had had at some time a too-intimate knowledge of others' petty pathologies and had rejected all that in favor of being . . . nice: a word much maligned in these competitive times, when it's taken generally to characterize the pushover or easy mark, but which should, at least in Lissa's case, suggest nothing less positive than a sunny disposition.

I was getting carried away. This was not the first time an open smile or a pointed glance had sent my imagination soaring. In fact, it's been soaring since third grade, when I was appointed class spelling monitor, a singular honor and

[15] This lack of pigmentation usually brings up a vision of my first girlfriend, Janet Bunson, and specifically her breasts, pale and translucent, and all the bluish circulatory geography seemed to point to and converge on the aureole, also lacking in melanin and itself blue-tinted, until the the nipple tightened up and became champagne pink: a digression I can't help but take whenever I see a redhead. Liz the shrink got excited when I first made this admission. She said it was a breakthrough and pantingly pointed out that I chase women who look like Ma, who also has red hair. This of course is nonsense. I'm not attracted to older women.

the first concrete indication Ma had that her son was, as she has been insisting for the last two decades, "something of a genius in the word department." The verbal prodigy was making his rounds during composition period, and Jeannie Kraepelien, an eight-year-old darling in patent leather pumps and a fount of fine dark hair, regarded me adoringly as I explained to her with all the authority of a sixth grader that "weird" was one of the few words for which one had to break the recently-imparted "I before E" dictum. It's because of The Look that I always trap myself, and even at that tender age it started me entertaining domestic fantasies: Jeannie Kraepelien accompanying me hand-in-hand to the weekend fright-show matinee where we'd share a box of Jujubes in the dark; Jeannie Kraepelien sitting demurely next to me on the living room sofa where we would suck on fudgickles and read comics in the afternoon; Jeannie Kraepelien smothering me with chaste kisses cool and all-enveloping as fresh linen bedclothes.

The same jejune idealizing, carried to the stupider extremes of which only grown-ups are capable, is the reason behind my having married by the time I was twenty-two and divorced within a year. Made real, the dream wears thin and the dishes take over, and the dirty clothes, and then another female gives you The Look. You see the present as a blank wall spray-painted with the dripping graffiti of regret, and in these enlightened times divorce is no big thing to do. Dump one slightly-used fantasy into the toy chest and find another. But the process does take its toll, as witness the three months after Brenny left, when I languished in bed, incapable of anything more strenuous than watching sitcoms and digesting Ma's soft-boiled eggs and buttered white toast.

When I recovered enough to take careful steps around the block, I decided that love always hurts, frequently stinks, and never lasts, and I insisted that I wouldn't ensnare myself again. But here I was anyway, less than a minute into my relationship with Lissa, already convinced of her utter nobility of character and previewing a lifetime of marital contentment. In my defense, there truly was something unique about her: Even the smartass, critical part of my psyche—the one that usually watches me play the infatuated swooning fool and makes snide comments like, "You really have a knack for picking 'em, don't you, Nails? That one looks like she'd be purring in three-inch spiked heels and goose-stepping across your chest; check her arms for cigarette burns or tattoos . . ."—had to stand open-mouthed, hand over heart, at the first sight of Lissa.

It was at this moment, as I was falling in love again, that the masked brute with the shotgun appeared in the scrotal catastrophe already related. That I had already, in my mind, had a brace of kids with Lissa, a station wagon to carry them in, and a shake-shingled summer cottage at Lake Arrowhead to carry them to, may explain a little better my rash leap into an onrushing gunstock. A male stands between his family and danger, and what better way, what more primally powerful instinct than to interpose the very simian territorial essence of his manhood, his evolutionary equipage, his symbols?

♥   EIGHT   ♥

The urologist examined my wounded symbols carefully. With gloved hands he probed, twisted and thumped ducts, reservoirs and vessels, requested and got the traditional cough, came up finally with a diagnosis of acute epididymitis, an inflammation of the ductile tissue of my right testicle. He recommended I wear a suspensory, a supportive device which he predicted wouldn't lessen the pain but which would promote faster healing by allowing more blood to the traumatized area. In this prediction he was half right: The device didn't lessen but instead focused the pain, which when I tried to walk felt like a meal sack thudding into my groin with every forward movement of my right leg, sending in turn a shock up into my lower bowel area, with the sensation of a long barb-legged parasite lodged and taking lusty nips at my appendix. In short, the suspensory was killing me.

I stayed in bed and took my temperature frequently, as I do whenever I'm bedridden. If healing oneself is passive, taking my temperature at least gives me a tiny attic window on my body and its autonomic processes over whose governance I have no vote, not even an absentee ballot.

With this latest malady I never went a degree above normal, but I kept on checking since constancy, at least in this one quantifiable corner of the human condition, comforts me. I took my temperature, did crosswords, checked my temperature again, watched a game show, ate, checked, slept, checked, and after a few days developed a bursitis in my right arm from shaking down the thermometer, a hypochondriacal variant of the fashionable tennis elbow, the pain of which took my mind off the original injury. The inflammation had begun to subside anyway. My movement was still severely restricted, but I could walk to the icebox now without wanting to retch.

I determined to confine my initial stabs at investigating the theft of *Doctor Syntax* to one location: Ernst's study, where I could, with a minimum of painful movement, uncover crucial clues,[16] and where I could get next to Lissa, who played a hot romantic lead in my dreams during the brief convalescence. I phoned Echo Park, and Ernst answered, "Cerrrtenlee, come oferr eni time. I enchoi to hoff a prrromising jung creetic arrround see haus." I didn't have

---

16 Everything I know about investigation—and most other things— comes from extensive firsthand experience with the succession of TV sets my family has owned over the years, from the first tiny oblate tube in the mid-fifties, to the huge, clunky color console in the early sixties, to our current sleek black solid-state Nanotron with oodles of microchip-generated frammies, digital remote control, digital tuner pad and chronometer. From TV I have an admittedly stereotyped and no doubt laughably naive view of detective work. "Dragnet" and "77 Sunset Strip" and "Kojak" taught me that you talk to people methodically and patiently, get the facts, eat burgers, and then the crook confesses or else tries to kill you and you kill him instead. But I've also spent enough time around my cousin Bradford the insurance investigator to have learned that success in detective work is usually the result of pure chance, lucky breaks, being at the right place, stumbling onto the right computer code: the same scenario as most successes in life's big crapshoot.

the heart or the physical energy—or even, at that time, the perspective—to explain to him that I was mired in a crisis of intellectual self-doubt, that my future life as a scholar depended on whether or not I could retrieve a ganja-induced revelation on a shred of paper, so I let it slide and said I'd be over the next day.

Everything was the same as last time. The books were fixing themselves breakfast or just hanging out, humanity filed away in what little space was left.

Ernst led me to the desk, where Lissa was typing a transcript from the dictaphone, and said, "Fie don't you tell Mr. Nels fot feef lernt so farrr about *Doktor Seentox*. I sink I shall rrretire to my betroom. I feel my afterrrnoon knap apprrroachng."

He shuffled off, picking his way through the stacks of cartons and leaving me alone with Lissa and a feeling that somehow encompassed both silly grammar school infatuation and supernal adoration. She said, "I'm glad you came back, Harmon. I wanted to thank you for what you did."

I said something rural like, "Twernt nothin' to it," and, too shy for further discourse along this personal line, I turned to business: "What's Dr. Gablonzer found out about my books?"

Lissa responded softly but with a fire born of evident enthusiasm for her work, "Actually, I did the research on this case. For some reason Ernst seems convinced the books aren't valuable. I think he probably wants to spare you the grief you'd feel if the books did turn out to be valuable but the police can't find them. I think Ernst has taken a liking to you. Or maybe he just empathizes with your . . . condition. Are you feeling better?"

She glanced toward my tenderized pud and smiled consolingly. My neck got hot and my face flushed. Out of consideration or pity Lissa pretended to miss my embarrassment and adopted the dry and practical tone I had chosen. "Anyway," she said, "I thought I owed you at least a good job of research. All I have so far is preliminary pricing data, which means I found what I could about your books from bibliographies and auction records available at the university library. But I'm hoping for more. There's a sort of underground network of collectors, bibliographers, rare book nuts, and they're the best source when you want to know about current demand. That's really how the prices are set."

As she spoke I rested my elbows on the edge of the desk, cradled my head in my palms and, hopeless romantic that I am, lost myself in her eyes, dark cisterns of boundless depth. Lissa's voice seemed distant, as though she were talking into a Dixie cup. I heard just enough of what she was saying to follow. Lissa opened a desk drawer and took out a folder. She opened it. "This is what I've got so far: *Doctor Syntax* was published early in the nineteenth century by the poet William Combe. It's the story, in verse, of a poor, eccentric scholar, Dr. Syntax by name, who goes out looking for adventures so he can write a novel about them."

This sounded like a good idea to me, although highly improbable. In real life people don't risk their lives for literature. Or so I thought then.

She continued. "The writing is considered second-rate by the few critics who bother to mention it. The books probably wouldn't be worth anything at all, if it weren't for the engravings. They're by an artist named Rowlandson, and they're quite a bit better than the poetry. In fact, it seems Combe wrote the poetry to accompany the pictures, rather than the other way around. Rowlandson would send Combe a sketch, and Combe would write verses to go with it. They went on like that for years, until all the books were done."

Still adrift in her eyes, involuntarily I made a moony face. Lissa looked unmoved, either positively or negatively, by it

and turned a page in the folder. "You wouldn't expect anyone to pay much for books of bad poetry, even if the pictures
were good, and until recently that's been true. Fifteen years
ago, you could pick up a mint set of *Doctor Syntax* at auction
for around three hundred dollars. Then for some reason
interest picked up. You can never predict the market. Within
three years, the price of the volumes more than quadrupled,
and a set went at auction ten years ago for around two
thousand dollars. Those are the latest figures I've found, but
there's no reason to suppose the books have stopped appreciating. At that rate, conservatively, your set might be worth
between fifteen and forty thousand dollars."

In spite of my mooning I heard enough of this for my
former nausea to resurface. Forty grand lost, maybe more,
and the thief probably had no idea: He just picked up my
tennis tote as a convenient receptacle for the pitiful little
tchatchkes he managed to bag on his way out, and *Doctor
Syntax* went along for the ride. I saw My Own Place reduced to rubble, my custom-tailored slacks rent to rags, my
kidney-shaped blue tile pool buried under muckslide, and
all by the theft of my books.

I croaked, "That much . . . for third-rate poetry? I could
understand that much for a really good writer—some engravings by Blake, maybe—but some unknown jerk like
Combe?"

With sarcasm light and pointed rather than cruel, she
said, "I guess some collectors don't share your sophisti-
cated tastes or care what the ivory-tower critics say is 'really
good' writing. And forty K is a lot of money for a set of
books, first-rate or not. But remember, that figure's just a
guess. It all depends on current interest: simple economics,
supply and demand. If demand has dropped, as Ernst
seems to think, your books are worth less; if demand is
higher, they could be worth more. A lot more."

# PART TWO

♣  ♦  ♠  ♥

*DÉJÀ VU*

# ♣ NINE ♣

Whenever I experience *déjà vu*, I expect my life to end. Neural researchers trash the terrifying mysticism of this phenomenon simply: One half of my brain is lagging just a nanosecond behind the other in reaction to some outside event, with the resulting illusion of passed time between the two acts of perception. Some Buddhists like my friend Chainsaw argue it's a faint recollection of a past incarnation, the intrusion of a former life—and death—on the present. Russ Thrasher has an even more absurd answer. I've plugged into a parallel dimension, he says, in which my life is unliving itself, in reverse, from future to past, like the Bizarro characters in the Superman comics, beings who live on a planet just like ours and look like clumsy metallic replicas of us and do everything backward.[17] Simultaneously

---

[17] Simple physical functions like evacuation must be extremely painful for such backward folk. They must have to suck their excreta up into their bowels like industrial-strength vacuum cleaners, which hurts, as you know. But on a backward planet, pain must be felt as pleasure and vice versa . . . which is often the case here on earth, too, if the Personals in the *L.A. Free Journal*'s classified ads section are any indication. Cf. Chapter 24.

I'm moving from present to future and from future to present, and the *déjà vu* is the point at which those two temporal planes intersect. Or so it seems to Thrasher, whose life is a Zap comic. Whatever . . . whether the ghost of an earlier existence, or trans-planar projection or jumped relay on this burnt-out circuit board my brain, *déjà vu* always carries the same disturbing piece of baggage: I get killed at the end of it.

The first time this happened, I was sitting at the dining room table with Ma and Pop and Brenny and all the maternal relatives at a Passover seder. It was a Monday evening, and I was still under the cruel heel of a migraine, the odious hangover from my first and last experiment with psychedelic drugs the previous day.

Thrasher had phoned and invited me to come over and watch a special unedited replay of the Superbowl, which the Dolphins had won a couple of months earlier. In those days Miami was our favorite team because they vindicated our freakdom: More than any other pro team they flaunted hair. It flowed down out of their helmets, peeked through ear-holes, napped out from under faceguards and chinstraps. The Csonka-Kiick Dolphins had hair and they kicked ass. We could project ourselves into that collective persona, envision ourselves as the misunderstood but righteous vanguard of a New Age bowling over the rest of the crewcut retrograde NFL rednecks who represented the blind respect for authority that we held repugnant.

Since Brenny was going to play duets with her flautist friend, Dee Trottoir (on whom I had a crush at the time), I had no trouble getting away for rerun football this Sunday. Brenny and I agreed—O rare and felicitous event—to get together with Dee and her husband early in the evening and go out for Italian, which sounded like a good day to me: televised sports, maybe throw the Frisbee after, a plate of linguine with clam sauce, longing glances at my wife's honey-blond best friend across a candlelit table, and maybe some snarling, butt-slapping sex with Brenny later on as a purgative for my unrequited adulterous lust.

Thrasher and his girlfriend, Lauren, rented a little place in the part of Venice that still had character, since it had not yet been reached by the condo blight that had germinated at the Marina Del Rey some fifteen years earlier and metastasized fast in all directions. From the airport to the sea, an unbroken expanse of two-level townhouses, self-serve gas stations, twenty-four-hour convenience markets and nine-hole pitch 'n' putts. Non-natives believe all of L.A. conforms to this cinder-block graveyard image, and the hungry developers work unrelentingly to prove them right, leveling quaint little sub-communities built in the twenties and thirties, displacing recourseless low-income residents, reaping huge, X-rated profits.[18]

Russ and Lauren's house and property had up to now been spared the bulldozer and backhoe, and on the dandelion-weedy front lawn Russ was bathing Moby in an inflatable polyethylene wading pool festooned with pictures of barnyard fowl waddling with umbrellas and canes. Moby, a cocker-mutt, mostly black except for the Rockwellesque white patch over one eye and muddy white booties, frequently scratched himself sore and bleeding because of a year-round infestation by unseen vermin, fat fleas and rat mites, which is why the insecticide dip. The ordeal over,

---

[18] Can I justify my tone of social outrage? Wasn't it my own father who supplied the linens to convention centers, highrise resort complexes, restaurants, and country clubs during the voracious, visionary salad days of urban circumfusion, the fiscal gains of which efforts paid for braces on my teeth, summer camp on the Trinity River in northern California, private tennis lessons at the Brentshire Country Club, and a trip to Europe after my high school graduation? A minor inconsistency: I accepted those gifts before my social conscience was fine-tuned in college. Would I accept them now, you ask? Would you?

Moby twisted from Russ' grasp and shook medicinal bathwater all over my Levis. Russ dried his hands on a towel and we went inside.

Unlike me with my bag of pharmacological allergies, bizarre drug reactions and exaggerated fear of losing control, Thrasher was never *not* stoned out on something. He smoked pot constantly, ate pills in handfuls from a lumpily overstuffed argyle sock he hid under the TV. He even managed to wheedle a five-foot tank of nitrous oxide out of a dental student friend of his. Thrasher kept the laughing gas by the living room couch. He would slip a little rubber five-and-dime balloon over the nozzle, fill it with gas, put it in his mouth and inhale until the balloon was empty, and then you could watch in horror and fascination as human self-abasement reached new depths. Thrasher's head would loll on his chest, his tongue would protrude from a corner of his mouth, from which he would drool down his chin while his arms twitched convulsively. All of this would last maybe ten seconds, and he would then awake brightly, shouting, "I've got it!" He said the universe revealed its mysteries during those seconds, which seemed like full hours to him. It was in one of his $NO_2$ reveries that he formulated his now-famous *déjà vu* hypothesis.

But the revelation would fade fast, so he'd have to do another balloon. If one happened to walk in on the end of such a session, he would see what looked like the aftermath of a twisted birthday party, with spent multicolored party favors all over the floor, Pepsi bottles, crumpled spittle-soaked tissues, seeds and stems and papers, Thrasher spread-eagled and burnt-out on the divan, and Lauren, who never indulged in but never seemed to mind my best friend's excesses, puttering around cleaning up the debris.

We sat on the floor in front of the TV, on what Russ called his "tubie seats," garish discount-store orange corduroy cushions with armrests and covered with just enough Moby fur and house dust to make my bronchial tubes contract asthmatically. I sneezed, and Russ passed one of the three or four boxes of Kleenex he always had nearby, mostly to attend to the mucous exigencies of his cocaine-ravaged nasal passages. He brought a small wad of tinfoil out of his pocket and uncrumpled it. Inside were four small white, purple-flecked tablets. Thrasher said, "It's psilocybin. The guy I bought it from said it's pure, pharmaceutical. Sandoz labs made it to experiment on convicts or prisoners of war or something."

Even I, a naïf in such matters, knew all homemade tablets advertised as exotic varieties of psychedelic were almost always garage-brewed LSD cut with some other medication, like amphetamine or Borateem. Dealers could get a higher price for what they called mescaline, which was supposed to imitate the distinctive psychoactive properties of peyote cactus; you would see beings' souls as glowing eggs and be able to launch yourself off cliffs and glide safely to the ground on cables of pure energy emanating from the power center in your navel. Or the dealers would hawk their acid as psilocybin, synthetic "magic mushrooms" famous for their ability to destroy the ego: In smaller doses it was rumored one could attain a profound and uplifting sense of one's place in the natural order, a role no more or less important than that of a dragonfly on a rock; in larger doses, you feel like your skin is frying off your skeleton as your essence rises to heaven in tiny sizzling soap bubbles.

Of course I knew all of this drug lore not from experience—my usual caution in the arena of pharmaceuticals had kept me from having allowed myself to trip—but from reading books. Since hallucinogens had the reputation of forcing one to let go of his constipative patterns of nonbehavior, I imagined they could be an immensely liberating influence, making me slip out of my too-tight wimp

wrapping. I researched the subject exhaustively, read all
the books on the subject, and learned that some psychiatrists were using acid as a means of catapulting clients out
of their neurotic impasses, like jet pilots ejecting from a
flaming wreck. I concluded that it would be worth the risk
to try some myself . . . a small bit, just enough to change
my point of view by a degree or two, but not enough to
make me freak.

Russ said he had saved the psilocybin for this football
game, to intensify his viewing pleasure. Televised sports are
better when you're high, he said. "It's like you're right on
the fucking field, you can hear the animals grunting, the
collisions are incredible, you really feel the impact, like a
JBL auditorium horn cranking Led Zep real loud . . ." He
offered me some.

Thrasher never forces his drugs. This is one of the reasons I've maintained my friendship with him beyond our
two years as roomies. He respects—or more likely doesn't
care one way or another about—my own reservations,
proffering his stash with the nonchalance of a smoker ex-
tending his pack. I considered the current offer and said I'd
eat a little bit. Russ gave me one of the pills, which I accepted in a piece of tissue paper, carefully avoiding contact
with my skin.[19] I broke off a tiny crumb, no larger than a
sesame seed. This I swallowed with considerable apprehension, while Russ blithely popped three of the double-
domes into his mouth, washed them down with Pepsi, and
settled down in his tubie seat with a translucent tar-black-

---

[19] Red-scare alarmists were at this time hysterically warning legisla-
tors that LSD can enter the body through the skin and suggesting
the commies might infiltrate Jergens plants all across the country
and render us helpless by drugging our strategic stockpiles of
moisturizing cream. While I'm not as gullible as Congress, I
bought the part about LSD entering through the semipermeable
membranes; better to be safe than psychotomimetic.

ened pink lucite marijuana carburetor at his side. American manhood watchful and prepared.

Nothing happened. The game started, the Broncos scored a field goal, Thrasher babbled no more incoherently than usual, and I hadn't seen God yet. After a half hour or so I told Russ that the drug wasn't working. He looked at me strangely, as though I were a hat rack that had somehow been granted the gift of speech. "The shit works," he said. He liked the way it sounded. "The shit works," he said again.

"Are you sure?"

"Try some more."

"Oh."

"Oh," he repeated, grinning at something on my nose, or at my nose itself. Reluctantly I unballed the tissue and broke off another crumb, this one a little larger than the last, and ate it. Another half hour and still nothing.

I became convinced that Thrasher's reaction to the so-called psychedelic was purely self-induced, that marijuana and the power of suggestion made him believe he was tripping. I took the rest of the tablet with confidence and then forgot about it.

Denver scored another touchdown.

I drank some Pepsi, remarking to myself that the corporation's Creative Department had made some interesting changes in the graphic design of their label. They were using some new and opalescent pigments in their printing ink, and the type fonts were tilted oddly. As I studied the cola label, the whole can began to stretch out like warm taffy and then rotate slowly on an axis about a third of the way down the can, leaving spectral, prismatic afterimages as it turned.

The words were animated now, crawling around on the can like escapees from an overturned ant farm. Sometimes they would roam randomly and other times arrange themselves in intricate patterns on the can, forming arcane religious messages that broke up quickly the instant before I could comprehend them and act on their instructions.

The sudden wash of stimuli confused me, and I probably would have been terrified at having thrown myself off the perceptual precipice in a flailing, free-falling header, but two things saved me. When I decided the drug was impotent I let go of my fear, and so what Leary used to call the mental "set" was clear. Also, even when I was at my most dissociated during the succeeding hours, enough of a kernel of superego remained to remind what was left of me that this was just a chemical, and that its effects would wear off—which turned out to be comforting but inaccurate, at least in the case of *déjà vu*.

Thrasher was right about one thing. Football was different. At various points in the proceedings I took on the roles of prosimian linemen, hyperactive referees with persecution complexes, fleshily seductive cheerleaders, Bermuda grass suffering with saintly grace the horrible trampling by the cleated herd above, a flea on Moby's ass. By the final gun the rush was well behind me, and I had settled into a groove wherein I straddled the noetic and the mundane fairly comfortably. I was hallucinating, but I knew I was hallucinating, and I could to my astonishment accomplish complex tasks like walking and even tossing the Frisbee, which would take forever to drift in my direction as though across a bruised blue galaxy, then loom up suddenly like a newborn moon whose orbit my hand would somehow manage to intersect through no conscious effort on my part but by a neuromuscular program visibly blueprinted in detailed superimposition over my field of vision.

"Good catch," Russ said, also impressed by my skill.

"Thanks," I said. "Watch this." I threw the Frisbee into the ivy, which swallowed it like a vast sea anemone.

"Good throw," said Russ.

Russ laughed when I got in my car to drive home. Lauren looked worried. No cause for concern, though, because driving was easy. I just had to steer my U-boat between mines while making sure I kept a safe distance from allied sub-chasers who lobbed depth charges.

Brenny knew something was up because when I came in, I stripped in the living room and went directly to the bathtub without so much as a hello. I filled the tub with steaming water, dumped in a double dose of Brenny's Sardo scented oil, grabbed Enzo and Rashid (the two kittens we had rescued from the gas chamber at the county animal shelter) and perched them on the closed toilet seat lid. I climbed into the tub and led a lucid seminar with the cats for two hours, covering topics ranging from kibble versus canned liver 'n' fish, to the elegiac conventions as reworked by Milton through Tennyson. We all came out of the discussion enriched, I think, and I smelled like a bower of wild jasmine or a hooker on Fountain Avenue.

When Dee and Peter Trottoir arrived for our dinner date, I was close to halfway sane and feeling a mixture of arrant exhaustion and silly good humor. I went into the bedroom to dress, while Brenny apologized for the situation to our guests. Peter—who, it turned out, was himself a freak in the late sixties, before he got married and settled down to write data-processing programs for a hospital service evaluation firm—was amused and supportive. The women clearly were not. They sat whispering on our rattan couch and shot what I interpreted to be disapproving looks my way. Thus, instead of spending the evening gazing longingly at Dee, I stuck close to her hubby, as an infant chimp does its mother, and he lavished an empathic, loving solicitude on me, leading me around by the arm, coaching me through dinner, explaining what I could expect to follow.

"You're still stoned but coming down pretty fast now,"

Peter said. "In a few hours you probably won't be able to keep your eyes open. You can expect to feel tired for a couple days, but then you'll be back to normal." A nice promise, but not true: At the seder the following night I had my first in a long series of acid-induced fatal premonitions.

It was a large gathering of "family" which, since most of my mother's family lived in Atlanta, consisted of cousins-thrice-removed, the spouses of some of them, and a couple of liberal gentile acquaintances who sought a taste of the "Jewish experience."

Bradford conducted the seder well, with relaxed dignity and not too much orthodox pomp, and it proceeded smoothly. We went around the table reading short passages from the *Haggadah*. Mine was the part about how God gave the pursuing Egyptians a case of boils. Still hung over, I read with such a lugubrious, cotton-mouthed delivery that Ma said to me in a concerned aside, "Harmon, you should take it easy with the Manischevitz."

We ate the eggs and bitter herbs in their time, and my cousin Martin Wolf, a lonely nebbish of forty extremely odd years and a man whose actual kinship to us is shadowy,[20] delivered his traditional "horseradish—the first Dristan" joke, and we all laughed ritually. Dinner over, we sang. Three choruses through "Dyanu" everyone was ready to stop, except Martin, who led enthusiastically into one reprise after another, and it must have been the peculiar endless circularity of the song that touched off my fatal premonition in the same way a stroboscopic light can cause a *grand-mal* seizure by synchronizing with the brain waves of epileptics. Suddenly I knew I had done all this before, and that on the previous seder I had died by choking grotesquely on a small, sharp fragment of chicken bone. I flushed hot with adrenaline, tensed up,

[20] He's the son of my Aunt Doreen's adopted sister Sadie Friedkin, by her second husband, Morris Wolf, in case you're interested.

nearly blacked out anticipating the mortal stroke.

It never came, of course. I cried out in relief, "Lo, I am delivered," or "Praise be on high," or some like, and all the relatives seemed to take this ejaculation as evidence of a rare personal appearance by the reclusive Jaweh through one of His less devout creations, because they nodded approvingly or beamed or clasped my hand. The evening broke up on this note of spiritual elevation.

I slept fourteen more hours to go with the eighteen of the previous night, and, as Peter had promised, the effects of the LSD faded, with the exception of one. Through the intervening years between then and now, *déjà vu* has always followed the same pattern with me: mortal terror followed by blessed relief.

So naturally, when I saw the metal-flake gray El Camino, the same one I had seen on my busted date with Diane, drifting dangerously close to me and my motorcycle across two lanes on the Hollywood freeway, I dismissed it as just another pseudo-paranormal ghost-vision, which would inevitably evanesce. This time I was wrong.

Dead wrong.

# ◆ TEN ◆

A nice day, like every other Santa Monica summer day, except this one ended with my near death by a silver El Camino. Slate-gray morning overcast, still and gloomy, followed by increasing heat in the afternoon as the clouds burn off and the sun mounts in the sky. On such afternoons I ride the Beezer, a classic BSA 250 with the stability of larger cruisers and the jumpy maneuverability of a dirt bike. I stuffed my army-surplus bombardier jacket in the saddlebag and rode to Ernst's, enjoying the cool sting of wind against my bare arms and under my T-shirtsleeves, and savoring a faint smog-ache deep in my lungs.[21]

I had passed much of the preceding week at Ernst's, not because I was making any headway in turning up useful

---

[21] If you grow up in L.A., you come to associate chest pain with happy childhood sensations, like playing touch football in a first-stage smog alert, when an end run is cut short not by opposing players but by your inability to extract any oxygen from the filthy air. Hands on knees, you bend over gasping from the exertion. But you think nothing of it; in the city, emphysema is as natural an adjunct to play as poison ivy itch is to a country kid. In a strange way the irritation feels healthy, a reminder that you've been out running around.

clues there, but because I had no idea where else to look. Ernst's was as good a place as any to wait for inspiration. Besides, I was feeling less awestruck by and more comfortable with Lissa, and Ernst had taken an almost paternal interest in me. Given the absence of my own pop, Ernst's attention felt good, as though in my brain a crucial neural receptor, agape like a starveling sparrow, had been filled. Ernst also appeared to condone and even to promote my blossoming (at least in my own mind) relationship with Lissa, because he made a point of leaving us alone frequently and for extended periods, under pretexts more and more exotic, as, "I hoff a suddn crrraving to sit on see porch unt lissn to automobile sounds," or, "I hoff been meeening to polish mein shoes für some time now. Phon't you two excuss me?"

Lissa's current project was typing up some taped criticism, dictated apparently by Ernst, who was aiming to prove that certain so-called "Lesbian Poems" were not only *not* written by Sappho, but that they are actually primitive folk-verse dressed up to look Sapphic, whatever that meant. I offered to help Lissa with her work, explaining that for my required classical language I had selected Attic Greek as an alternative to the tedium of reading Beowulf in the original Old English,[22] and that I still remembered some of it.

Mercifully, Lissa declined my offer of help and said she'd rather we spent our time alone getting to know each other, at which suggestion my heart leapt up. She asked me

[22] As it turned out, Greek literature, with its inane declensions and grotesque conjugations, was far dumber than anything composed by even the most superstitious, grunting, greasy hartskinned and soot-blackened Pict. I had to repeat Classics 10 twice before I passed, as I never saw any percentage in knowing that frogs say "brekkekekek-koax-koax" in Thebes, nor could I manage to stoke up even a little interest in following Xenophon from one killing floor to the next.

about my past, and I regaled her with the usual packet of true-life adventures: my first bicycle, near-brushes with fatality while surfing and motorcycling, Pop's long terminal illness that resulted in my devout existential nihilism, high-stakes poker, my attraction to my recently-deceased kitty named Newton, my marriage, divorce, and subsequent utter nervous explosion, the missing scrap of newspaper that could change my life if ever I could find the maggot who'd stolen it along with *Doctor Syntax*.

Lissa was a good listener. She didn't interrupt except to laugh where appropriate or to offer a murmur of consolation during the sad parts. She seemed truly interested and, at times, moved. Surprisingly, the process was cathartic for me, too, in the way I suppose psychotherapy should be but rarely is because you always know in the back of your mind that you're forking over a dollar a minute to this schmeckeleh who's nodding attentively while thinking of tasteful ways to tile the bathroom in the new wing of his house, which construction project your shrinkage over the past six months financed. Talking with Lissa lightened my psychic burden instead of my billfold. I told her I was grateful for her attention. "Now it's your turn to talk," I insisted.

She began slowly. Of her past she said there wasn't much to tell. "Pretty normal midwestern stuff, I guess. Nothing to complain about, but nothing memorable, either. I came to California to go to school. I wanted to find out for myself if everything I was hearing about this place was true . . ."

"Is it?"

"Yes, and much worse." Her narration picked up momentum. "I was sharing a studio with a bio major. She had *birds*. Never have two birds at one time, by the way . . . at least two parakeets."

"Parakeets have never been high on my list of life's goals."

"Mine, either, but there I was, stuck in a little studio apartment with two of them. One, she called him Leonard, the little flyaway fringe of feathers on his head reminded her of Leonard Bernstein conducting. Leonard used to fly around, usually into the bathroom. The other one, Dukie, had his wings clipped, so he had to stay on his perch. There they'd be, Leonard in the bathroom, Dukie on his perch, screeching at each other across the room."

"It sounds delightfully cheerful. Did you kill them?"

"I felt like it. They made this annoying 'chit-chit-chit' scolding noise all the time."

"I know that sound. My mother makes it when I scuff the kitchen linoleum with the heels of my dirt-digging boots. It's like an old washing machine in the spin cycle."

"With an unbalanced load," she extended the metaphor.

"Precisely. And shot bearings."

"It was driving me insane. I spent all my free hours in the library, just to get away from the racket, so I ended up studying a lot. I got good grades, thanks to Leonard and Dukie."

"Maybe I should borrow those birds next quarter."

"I'm afraid Leonard and Dukie are in birdy heaven now. The neighbor's cat got them."

"Too bad. I could really use their help. I have to take Dr. Brunkard's Browning seminar."

"Browning is good. You'll enjoy it."

"Browning's all right, he limps along. But you've never truly suffered until you've read Peble's simpering essays on the prosodic style of his later dramatic monologues. Most literary criticism is unreadable, but . . ."

"I like criticism." At this admission my adoration of Lissa eroded a perceptible bit, like a chunk of aquamarine-flecked plaster falling from a Giotto fresco. Unaware of the offense, she picked up the thread of her story: "Anyway, last year, when I graduated, I didn't know what to do with myself. A bachelor's in comp lit, high honors, fluency in ancient and modern Greek, Latin, some French. Everyone warned me my skills wouldn't be marketable, but I didn't want to believe it."

"The higher and more specialized your degree," I observed, "the less employable you become. All you can do is teach or wait tables, and restaurant work pays more."

"So I found out. When I ran out of money, I went to the school placement center to look for work, anything—cocktailing, babysitting. I found an ad for an 'Editorial Assistant: must be versed in the classics, flexible hours, salary to be arranged.' It turned out to be Ernst. I found him irresistible—dedicated, brilliant, demanding, warm—I'm sure you've seen the same qualities in him." I said I had. "The work isn't as creative as I'd like, but it's a challenge. He's giving me a research acknowledgment in his next article."

"I didn't know he published."

"Actually, he's considered a kind of authority in his field. Which isn't easy for someone who's not connected with a university."

"With a reputation like that, why can't he land himself a professorship somewhere? Then he could afford a house big enough for all these books . . . and hire an interior decorator."

"He doesn't notice the clutter. He likes it here. It's familiar. Besides, he did teach in a university once, in Europe, but he gave it up when he came here."

"Why?"

Lissa paused, as though to consider the morality of discussing at greater length a history revealed in confidence, even if our conversation didn't exactly fall in the category of gossip. Picking words even more carefully than at first, like an outlander working from a dictionary, she said, "I've pieced together what I know of Ernst's life from conversations I've had with him and his colleagues. He's had a hard life, the kind that would destroy most people, and that's why I respect him all the more. I don't want to betray his confidence."

I wavered between respect for Ernst's privacy and a dire need for facts. At this point, almost a week into my so-called investigation and nothing to show for it, even irrelevant information would feel like progress. I assured Lissa I would never say a syllable to hurt him.

She allowed, "Maybe I'm a little too careful when it comes to Ernst. But if you knew what he's been through, you'd be more protective than your mother."

I protested, "If I devoted every erg of my vitality to the project, I could never be more protective than my mother. Her protectiveness is absolute, perfect and complete. Like death."

Hyperbole always wins the day, which, I suppose, is how advertising agencies stay in business. Her story came out:

Ernst Gablonzer was born in Austria but went to England to pursue his education. After receiving his doctorate he accepted a position teaching classics at Kent University. He met and married a girl from the nearby village, a milliner's daughter who was said to be incredibly beautiful—flaming red hair, ivory skin, mysterious dark eyes—but naive and inexperienced. They had a baby girl, and for the first few years everything was blissful. But it all fell apart. Ernst was working on a series of translations with a female colleague, and he was away from home a lot. At the same time, his wife met this charming man, Laurence Sterne, descended from the famous novelist of the same name.

Sterne was rich, some kind of a religious figure, and a collector of rare things—art, rugs, books, stamps. If it was scarce and valuable he either owned it or coveted it, and what he coveted he eventually owned. He took one look at Ernst's wife and decided he had to add her to his collection. Over the course of several weeks Sterne managed to plant in her mind the suspicion, then the conviction, that Ernst was having an affair with his female colleague, that he wasn't worth her fidelity. Sterne invented proofs, going so far as to show her love letters allegedly written by Ernst. Too gullible, she believed him. Sterne wooed her and eventually took her to America with the child, no forwarding address.

Ernst followed them across America, determined to show Sterne for the charlatan he was. He got close, but Sterne protects his possessions. He had two of his religious "converts"—thugs, really—confront Ernst in his hotel room. They warned him to lay off, but Ernst refused. To scare him they tied him to a chair and held a bottle of some kind of cleaning fluid over his face, threatening to pour it in his eyes if he didn't leave Sterne alone. Ernst struggled and upset the jar. The caustic solution got in his eyes. The two guys panicked and ran, leaving Ernst helpless. By the time someone found him, it was too late.

Not comprehending, or more likely not wanting to comprehend, I said, "But his vision is perfect. He gets around here fine . . ."

"He knows this place by heart. Otherwise, I do his seeing for him. I'm his eyes. Ernst is blind."

# ♠ ELEVEN ♠

Shaky and distracted, I eased onto the Alvarado entrance to the Hollywood Freeway and headed east, on a roundabout route that avoided the densest commuter traffic on the Harbor Freeway by taking me east to the Pasadena Freeway, north to the Golden State, south to the tangle of concrete fettucine the radio weather-and-traffic-condition jokers call the "downtown four-level interchange," then west on the Santa Monica Freeway, toward the beach and home. It was almost dusk, the sun a cherry Necco behind bad air, the day cooling down. I had on my old leather bomber jacket for warmth.

The heartless mistreatment of Ernst, a man I was sure had not an ounce of evil in him, sickened me. Under my mantle of southern California mellow, and deeper, below the thicker crust of my nihilism, flows a secret molten hope: that Camus and the rest of my modern anxiety-age heroes were wrong in positing a universe that snickers quietly at our annoying little toe-stubbings and ghastly suppurating buboes, our catty back-stabbings and atrocious mass exterminations—or worse, that has no consciousness at all, sadistic or otherwise. I secretly want twentieth-century philosophy to be disproved by a sudden and unprecedented epidemic of righteous deeds, a universal power-spike of goodness. But more often than not my closet optimism gets a poetic jackboot in the teeth or a too-real gunstock in the kishkas, and I want instead to puke, or weep, or lash out.

In such a mood I wound the Beezer out hard, got up to cruising speed, and stayed in the right lane of the freeway. Even though the 250 is a solid enough road machine under sixty or so, there is a noticeable loss of stability at higher speeds, and you start feeling as though the tires are touching the pavement only as a grudging concession to gravity. I've driven mad enough times to know that I shouldn't, because I get crazy. In my current disturbed state it would be easy to find myself airborne, and—as Thrasher says—it's not the rush that kills you; it's the abrupt stops. I kept to the slow lane, which in L.A. means sixty instead of eighty.

In the fish-eye mirror I saw the silver El Camino coming up fast, but I was too preoccupied with moral outrage over the blinding of my new father-surrogate to accord the pickup more than desultory attention. It pulled alongside me in the next lane, and the driver and passenger both leaned over and peered out the passenger's side window, as though to check me out. I rode on, barely noticing.

They backed off, fell in with the traffic behind, and the next time the El Camino came into view, it was running parallel with me, at the same speed, but in the fast lane. We continued in his way for a mile or two, traffic thinned out as we passed over Sunset Boulevard and made the transition from the Hollywood to the Pasadena Freeway, and I was still only vaguely aware of the truck, when with alarming suddenness it veered in my direction. It was here I made the instantaneous connection between this silver El Camino and the silver El Camino I had noticed while driving back from the beach with Diane Droddy. I judged that it was just another one of my chicken-bone LSD flashbacks playing cute tricks, that the sudden terror I was experiencing as the car got dangerously close would soon pass, as had all my previous *déjà vu* premonitions.

When the right fender nudged my thigh I knew this was no flashback. I had by reflex swerved to the right, thus lessening the force of the impact, but the pickup hit my left leg hard enough to bounce me in the direction of the concrete retaining wall flashing by fast to my right. My initial horror didn't leave—even with the twin headers howling I could hear, or feel, my heart racing wildly under the leather jacket—but merged with my fury at the abuse of Ernst into a kind of savage determination to survive.

There wasn't much shoulder to work with here, as this section of freeway was one of the earliest built in L.A., before a mounting death toll hinted to planners that wider easements might provide speeding motorists a little more margin for error—it piqued me momentarily that no amount of reasoning, no matter how irrefutably documented, will budge Highway Department and earthquake-safety paper-pusher types off their plush, stuffed-leather status quo; it takes the grisly evidence of what they euphemize as "sustained creatural spoilage," or something like that, to get them to make sensible changes, always too late. I dropped the thought, braked hard, threw all my weight into my left hip, cut the handlebars sharply and, smoking the rear tire, slowed my sideways drift enough so that when I hit the wall, I didn't flip. Instead, I ricocheted back onto the highway.

I had slowed to a wobbly twenty or so, and the flow of automobiles was moving considerably faster, a dense clot of traffic bearing down on me from behind. The El Camino was up ahead now, its broad panel of brake lights warning me they were going to wait for me to regain speed, traffic be damned—it's easier to be cavalier about getting rear-ended when you have the cushion of a truckbed between you and a cresting wave of Detroit and Osaka steel than it is when you're bum-to-the-breeze on a motorcycle. If I kept at this speed in this lane, I would be mushed in seconds by the fat primer-red step-van at the vanguard of the onrushing pack, its driver already honking frantically and its tires squealing. If I sped up, I would catch the El Camino, and they would probably dispense with the kicky stunt-driving this time in favor of the less flamboyant but more reliable alternative: Just stick a gun out the window and blow me away.

Danger on all sides, my leg throbbing from the collision, vocal cords raw from screaming wrathful imprecations, I clicked involuntarily into a kind of auto-pilot trance state, not all that different from the pointed focus Buddhist monks and video arcade trolls achieve on their better days. The sensation wasn't unfamiliar to me: I had had it once before, the day I almost drowned at Point Zero.[23] By instinct I got control of the bike, managed to swing right enough to avoid the first car, which sped by just past my left shoulder, and threaded my way somehow between the wall and the traffic. Time slowed, the world got quieter, a cool wind touched my hands and cheek and ruffled my hair like a lover after the act, a weed determined to grow in a seam of the concrete retaining wall was in bright lavender bloom, and there came over me a strange sensation of invincibility, the kind that chronic gamblers are said to get during a winning streak, when they know as surely as their next heartbeat they are going to jam up that inside straight in jacks-or-better draw or, letting ride a stack of casino black, double down on thirteen and then catch the eight they need to squeak past a dealer showing two paints, while a tight semicircle of fans oohs over each succeeding coup.

I twisted the throttle grip hard. Because the Beezer is

[23] Cf. Chapter 29.

geared almost as low as an off-road bike, the full thrust of its acceleration is instant and almost impossible to control, and the torque lifted the front wheel and nearly threw me over backward. I let off the gas just enough to check the wheelie and outran traffic until I came up directly behind the El Camino, so close that I could read the cryptic message on the customized license plate: JQGENUS. We passed over a dry L.A. River,[24] still heading north on the Pasadena Freeway toward the San Gabriel Mountains, invisible now in the failing light.

I had kind of a plan: not one which I had laid out carefully, given the milliseconds I had to work with, but more akin to the instinctual series of moves roundball players can somehow anticipate and then put on as they push the dribble downcourt on a fast break. When the El Camino's driver hit his brakes hard, throwing the truck into a controlled four-wheel skid—no doubt in hopes I would rear-end them, lose control, fall, and be buried by the thick mass of vehicles behind us—I was ready. I veered right and pulled up alongside the El Camino as we passed under the green sign for the Avenue 50 offramp. Just inches from the passenger's window, I got a good look at the two this time. The driver was dark, with oiled-back black hair and Mediterranean pigmentation, and he was staring intently ahead, absorbed by the rigors of life-and-death pursuit. The rider, larger and bleached blond, was slipping on a ski mask remarkably like the one our assailant had been wearing at Ernst's. Here I made my fledgling deduction in my new role as investigator, a logical conclusion that would have knocked Holmes' socks

---

[24] The River has been the unfair butt of too many easy jokes. I've seen days of sudden rain when the concrete aqueduct runs awful with a muddy turbulence, the surface littered with uprooted trees, a thunder of sandstone boulders carried along by the current, and it's as impressive in its power as any of your major rivers, or at least any of your major sewers.

off: This was the same guy that had stolen *Doctor Syntax* and wounded my *cojones*, and he was lifting the same (at least it looked pretty similar) shotgun and pointing it at me through the rolled-down window of the same El Camino that had followed me at least once before. I geared down, lifted the front end off the ground once again, and rabbited away from the pickup.

I heard the gun go off once.

Mere survival was no longer my goal. I was too angry with fates who had not only had the bad taste to dump on a sweet guy like Ernst, but who were now sending geeks to kill me artlessly. If there really exists collectively within each culture the body of unconscious drives on which post-Jungian and neo-Reichian psychologists base their occult brands of faith-healing, then my Italianness was getting pricked here. I wanted *soddisfazione*, soul-purging Black Hand-style revenge that encompasses your basic eye-for-an-eye Mosaic civil justice and ritual retribution by one whooping heathen tribe on another.

I headed for the Avenue 50 offramp, making sure the El Camino was on my tail while weaving and positioning myself ahead of the driver's side of the truck, to avoid any direct shots from the masked rider. I sped up gradually, so that by the time we hit the offramp, the Beezer was going pretty much full-out, and the El Camino was gaining. All part of the plan . . . such as it was.

I eased off on the throttle, and, just when it looked like the pickup would smash me and my bike to spare parts, giblets 'n' sprockets, I dumped the Beezer. I hit the pavement smoothly and slid on my side, the bomber jacket absorbing most of the friction from the gravelly asphalt. I rolled onto the shoulder of the offramp, which was covered with a thick mat of low-maintanance succulent ground cover. The iceplant cushioned and slowed me, and I came to a stop on my back, among yellow flowers, with some bees circling and stoically relocating.

The Beezer, meanwhile, accomplished the sacrifice I had planned for it. When I laid the bike down in front of the speeding El Camino's right fender (a maneuver I had practiced to a polished smoothness by falling down repeatedly while exploring dirt-and-gravel firebreak roads in the San Gabriel foothills, but which I had never before performed on pavement), the pickup's driver didn't have time to override his natural inclination to avoid the obstacle, and so he cut left. But unlike the gently sloping and densely planted right side of the offramp where I chose to land, the left side had just a raised tar-and-gravel curb, a few feet of dirt plateau, and then a steep drop down to the freeway. The truck caught the curb, lost contact with the ground for a moment and landed, atilt on the two left wheels, at the summit of the incline. There it teetered for what must have seemed to the occupants of the truck a nauseating eternity, until it began to roll, at first with dignified restraint and then with jarring, bone-snapping rampancy. It rolled out of my sight, but I heard it hit bottom with a curiously soft sound, like the crunch of a single footfall in hard-packed snow. [25]

As much ill as avenged (after all, I'm only half Italian) I got up and tested my legs. They ached, but seemed otherwise functional. I limped my way to the bike and righted it. Same story as my legs, a little bent but still in working order. The front wheel was out of true and wobbled, and the front brakes were shot. The gas tank was flattened on one side and leaking at the stopcock valve. The muffler hung limply, held in place by a rivet, from the right header. No one was around to help or even observe me, since morbid curiosity and humanitarian concern centered at that moment on what sounded like a multiple-car pileup down below: honking and screeching, dull impact

[25] I've never actually been in snow, but I imagine that's what it sounds like.

sounds, sirens in the distance. I didn't much feel like waiting for the Highway Patrol, reports in triplicate, and the probability that I'd get hauled downtown and locked up on suspicion of failing to yield the right-of-way to a truckful of homicidal maniacs, so I numbly kick-started the bike and took off into the city. I glanced into the rearview every few seconds, fully expecting a posse of black-and-whites to be closing in on me, but no one cared. For a change, alienation was a blessing.

Somewhere around Fairfax—I could tell by the proliferation of signs in Hebrew—the bike started showing signs of giving up the ghost. The muffler was dragging on the ground now, sending up little fans of sparks, and the unmuffled engine noise was starting to draw stares from pedestrians. The fuel leak had grown to a steady trickle, gas was spattering and hissing on the cylinder head, and it was only a matter of time before we would have to call the fire department to put down a two-alarm blaze on my right shin.

I pulled off the street and made a call from a phone booth in an obscure corner of a Mobil station, and a few minutes later Thrasher arrived in his old VW bus, the rear two-thirds of which he had blowtorched a few years previous into a kind of makeshift truckbed. He looked at me, looked at the bike, and smiled with sympathy and admiration. From the condition of me and The Beezer, it was obvious to him that I had spent an afternoon of unprecedented radicality. Thrasher approved. According to his worldview, the closer to the edge, the better. He heaved my mangled Beezer into the back of the van, and we rode back to my house, wordlessly.

♥   TWELVE   ♥

Ma's objections to his job aside, my cousin Brad is one of my favorite people in the world.

This was not always so, because Brad was a nasty kid. At family get-togethers I built houses of Lincoln Logs with him, a forced partnership in which I did the laying of lapped walls and carefully imbricated green cardboard-shake roofs while Braddy laid my creations to scrap with gleefully malicious swats. I hated him for that and dreaded the major Jewish holidays up until my teens, when the roles reversed: I became the brat surf-punk shoplifting teenager, and Brad started turning into a regular guy—as is the curious case with a lot of juvenile bullies, even some of the most vicious, the kind who build elaborate little wooden guillotines out of ice cream sticks to chop earth-worms in half, or who ally themselves with other nasties to pin down the class wimp and masturbate him at recess.

A few years ago, Brad was still "trying to find himself," as his mother, my recently-passed Aunt Doreen, rationalized it to clucking family. He was volunteering hours acting at a small repertory house in Venice under the stage name Dan-iel Woodlawn, crashing in a loft above the theater—an unconverted warehouse, really—with six other actors and actresses, waiting tables at a coffeehouse called the Busted Snaredrum ("It's Unbeatable!") and using his primary teaching credential to do a little substitute teaching at a local public school. The combined income from these jobs couldn't keep his ringworn Datsun in Pennzoil.

At length exasperated with his self-imposed rich-kid squalor, and convinced that he didn't have the clawing, screw-the-competition drive or the physical stamina or the reliable coke connections necessary to be a success in Hollywood, Brad succumbed to his father's pressure and joined the family business: Global Casualty, a small firm and probably shady even by insurance industry standards, catering mainly to clients who, due to a surfeit of drunk driving convictions, could no longer qualify for coverage with the larger and more reputable companies.

My Uncle Ed, Global's founder and a man of rigid traditional values, said his son had to work himself up in the business, "just like any schnook off the street," so Brad now finds himself on a rung maybe a little higher than halfway up the corporate ladder, a Global policy salesman who has to follow up on an occasionally questionable claim, like the time a client, shitfaced drunk and speeding in the rain, spun out and plowed into a disabled Camaro on the shoulder of the southbound Ventura freeway, then compounded this inanity by submitting a claim in which she accused the Camaro's driver of backing into her. Brad investigated. She lost.

Finally settling on a career niche seems to have made Brad genuinely satisfied with himself, probably the main reason why he's become such a pleasant, easygoing companion. He now has a wife, Margy (pronounce the "g" hard), a darkly chic but not overly narcissistic Vassar graduate, raised Catholic, who baby-talks under social pressure of family gatherings but who has down-home common sense and is extremely supportive of Brad. Brad also has two Great Danes and a newish split-level in the valley, a little kidney-shaped pool and a Ping-Pong table, and a new Sony TV with which he pursues his second passion (after Margy): watching sports and murder mysteries. Brad's recall of sports trivia is total, and he can remember the characters and recite the story lines of all the major crime shows, going back as far as "77 Sunset Strip" in the early sixties, with an attention to intricacies of plot rivaling that of the pickiest Restoration drama professor.

It embarrasses Brad to tell people, especially his self-righteous theatrical crowd, that he's happy—that Daniel Woodlawn is once again Bradford Lesnick, with a tract house and a color tubie and a lifetime no-cut contract to play the indemnity game. But he is happy. He appreciates the money (his first act as a man of swelling financial substance was to trade in his Datsun for a new root-beer brown BMW sport sedan) and admits he enjoys the personal contact that comes with the territory: ". . . being up there on stage performing for a bunch of faceless people always made me nervous, but I like talking one-on-one with clients. Maybe I should have gone into psychology." Further, he's surprised himself and thrilled his parents (who always thought him hopelessly thickheaded in areas they considered practical: pre-med biology, engineering-track calculus and physics, legal-prep political science) by becoming a bit of a computer nerd. At the office he has learned how to code into the most far-flung modem-accessible data banks, with a facility that would inspire envy in a CIA operative with years of experience spying electronically on innocent citizens. Brad loves his new digital toy. With it, he can access (often illegally, I imagine; I'd as soon not know) Department of Motor Vehicles records, bank credit ratings, state and federal tax returns, police and FBI rap sheets, news services, aviation weather reports, a gourmet cooks' recipe service, and a personable but nearly unbeatable backgammon program on a main-frame somewhere in Kansas.

I subscribe to the motto that if it relaxes you, do it; if it relaxes you and pays well, make a career of it. So, even if I could never stomach insurance work—neither the tedious keypunching nor the hours of filling in all those morbid little boxes on carbon-paper forms nor the hyper-pushy Sta-Prest image the job conjures—I approve of Brad's work, for Brad. Besides, still wobbly from the episode on the offramp, I desperately needed his investigative expertise. Something I had done or was doing—hanging around the star-crossed Ernst? wooing Lissa ardently? digging up skel-etons in George Eliot's closet? annoying some hyper-sensitive psycho by hawking too loudly when an unseen cloud of ragweed pollen stimulated my postnasal drip?—was clearly putting me in harm's way. I needed answers, fast, before someone else tried to do me in. The same day on which I demolished my BSA and nearly myself, I made an urgent call to Brad.

Dispensing with our usual talk of the Dodgers' pennant chances, I filled him in on all that had happened. I related details of the inheritance, the theft and assault, my new friendship with Ernst and Lissa, and the recent near-calam-ity on the freeway.

"Jesus," he shouted, "they shot at you. They tried to run you off the road. You have to tell the police."

"You really think they're more likely to take this com-plaint seriously than my last one? Lissa nearly got raped, I got my balls mashed, and the police rushed off like they were late for their next bribe payment. If I report this one, they'll probably bust me and throw me in jail for driving my motorcycle with a faulty muffler."

"Suit yourself. But an El Camino's a deadly weapon, and the police don't take assault with a deadly weapon lightly."

"Tell that to my balls."

"I'd rather not address your balls directly, if it's all the same to you."

"Suit yourself." I mimicked. "But the suspensory's still killing me, and I haven't heard word one from headquarters. I'm going to follow up on this one myself. And you're going to help."

I asked Bradford if he had the inclination to do a little computer-assisted "background research" on all this. Brad positively jumped at the prospect of unraveling a mystery instead of just watching it on TV. "Inclination? Sometimes I have computer dreams. Weird, huh? Real vivid, too, like they're real. About, you know, plugging into a bank account with unlimited funds or tracking down a killer the police haven't been able to find, and I end up rich or famous or both . . ."

I cut short his effusion. "Calm yourself, Braddy, this probably won't be real exciting. What we're dealing with here is a blind antiquarian and a research assistant from Nebraska. Not the stuff your high-tech wet dreams are made of."

"Maybe, but the El Camino, the plates, the shotgun . . . we might turn up something really good. Anyway, it's worth a try. How soon do you need it?"

"Soon," I told him. "I have a feeling I'm going to keep having 'accidents' until I can figure out what's going on."

♣　　THIRTEEN　　♣

Brad buys two sets of season tickets to the Dodgers every year, good seats, halfway down the third-base line and not too high up in the second deck. He gives most of the tickets to his insurance clients as gifts, having found they enjoy baseball more than the Global Casualty logo-embossed polyethylene pitcher-and-glass sets he passed out at Christmas during his first couple of years with the business. But he always saves the primo games, like the Astros, for himself and his wife, or himself and his former Lincoln-Log partner.

We parked outside the stadium—an old trick of Brad's; saves money and beats the crowds leaving the game—on a hill not far from Ernst's house, in fact. I had a pang of tragic yearning, knowing Lissa was nearby, but I displaced it with the compelling image of a foot-long kosher Dodger-dog, heavy on the chili and relish. We took the elevator to our level, stood in line, and bought our dogs, drinks, and nacho chips covered with a drippy yellow "cheese food" that looked like bathroom tub caulking and had no taste. But the junkier the food the better at baseball games. It contributes to the ambiance of guffawing, bearded blue-collar joy and stupidity, of beer spilled sloppily from whopping waxed-paper cups and nylon mesh Caterpillar Tractor caps. We found our seats and ate. I got ketchup on my Harley T-shirt. I fit right in.

It was a day reminiscent of the immobilizing, sticky Julys I spent in New York visiting the grandparents during my childhood. The northern edge of a tropical storm had spun itself over the L.A. basin in a thick, pale gray quilt of cloud, which trapped and concentrated the heat and humidity and pollution. By the time Enos Cabell rolled a little groundout to Russell to end the Astros' first inning, our shirts were soaked with grimy sweat. We took them off. Around the stadium all the patrons, or at least the menfolk, were doing the same thing, sweating and stripping. There was no breeze. The place smelled funky, like an elevator filled with militant soap-resisters.

Removing his Izod alligator shirt revealed a wide white bandage wrapped tight around Brad's upper torso. I contemplated it for a moment and then commented, "I'm the guy who fell off his bike. What happened to you?"

He said, "Oh, softball last weekend. It was the last game of the season, city 'B' league, you know. One away, bottom of the ninth, we were up by two runs, and they had the bases loaded. I was playing third, and the batter hit a shot right up the third-base line, and . . ."

"Always the star . . ."

"Yeah, right. I dived for it, a real Graig Nettles-type circus play, and I caught the ball, too, but I came down on top of my glove and ball, and I got knocked out. They said I was only unconscious about a half a minute, and I felt OK enough to finish up the game, but the next day it was like I couldn't breathe, and I knew something was wrong."

"That's always a giveaway something might be wrong, when you can't breathe."

"The doctor said I had bruised ribs, nothing cracked,

and he taped them up. Happens all the time, he said."

"It's real attractive. You look like you're up for the lead in 'The Mummy's Curse.'"

"Yeah, I know. It doesn't hurt much anymore. Most of the time I forget I have it on."

"Big mistake. You should be milking this for all the sympathy you can."

"Good idea. Could you get me another Coke? My ribs hurt."

"Get it yourself," I said.

Houston up in the fifth, Sutton working on a one-hit shutout, Cruz hit a long fly ball that turned Reggie Smith around, but he made an over-the-shoulder catch at the warning track and the crowd went wild. We ate the last of the nachos, schvitzed like pigs, and, small talk spent, I brought us around to the crucial topic. "So did you find anything out about my . . . situation?"

Brad spoke slowly at first, with a worrisome solemnity. "I was afraid you were going to get to that. I found out quite a bit, actually, and you're not going to like it very much."

I tried to lighten his tone of pending calamity: "Spare me the suspense, Woodlawn. Did I ever tell you 'Woodlawn' sounds more like a cemetery than an actor?"

"Probably. I've heard every lame joke you know at least ten times. You repeat yourself a lot."

"That's what she said last night," I said, aping the obnoxious commentary of macho dudes in YMCA locker rooms.

"You're dreamin', Harmie. The way I hear it, last time you were with a woman you got your peepee whacked by Aunt Fay." That's what he called my mother, because she's his aunt. "Have you ever thought about moving out and settling down . . ."

"Like you. Suburbia, one-point-eight kids, picket fence, Toyota in the driveway . . ."

"Datsun."

"I know."

"You could do worse."

"I suppose. It's just that I'm a husk of my former self since the Brenny business, plus I've got this fucking dissertation hanging over my head all the time. Right now settling down seems like a remote possibility." I paused. The DiamondVision scoreboard was flashing an unrecognizable digitized image of the Astro who was currently at bat. The San Bernardino foothills lay beyond, an unevenly ripped chaparral-gray horizon under red-brown monoxide haze. "Extremely remote," I repeated emphatically, "like one of those trees you can barely make out on Mount Baldy, you know what I mean?"

"All I know is if you wait much longer it might dry up and fall off. Use it or lose it, like they say."

"Oh, super advice, Brad. I'll take out an ad in the *Freege* tomorrow. 'Single white Wop-Kike, divorced, twenty-eight, seeks bitchin babe for ingenious experiments in nuclear family fusion. Send photo, fems only.' I ought to get tons of letters."

"You couldn't do any worse than you're doing now."

"I appreciate your concern for my psychosexual well-being, Brad, but to tell you the truth, right now I'm more worried about just living through the end of the week. Could you just tell me whatever you found out."

He began, "Well, I couldn't find any special meaning for JQGENUS or GENUS or ENUS or . . . Anyway, I checked a lot of combinations against telephone records of individuals, groups. Nothing. But the El Camino is registered to a guy—wait, I brought all this stuff with me . . ." He unzipped his brown daypack, dug into it and brought out a small, vinyl-covered ring binder, which he opened. As he flipped through its contents, he continued, "By the way, you'll be relieved to hear that the accident report said neither guy in the El Camino was hurt bad. The truck was totaled, a few other cars got some dings, but it landed upright, on its wheels, and the guys walked away. They got taken in for carrying a concealed firearm and suspicion of drunk driving. Your would-be murderers are out now. On the streets. Maybe if you had filed a police report . . ."

"I don't want to hear about it, OK? Ever since that time they hauled me in and worked me over, the police make me nervous."[26]

"Here." He stopped his paging. "The El Camino's registered to a Robert Sweeney, who it turns out has a record as long as your arm—no, longer, 'cause you're a runt. Nasty stuff, too, armed robbery, assault, that sort of thing. In case you're interested, he has also gone by the aliases Bobby Sweet, Dick Sweeney, and Sid Dickey . . ."

"Did you get anything on him?"

"Sure. I can tell you how many parking tickets he had in 1959 if you want."

"Anything a little more relevant?"

"This Sweeney reported yearly earnings of over fifty grand the last few years, and—here's the cool connection— he works for one Laurence Sterne, as his gardener."

"Sterne! The guy who had Ernst blinded?"

"The same. Sweeney works for him. His *gardener*. I'd call fifty grand pretty good bucks for picking weeds, wouldn't you? The accident report said Sweeney was the passenger in your El Camino."

My steel-trap sleuth's mind was already snapping at inductions: "Sterne ran off with Ernst's wife something like thirty years ago, and now he's sending thugs to rough me up. What possible reason . . ."

[26] I was exaggerating here. Until I started pursuing *Doctor Syntax*, no one had ever worked me over. But I had had some unpleasant run-ins with the authorities, which made me more than a tad mistrustful of our men in blue. Cf. Chapter 19.

"Wait, there's more, and this is the part you're not going to like."

I waited.

"I couldn't find any record of a Lissa Sturm in L.A. or in California, or in any midwestern state, for that matter, until . . ."

The former Dame David Woodlawn couldn't resist the dramatic pause here, and an imaginary audience hushed in expectation of a shocking revelation, ". . . until I made the connection: Sterne's old tax returns, real old ones, listed a daughter as a dependent: Lisa Sterne, around twenty-two years old. Her most recent address is also Sterne's."

I started gasping, foaming.

Brad concluded, "From the few descriptions I could get of this Lisa Sterne—driver's license stuff, mostly—she sounds an awful lot like the Lissa Sturm you described to me. It adds up to this, old cuz: You may be in love with the stepdaughter of a guy who's trying to kill you, and she's working for her real father under a fake identity. Way to go, Harmon."

Top of the ninth, Cruz got all of a Sutton slider this time and sent a towering homer into the right field pavilion with men on first and third.

The Dodgers lost by a run.

## ◆ FOURTEEN ◆

I have days, usually after troubled and sleepless nights, when I can't wear my contacts—when I need the world to have softer edges, a uniform field of diffuse color on which my imagination can paint its own soothing detail in ferny greens and pastel blues. This day was one of those. Never mind that I see double and bump into things, upsetting the old, wrought-iron art-deco lamp my parents bought shortly after they were married, and bruising my hip on the sharp corner of the dining table. Small surcharge indeed for a world that appears balanced and hospitable.

Lissa lied. Whatever else she might be up to—whether spying on Ernst, plagiarizing her real father's scholarly discoveries, conspiring with her stepfather and his henchmen to steal my inheritance (and staging a damned convincing near-rape in the bargain) and dispose of me—all this was less than a grain in balance against her simple absolute betrayal of my trust. Boring midwestern upbringing, she said; get to know each other better, she cooed; too protective of poor blind Ernst, she protested! I was bumping around blind, bulimic with anger at the treacherous bitch, even more furious with my own pathetically predictable weak self for doing it again. You can get away with stupid mistakes, like my marriage, when you're young, because you still have a reserve of regenerative energy with which to put back together your shattered nervous core, like a lizard sprouting a new tail. But when you're older and the reserves are shot, you need to be more cautious; with Lissa I had jumped in even more recklessly than I had done with Brenny.[27] But at least this time the inevitable withering truth came sooner, before I had played out the sordid script one more time. I could let Lissa go now, and I would do it in coolest private-I style, with a glacial passive-aggressivity: just walk in, take my books and stuff, a chill-breezy "See ya," and leave under some preposterous pretext, like, "I have to work on my dissertation."

I frequently rehearse such confrontations with imagined enemies. Usually this happens after English department meetings, where the fatuous bullshit of certain professors runs so deep that I can't help but lie wide-eyed at night and cycle through my mind a whole spectrum of violent fantasies. This morbid form of insomnia is piqued most deeply when Dr. Pulsinger asserts and defends hawkish positions, like his most recent, that inner-city minority students should get no credit for the remedial "bonehead" composition courses they invariably have to take: "If they knew they were coming to college," Pulsinger says smugly, "they should have had the maturity to prepare themselves for it. In my day we managed our schedules so well we had time to

[27] I had apotheosized the musical Brenda Garbacs as the soul of easygoing cool, only to have her emerge shortly after the wedding as a carping neatness-freak who complained when I left the toothpaste on the wrong side of the sink. Before we got married I couldn't keep my mind or my hands off Brenny, who was all secret love-flush and public tushy-grabs. A month later she cut out sex with astonishing thoroughness, blaming pain in her Bartholin's gland, an organ so tiny and insignificant I had never even heard of it until one day it swelled up to wreck my sex life.

prepare for each of our courses, attend debate club meetings, play in the marching band, and still have time in the evening for the little ladies, heh-heh." Three A.M. and still fully awake, I imagine I might, on the conservative and rational end, explain to Pulsinger in an assertive (but not, as Liz warns me, aggressive), adult-to-adult manner that in his day, during his bone-white East Coast prepsterhood, you didn't have to concern yourself with six-shot Saturday night specials concealed in the classroom desk well or with incessant pressure to smoke angel-dusted Sherms and gang-bang after school. Or, at the more radical end, I might dispense with the futile chitchat and, catching Pulsinger in the faculty parking lot, pump several dozen rounds from a silenced AR-16 into his belly, enjoy the dull splat of lead alloy in soft flesh, the convulsive jerk and horror as his smug facade crumbles . . . a picture that invariably relaxes me into sleep.[28] So I rewound and played back my cruel exit scene over and over, imagining Lissa's inconsolable grief over losing me, the bitchinest guy she would ever meet. But as soon as I walked in Ernst's door and saw Lissa, I was disarmed—as almost always happens to my terrible dark fantasies in the light of day, luckily for the integrity of my teeth, I suppose; there are

[28] Whenever I hear a news story about one of those innocuous types, "He was a nice guy, kept to himself, didn't talk much," who walks into a restaurant and guns down customers dcing nothing more offensive than standing in takeout lines or sitting in booths, I give myself a powerful adrenaline-squirt of fear: *I could belong to that elite group of crazies who plod along in life, taking thump after thump and only dreaming their bloody getbacks until, after one thump too many, they snap and make their dreams come true.* I console myself by recalling the words of Thrasher, who used to drive us up the coast to Fiesta City in the old Austin America he named the Octopus (he had glued a clump of junked vacuum cleaner hoses to the roof of the car, so that they created an absurd Medusa-head effect as we rounded the curves by Point Mugu). (Note continued on next page.)

a lot of people out there, bruisers with hands like butt-steaks, just waiting for some little feist like me to start yapping in their face so they can act out their own violent dreams, and more devastatingly than I ever could act out mine, I'm sure.

Lissa greeted me bouncily, seizing my arm and dragging me inside. "Harmon, I'm so glad to see you," she effused. "I saw a picture in the paper today of this college professor, he's really a retired navy officer, one of the founders of modern electrical engineering, the paper said, as if there's such a thing as ancient electrical engineering—Myceneans processing data on sheep grazing patterns or something. Anyway, this guy was holding a strip, a piece of wire about a foot long, and he said, 'This is how far an electron travels in one trillionth of a second.' I thought, 'Wouldn't that be a good way for Harmon to open one of his classes on some cosmic Romantic poet?' Instructional aids for Wordsworth's 'vision splendid.'"

This unexpected excursion into theoretical physics and experimental pedagogy took me by surprise. I was ready for

(Continued from previous page.) We were overriding the agricultural monotony around Oxnard by discussing New Age heroes like Fritz Perls, father of the don't-push-the-river Gestalt ethic that was in vogue less than a decade ago but which has been supplanted by a more traditional American frontier spirit: Grab everything you can before the next asshole does. We were talking morality. I was in the twilight glow of my "love is all you need" phase, and I said something vapid, like, "The only thing that really matters is to leave behind you a wake of good deeds dancing in life's polluted bay." Thrasher warned me, "No good deed goes unpunished," quoting Perls or improvising his own homily which sounded Perls-like, "and every violent fantasy is a murder averted. The more brutality you think, the more you purge the world of it." At the time, I thought this heresy. But as the seventies wind down, his words help get me through evil times like these: I can see my frequent dreams of vengeful mayhem as nothing worse than a healthy form of discharge, self-inflicted psychotherapy rather than rehearsal for mass slaughter. I hope.

fight-or-flight on my terms, not cheery wordplay, so the best I could muster as a response to her bubbling was a disinterested-sounding, "Where's Ernst?"

"I drove him over to Dr. Zacky's, a colleague of his. He'll bring him back in a couple of hours. So what about my idea, approaching poetry from an angle kids can all respect, electricity, technology?" she persisted.

Struggling to stay mad, I played dumb, "What was the point he was trying to make with the wire?"

"I guess that an electron goes pretty far in a second, although I think it must really go twice that far, since it's traveling back and forth between here and Hoover Dam or . . . where do our electrons come from?"

I was hooked. Lissa made absolute non sequiturs seem connected by an irrefutable logic just beyond the grasp of even the most synthetic of minds, like my own. I love that kind of stuff and had to play along now, even though I didn't want to. Still enunciating woodenly, in the robotic, end-stopped monotone of locked-down hebephrenics, I said, "That's a really good question. Everyone should know where he gets his electrons, in case he has to return a defective one to the factory or something."

She agreed, "The first thing I would do if I were teaching a computer course would be to load the class into a bus and take them to Hoover Dam . . ."

"And show them where their electrons come from. That would make a good one-act play, a couple of electrons talking about their origins, and then this college class comes, and *what's all this shit about you being Sterne's stepdaughter?*" I blurted out in a quavering strangled falsetto.

She stared at me in astonishment, then lowered her eyes. "How did you find . . . never mind, it doesn't matter." She looked pissed.

Still a couple of octaves above my normal range, I shouted, "Doesn't matter? You tell me this guy got Ernst blinded, you intimate that you're some innocent cowgirl from the corn belt, dirt still under your fingernails . . . and it turns out Sterne's none other than dear old stepdad—who's also, in case you didn't know, and I'm sure you do, trying to . . ."

She interrupted my blathering with tragic quiet, "You don't know anything about this."

"No, and I'm sure there's some perfectly logical explanation for why you're in cahoots[29] with your father to fuck over Ernst and kill me."

"Nobody's out to kill you, Harmon. Besides," her voice was rising now, too, her tone stoked with indignation, "where do you get off judging? While I was getting dragged across the country, town to town, hotel to hotel, you were growing up in pampered luxury under palm trees, getting spoiled rotten, making a religion out of worrying about your petty little problems because you had all the comforts and lots of leisure time to kill. You're always putting your parents down because they loved you, they protected you. You call that destructive. You don't have the first idea how destructive parents can be. You've had it easier than anyone has the right, and you dare to draw conclusions about my life?"

I couldn't argue.

Her fury spent for the moment, Lissa softened: "You think I didn't want to tell you? I've been dying, keeping this thing inside, with no one to share it with. From the very first, I thought maybe I could open up to you. But we're on dangerous ground here, and I couldn't be sure. We haven't really known each other that long . . . but it really isn't what it looks like, Harmon. You've got to believe me."

[29] I really did say "cahoots" and blushed at my reversion to Hopalong Cassidy matinee cowboy dialogue under pressure.

♠   FIFTEEN   ♠

I wanted to disbelieve.

I've seen too many Late-Nite Movies on Channel 13, where the stereotypical scheming broad wrings out a few tears and then cons an infatuated paramour into murdering her fat husband, for which chivalric act our hero spends the rest of his days lettering street signs in the prison metal shop while she lives it up in Rio with a tanned boating instructor. But if you're going to have a tragic flaw, it might as well be a too-complete trust in the woman you love. And if she takes you down, then you go down true to your sense of romantic honor, a nearly-extinct moral code which should have been shoved downriver in the funeral barge next to Arthur but which lives instead in a few starry-eyed throwbacks like me. Skeptical, knowing that I was risking a fall that would make my marital failure seem a love slap by comparison, I chose—because I couldn't do otherwise—to take a chance that my initial impression of Lissa was accurate.

"All right," I challenged, "make me believe you."

Where she had been deliberate and plodding as she invented lies, quick and rambling when happily absorbed, she now began tentatively, taking little stabs at speech as though trying on a new set of vocal cords. She began, "I don't know. You're right. I did. Lie I mean. But as for being in cahoots . . ."

"Let's try to forget I said 'cahoots,' all right? It's embarrassing."

"I'm trying to tell you, I'm not working *with* my stepfather. I'm working *against* him. See, Harmon," she started gathering momentum, "when I was a small child all I heard from my stepfather was that Ernst, my real father, was a wife-beater, a philanderer, a pederast, and on and on. Over the years Sterne told my mother and me some dreadful stories about him, and they couldn't help but make an impression. I mean if my mother, a fully grown woman, believed him, it's not surprising that I would, too. Sterne eventually got tired of his little family and abandoned us when we moved to the West Coast, but by that time those stories had their own life. My mother died a couple of years ago, still convinced Ernst was a degenerate.

This new story sounded even more improbable than the last one, but I held the Nails tongue in order that she might have a chance to finish, thereby either hanging or vindicating herself.

"When you think about it, my mother had to keep believing Sterne's story. Otherwise she'd have to admit to herself the unthinkable, that she wronged a good man, Ernst, to go off with a corrupt one."

"Sterne," I said in a tone that implied cold rationality, a dispassionate need to assemble the facts as she presented them and thus to derive my own conclusions about Lissa's sincerity.

"Right. But I inherited my real father's independent nature, I guess, and I always nurtured this secret seed of love and trust for him in spite of all the stories. So when I turned eighteen, I decided to find out for myself. I moved out of the house to go to college . . ."

"The bio major and her aviary."

She nodded in affirmation.

"Was that all made up, too?" I asked.

"No, the business about the birds really happened."

"Leonard and Rexie really are dead?"

"Dukie, not Rexie."

"Dead?"

"Dead."

"Damn." Against my better judgment I was already letting down my guard a little, even if there were huge hunks of the puzzle still unexplained. For better or worse, there was no way I was going to mistrust Lissa when she waxed sincere. I said, "I suppose even a compulsive liar like you couldn't make up that stupid bit about Bernstein's hair."

"We all have our limitations, Harmon."

"So let me get this straight. You move into the studio, hide in the library to get away from the parakeets, graduate with honors and end up on the doorstep of Ernst, your father. He must have been a little shocked; long-lost daughter shows up and asks Daddy for a job."

"I didn't do it quite that way. I really didn't know whether Ernst was the soul of evil Sterne described or the good guy I hoped and suspected. I thought it'd be better if I got close to him and checked him out, instead of showing up and saying, 'I hear you're a cruel pervert. Tell me about it.'"

"Yeah, I see your point. That might not go over real well."

"No, it might not. So I did some work for Dr. Zacky and got him to introduce me to Ernst as a graduate student interested in old Greek poetry. After a while, I offered to help him out with his research, and he hired me."

"You mean Ernst still thinks you're just an employee?" My skepticism was starting to resurface, in the same way that a lunch of chile relleno resurfaces when it's followed too closely by several sets of situps and oblique crunches.

"You still haven't told him you're his daughter?"

"Yes. I mean, no. I mean, I haven't."

"That's dragging out the role-playing a bit far, don't you think? I mean, you must know by now if he's a cruel pervert or not."

"Oh, there's no question that Sterne was lying all those years. And I have every intention of telling my father, only I don't know how to go about it gracefully, so I keep postponing, and it gets harder and harder. Every day I say to myself I'm going to tell him, and then I just . . . don't. He's not strong, physically, and I don't know how he'd take it. That sounds so selfless and noble, but really I don't know how I'd take it, either, his reaction when he found out I'd mistrusted him and spied on him. I'm not the pillar of granite you seem to think . . ."

This admission of vulnerability worked to soften my resistance. I suggested, "You could tell him the same story you just told me. Anyone with an ounce of compassion would have to understand why you did what you did," and offered, "I'd be glad to be there when you tell him, in case you have to faint into my arms or something."

"How *gallant*, Harmon. I may just take you up on that."

Disburdening herself of a portion of the awful secret she had been carrying for months seemed to swing Lissa's mood abruptly to an exhausted giddiness, like the weird high one experiences after sitting at the bedside of a dying parent for days and nights: coffee, no sleep, fast-food malteds for nourishment, finally the death, and one's first reaction is not a wailing grief as one expected, but instead a paroxysm of uncontrollable giggling in the face of a somber and well-intentioned attending physician and several shocked nurses. In such a state Lissa mock-swooned at my suggestion, and I caught her up. We were both laughing, I mostly out of wonder at the physical contact between us, two friends who had never gone beyond the intimacy an introductory handshake.

We became quiet. Lissa opened her eyes and we regarded each other strangely, as though across a long gallery hung with panels of the abstractest sort. Time suspended its fierce shaking, and when we kissed at last the stars sang in their spheres—or at least they hummed and whistled and cleared their throats and shuffled their big awkward feet. I was struck so hard by a mixture of shock, elation and apprehension that I actually did begin to feel faint, and I let Lissa slip out of my arms, for which she was wholly unprepared. She fell hard on her rump, a small cloud of house dust rising around her thighs. "I take back the part about *gallant*," she said.

"I guess I can't stand up and kiss at the same time. As I heard someone say recently, we all have our limitations."

"Then come down."

Everything was moving too fast. Certainly I had entertained fantasies of ecstasy with Lissa on the floor—also the bed, the sofa, tables, bookcases, chair-backs, coatracks—had wondered about the private vectors of her breasts, the possible lineations of aureoles—darkling nubbins? alert rosy buttons? translucent domes with faint red mottlings?—had imagined prolonged sessions of post-coital languor and silliness followed by explorations of other furniture, of other anatomical flexures long kept secret. But since bitter experience has shown me that dreams fall apart when they become real, I couldn't risk having my love blasted again so soon, like a sapling willow struck twice by lightning in the same fierce storm. To stall for time I improvised a feeble excuse, "I can't, not on the floor . . . dust makes me sneeze."

Lissa reached up and took my hand. She said, "I'm not ready to be lovers either, Harmon. I like going slowly. I've been in too many train wrecks myself. Just hold me while I finish the story.

"I can do that," I said, relieved but at the same time disappointed.

"Good. I haven't even gotten around to *Doctor Syntax* yet."

The mere mention of my lost books projected me back into more mundane dimensions. It seemed eons had passed since I had even thought about investigating *Doctor Syntax* or researching George Eliot. I sat down next to Lissa, put my arm around her shoulders and lay back on the hard floor. She nestled under my arm and I was surprised by the almost doughy quality of her embrace, not the throttling ivy wrap I was used to suffering—and, I suppose, inflicting sometimes—but more a paradoxical yielding with force.

After some moments of silence, she said, "*Contenta*," and then, "How much do you know about the poems in *Doctor Syntax?*"

I responded by writhing as though tormented by night terrors and pleading, "No, no, Dr. Brunkard, don't make me talk about poetry now, I meant to do the reading, but the parakeets ate my *Cromden Anthology* so I didn't have a chance, but I promise if you give me another month . . ."

"I take it that means you haven't read them."

"I skimmed *The English Dance of Life*, but mostly I looked at the pretty pictures. You can pick up most of what's happening that way, and it saves you from having to read Combe's vile couplets."

She agreed, "His poetry's not my favorite, either," adding, " but it helps if you think of it as reflecting the sensibilities of a period. Helps me, anyway."

"You can call me an effete snob again if you want to, but bad writing is bad writing, and if I don't like something, I can't trick myself into reading it. It's kind of like impotence, I think. The harder you try, the worse it gets." Reflecting upon the analogy, I added, "Not that I've ever had that particular problem, of course."

100 ♠ Doctor Syntax

She shot me an ambiguous semi-smile that suggested either skepticism, mild curiosity, or utter disinterest.

"Anyway," I continued, dropping the subject of sexual dysfunction posthaste, "with a boring book I start thinking about food, or my tennis serve, or . . . you. You've been my main distraction lately. Before I know it I've turned five or six pages without comprehending a word."

"You have to make an exception with *Doctor Syntax,* even if it means taking your mind off me for a few minutes. It's important that you read it, and carefully. There's a lot more going on there than the pictures, which is why my stepfather wants the books: To Sterne, they're more than just collector's pieces. They're sort of . . . sacred . . ."

My wild laughter was interrupted by the sound of a car driving up and stopping out front, the slamming of one car door, then another, voices approaching. Lissa said, "My father's home."

We jumped like teenagers caught petting, brushed dust off each other's backs, smoothed out wrinkles. Just as the front door opened, Lissa gave me some words of advice: "Get a copy of *Syntax* from the library and read it, Harmon. It's the key to getting at Sterne."

# PART THREE

♣   ♦   ♠   ♥

## THE DOUBLE
## DOUBLE LINE

# ♥  SIXTEEN  ♥

Toward the front of our family album are pasted a few antiquated metallic-gray snapshots of Ma as a college-age camper, the wild-haired urban intellectual at play in knee-length clamdiggers and workshirt. But in spite of this incontrovertible photographic proof, I have always found it impossible to imagine Ma sleeping on a cot in a wood-slatted open-air dorm, or cannonballing into a frigid, snowmelt-fed lake, or taking the point on a nature walk through bunchy, fulsome thickets that could conceal biting snakes or weasels. Yet she did it. Pictures don't lie, especially when there's no percentage in it.

On this morning, I was having more trouble than usual imagining Ma roughing it, as I helped her get ready for her pilgrimage to Tucson. Every year Ma visits Ruth Wrightson, née Velcoff, her former bunkie and best friend at Civitauqua, a progressive, Indian-theme Jewish summer camp at which they worked as counselors several successive summers before the war. I never attended one of their reunions, but I imagine they spend most of their two weeks lying around the pool and reminiscing about the good old thirties: boyfriends, socialist causes, bobbed hair.

Today my "helping" her involved listening to Ma fret while she cleaned out whole closets with the sweep of an arm: winter dresses, woolen scarves, tweedy wraps, and all for Tucson—in *summer* yet, when locals welcome 110 in the shade as a break in the heat, a cold snap. Ma was only going to be in the desert ten days, but she had to cover every meteorological contingency that could possibly arise, including blizzards. "With the weather you never know," she said. "It can change any minute."

"Right, Ma. You don't want to be caught without your coat when the next ice age sweeps down over Tucson."

"Make jokes. Better to be prepared than catch pneumonia."[30]

Ma was on her second valpack, with two or three more to go. The thick redolence of Chanel and mothcakes from her closet was overwhelming. I couldn't take any more. Gagging, I excused myself, promised her I'd get back in plenty of time to drive her to the airport by 5 P.M., and betook me to the lighthouse jetty to be alone with *Doctor Syntax*.

The lighthouse jetty is the southernmost, and the longest, in a series of nine scrap-granite promontories built by the Army Corps of Engineers to keep the sand on Santa Monica beaches from being carried away by the powerful north-south current and deposited in the boat channel at Marina Del Rey. Until a few years ago the lighthouse jetty had a lighthouse. Built in the style of New England lighthouses, stocky at the base, and tapering gradually to a halo of massive glass blocks, it had a basso foghorn blast

[30] I do make jokes, but to this day, following my mother's example, I can't go to the movies without at least two extra articles of warm and impermeable clothing, just in case a cloud of warm, moist air from an unusually sweaty filmic clientele rises to collide with an arctic blast from the air-conditioner, creating an occluded weather front inside the theater, with resulting thunderheads and rain squalls.

so forlornly piercing it would wake me before sunrise, through two overstuffed down pillows clutched to my ears, even though we lived at least five miles away. I'm a light sleeper, no question, but that's still one loud fog-horn, baby.

Surfers used to use the lighthouse as a landmark by which to line up the perfect spot for taking off on waves. But around the time my father died, someone decided to tear down the lighthouse and replace it with a snack bar so that bathers wouldn't have to walk so far for their Sno-cones. All that remains of the original structure is the block foundation on which the lighthouse perched, converted now to a storage facility for lifeguard gear: four-wheel-drive sand cruisers, surfboards, orange bubble markers on nylon ropes. Of course the jetty remains, too, and when the tide is out you can rock-hop to the end of the spit, a good hundred yards from the surf line, sit hidden among the craggy boulders mottled gray-white and blued with mussels below the surf line, hung with clinging kelp and seagrass. You are cooled by the afternoon on-shores carrying a fine salty mist from waves spending themselves on rock. You study thumb-sized fiddler crabs clinging hard under the onset of each tidal surge, then moving on about their crabby business. And if you look out through spray-haze, across the water, to the scarcely perceptible arc of the horizon, you frame a vastness that can provide answers to profound and unanswerable questions—such as how Combe's poetry could be considered "sacred," or anything more than emetic. I hunkered down at the end of the jetty, my backpack burdened with turn-of-the-century reprints of the three *Syntax* books. I had checked out the volumes from the university library, which held a set of originals locked in the Special Collections section but never let the old hidebound volumes out of their glass casement—one more confirmation that my stolen heirloom must be of considerable value.

Lissa had hinted that certain holy secrets might be couched within the text of the *Doctor Syntax* series. While this seemed no more likely than that the prophet Elijah was going to visit the lighthouse jetty today with a channeled tri-fin thruster under his arm, I had nothing to lose by following Lissa's urgently delivered counsel. Besides, I had everything to gain by staying away from home while Ma packed. I therefore started reading *The English Dance of Life*, the volume I had skimmed earlier and dismissed as artless tripe.

A second, closer reading did give me new insight. The writing was not artless tripe. It was artless, morally self-righteous, and occasionally anti-Semitic tripe, and the other two volumes came off no better. The rhymes were facile and arbitrary, the meter arthritic. It was obvious that Combe had written the lines to fit the rhymes, instead of the other way around, which, as you know if you've ever read or written poetry, is dangerous practice.[31] The result of Combe's relentless devotion to couplets was nothing less than catastrophic: The syntax of *Syntax* is often so painfully inverted that it really does cry out for a doctor, with a hypo full of Demerol to put the lines out of their misery. Every poet, even the best of us, can be forgiven a few shoddy or cloddy phrasings,[32] but with the *Syntax* books you can close your eyes, flip to any page and point your finger randomly at any line for a verse disaster, thus:

[31] I dabble in poesie myself from time to time but had to give up rhyming almost entirely because, like Combe, I kept forcing the enjambments—a painful practice even with the advent of K-Y Jelly in these modern times.

[32] Didn't Hopkins write, ". . . nor can feet feel, being shod"? Didn't Blackjack Keats pen, ". . . every man whose soul is not a clod / hath visions . . ."? Didn't Shakespeare himself get away with whining, "O senseless linen . . ."?

*A rising mound points out her grave, / The cropping sheep its verdure shave.*

As for Combe's spiritual message, it was nothing more than a rehash of the usual Anglican preoccupation with humility, chastity and other forms of extreme self-abasement: self-consciously moral, but nothing you could call inspired or inventive. The most ingenious part, and the only one I liked, was where rats stole Doctor Syntax's wig and ripped it to shreds, and Syntax was *"All decomposed awhile he strutted, / To see his peruke thus begutted."*[33] But when I got to the part in the third volume about Jacob Levi, the Money Lender, a *"keen, cautious Israelite"* [34] who takes advantage of poor, honest, hardworking gentiles in his "usurious dealing," I realized that Sterne and I must have such divergent definitions of "sacred" that it was pointless to look any further for clues. I'd have to get more information from Lissa when next we had a chance to be alone. I read a while longer, waiting for the tide to come up a little. I got cooled by spray, tasted salt, watched crabs, checked the horizon one more time for answers and got none. I went back to the car and grabbed my board.

The waves were small, two to three foot and a little blown-out, but they were sucking out nicely over the sandbar created by the jetty's interposition in the southward flow of sand, creating tight little barrels with enough juice for me and a couple other locals to tuck into if we took off right by the rocks. I got tubed, paddled until my arms

---

[33] Combe, William, *The English Dance of Life*. I forget the date and publisher and page and so on, but you can check it out from your library and then flip through the book until you find a picture of some mean rats running away with what looks like the business end of a dust mop, and a baldish dude chasing them futilely.

[34] Op. cit., I forget the page here, too, but it's somewhere after the part with the rats.

became rubbery[35]and until there wasn't an erg of the previous days' confusion, pain, frustration, fear, sexual tension left in my body. For the first time in what seemed months, I forgot about rare books, traumatized soft tissue, wrecked bikes, true love, mystery.

The tide kept coming up and the waves eventually got too mushy to ride. I rode the whitewater of one last wave onto the beach, climbed the dirt embankment to the parking lot, unlocked the car and laid my board wax-side down across the back trunk ledge and the front passenger's seat. I got in the driver's side and peeled off my wetsuit. You're subject to a "lewd conduct" citation and a stiff fine if they catch you on the beach or in your car with your pants down, so you get skilled at doing the quick change in the front seat. The brief, illegal moments of nudity, as you arch your back and shove your hips forward to pull down soggy boxer shorts, usually go unseen unless one of your buddies happens to be standing by the car and yells "choner alert!" gesturing hysterically for all passers-by to check you out. This day I was alone, and so without embarrassing incident I pulled on dry boxers, a pair of Hawaiian-print walking shorts and my favorite T-shirt: it's gray with Grateful Dead in snaky letters on the back, and over my ribcage a dancing, top-hatted, pipe-smoking skeleton holding up a hand of cards in his bony fingers and grinning, as though to suggest he had just drawn out on the world in a game of California Lowball, no limit. I think it looks rad on me.

I made it home in plenty of time to load Ma's luggage into the trunk of her Volvo and cruise to LAX, where, as the skycap loaded her luggage on a metal handcart, Ma

[35] Only about five percent of surfing time is actually spent surfing. The rest of the time you're digging out through the shorebreak and back to the lineup, or belly-paddling around for better wave position. All this paddling accounts for my legendary upper-body strength, which makes me an awesome physical specimen despite my shortness and legendary asthma.

hugged me and kissed me on both cheeks and gave me this parting advice: "Harmon, you're a mature adult. I trust you and I have no doubts in my mind you'll behave like a responsible young man while I'm gone. Just be sure you check the stove every time you leave the house in case you should leave a burner on and take off your motorcycle boots before you walk in the house, keep the kitchen counters spotless, remember to separate the whites from the coloreds and turn off the faucet behind the washing machine after every wash, lock the door behind you whenever you leave, I've left salad fixings in the crisper so you won't forget to eat your leafy greens, take your MegaMix[36] and get some roughage every day for your stool, don't open the door to strangers and work hard on your doctoral (she pronounced it doctóral, heavy on the "o," which always sounded to me like a species of mucus-solvent allergy medication) thesis, I haven't seen you working on your schoolwork[37] much lately, don't forget you've got a deadline, I've left Ruth's number for you by the phone and you know the emergency numbers, my will is in the safe deposit, I'll call tonight to let you know I got there safe."

I let her words wash over me like a Novocaine shower;

[36] Ma is big on vitamins. She's convinced that taking a combination of the trace mineral Germanium and a recently discovered nutrient called Co-enzyme Q-170 is going to take her well into her hundreds, and she swears by a potent multivitamin-mineral supplement called MegaMix, whose only noticeable effect is that it turns my urine a healthy gold against the powder-blue porcelain of our decorator toilet bowl—the school colors of UCLA, by the way.

[37] Whenever Ma talks about my Ph.D. thesis, she uses the same language with which she used to talk about my math worksheets in fourth grade. This makes sense; I used to avoid doing my math worksheets, too, usually by faking a bellyache. Nowadays such scholastic dodging requires more ingenuity taken to greater lengths, such as chasing after baddies who stole your antique books.

accustomed though I am to my mother's neurotic soliloquies, they never fail to have a numbing effect on my vitals. Still, her heart has always been in the right place, her only abuse that of doting excessively, and I couldn't fault her that impulse since I was currently guilty of it, too, with Lissa. I gave my mother a real hug and kissed her cheek. "Have a great time, Ma," I said. "I promise I won't burn down the house."

"That's something," she said. She kissed me again and beetled down the concourse despite being a good half hour early.

With the elation I used to experience as a teenager when the folks would go on vacation, leaving me alone for a week of all-night poker games, frozen pizza, little imported Schimmelpennick cigars and Cinzano highballs in front of Johnny Carson, I rolled down the windows of the Volvo, slipped on my shades even though the sun was already down, and ran the needle of the AM-FM up to K-Jizz at the top of the dial. Usually they play decent acoustic stuff, lots of bebop and cool classics—Bird, Monk, Miles, Trane before he got too weird. But every once in a while they slip in some overproduced pop-fusion, I suppose because corporate marketing execs can't help pandering to the malignant multidenominational cult that is mass taste. The tune currently being aired was one of these, a turdlet of predigested piano-bar schmaltz that all the radio stations were playing. The song's hook, which went, "We're lost . . . in a masqueraaaaade," along with some other instantly forgettable lyrics, burrowed deep into the subconscious, where like some nocturnal arachnoid it took up residence, spinning out infinite loops of fatuous chorusing. Undaunted by the unfortunate selection that Chance had punched up from the empyreal jukebox, I cranked the tune real loud anyway and, drowning out the lead singer's sappy Vegas lounge-act phrasings, soulfully sang my own liberation in a universe of infinite possibility and a house vacated by my mother.

"We're lost . . . in a masqueraaaaade," I sang over and over, as dusk turned the sky redder and redder.

# ♣ SEVENTEEN ♣

While the brat teenager that slouches and revs inside my breast still loves the Euro-groovy image conjured by Schimmelpennick cigars and dark Italian vermouth, the rest of me—the Real Harmon, if you will—must be maturing, because smoke and alcohol both nauseate me in a way neither did before I turned twenty-four. This seems a shade young for the metabolic change-of-life, but when the first symptoms of your mortality drop by like distant relatives with overstuffed suitcases and plans for a protracted visit, you can resent their intrusion bitterly or accept them with humility as I do. Entropy always has the house advantage anyway and will grind you down in the end, so why fight it, is my motto. Besides: Humility, which usually comes cello-wrapped with the wisdom of age, is a much more useful quality learned young, when its application can save you from bragging in bars and having stool frames bent over your skull.

At least gambling still agrees with me. So when I got home after leaving Ma at the airport, I went directly to the front house, made a dozen calls and rounded up enough players for a medium-stakes game. These days we played

Pineapple, a high-low variant of Texas Hold-'em, especially nerve-shattering because you need an eight or lower to qualify for taking half the pot with a low hand, and if nothing but high cards come up on the flop—which happens frequently—your low cards are rendered worthless. You can pay plenty to see those last cards turn, and you often do.

Playing hand after hand of Pineapple, you lose all sense of time as you fall into a rhythm of dealing, betting, splitting up pots, scarfing munchies, shuffling up the spare deck, kibitzing. As the game got under way, table talk was sparse and superficial, the way guys like it. We played a few hands and heard from Joe Lineholt, a local marriage counselor and hypnotist, and a sensible man; the less generous in our circle call him deadly boring. Last time I was sunk deep in the self-loathing that is the dominion of all A.B.D.[38] grad students, Thrasher consoled me, "Don't feel so bad, Harmon. Just think, you could have been born Joe Lineholt," and I did feel somewhat cheered. Tonight Joe spoke in glowing praise of his old Honda Civic's engine, and everyone yawned and agreed with Joe that a hundred thousand miles without so much as a valve job is a miracle, right up there with virgin birth and pasteurized cheese spread.

A few more rounds, and Chainsaw Chuck Selvy asked me about college girls, as he always does. Chainsaw is a tree surgeon's assistant, a city kid who has assumed the persona of the outdoorsman and plays it to the hilt—untrimmed beard, plaid shirt, cracked and callused palms. Sometimes I imagine he spends hours working on his hands to achieve that weatherbeaten look, making tiny lacerations with an X-acto knife, painting in the dark

[38] Stands for All But Dissertation, a designation they assign to doctoral candidates who have long since finished their coursework and are terminally enmired in research, like waterfowl in an oilspill.

ridges with liquid eyeliner, then tinting the whole hand with brown shoe polish. A practicing Zen Buddhist for enough years to call it something more than a passing phase, Chainsaw is devoted to his meditation. But he's also intensely competitive, an inveterate gambling addict, and the dirtiest backgammon player I've ever met. He never cheats, but his cries of "Kill, kill!" while he rolls the dice, or "Geek, geek!" while I'm trying to come in off the bar, always throw me into into a pre-ulcerous dither, so that I calculate odds inaccurately and lose big. I rarely play with him anymore, because I don't take losing well, and I can't afford any more citations for speeding or reckless driving, which is what I do when I'm mad. Chainsaw brings this same competitiveness to his spirituality, so that Zen in his hands takes on a militancy that I'm sure contradicts the pure intention of the religion.

But as overzealous as he is, Chainsaw is sexually repressed to an even greater degree, which is why he always asks me about girls. He harbors this soft-porn stereotype of college teachers as having unlimited erotic access to legions of willing coeds, an attitude I find so censurable that sometimes I can't resist unsettling him with preposterous yarns about campus perversion. Tonight I told him about Dana DiSipio, lithe, brown, and nineteen: ". . . she shows up at my office after hours with a rough draft of her persuasive essay on improving dorm food. She's wearing a light, low-cut cotton T-shirt with little red and pink hearts all over it, no bra, and when she bends over to examine her thesis statement with me, she puts one hand on my right thigh, right here . . ." I put my hand on Chainsaw's leg, three inches above the knee.

Chainsaw's cheeks turned a homophobic pink, and he slapped my hand away. "Yeah, so . . . ?" he said with hoarse impatience.

". . . so then," I continued, taking my time, "she

showed her dusky breasts, swaying ever so gently from the momentum of leaning forward, an unmistakable invitation to sex . . ."

Actually, the story is true up to this point. Dana DiSipio did in fact come to my office, close the door and dangle herself in front of me. But my overriding sense of propriety, my distaste for abuses of power in any form, and my staunch professionalism—not to mention my fear of being drummed out of the university on charges of sexual harassment[39]—caused me to roll my chair out of eyeshot of her swelling bosom and out of reach of her lovely long fingers . . . for which missed opportunity I still kick myself sometimes when I think back on it.

For Chainsaw I invented a more primally satisfying conclusion to the story, one in which Dana lifted the T-shirt slowly over her head and stretched herself out like a cat waiting to be scratched, which tightened her breasts against her ribcage and made her nipples harden and protrude, an unsubtle gesture that she followed directly by lifting her little pleated skirt and simultaneously bending over my desk while resting one of her forearms, fragrant and glistening with coconut tanning oil, on my open gradebook, and so on. In response to my ripe invention Chainsaw's eyes got big, and this time his face turned the bright red of Dana DiSipio's fictive panties. He blithered, "Shit, some guys have all the luck."

Although the cliché didn't apply to me in the case of Dana DiSipio, and although I doubted its validity in universal terms, I couldn't argue with its applicability to certain guys—myself included —who from time to time find

[39] This would create a scandal, which would find its way onto front pages of supermarket tabloids, "PRIAPIC PROF PRODS PUPIL," ruining me professionally, making my mother a laughingstock, and rendering it even more difficult in the future for me to interest women in visiting my studio for maternally interrupted sex.

themselves swept up in occasionally prolonged but always fugitive lucky streaks. I therefore agreed with him. "Some guys do," I said.

More cards and more small talk, and around five-thirty, as a peach- and champagne-hued morning light was breaking over the pittisporum hedge, the winners started suggesting we break it up. Thrasher was the big winner. He was up about three hundred but too burnt out from pot and beer and no sleep to do his usual gleeful gloating. I had played my usual steady, clear-headed game and was up a modest sixty-five bucks, not counting the twenty or so I collected by raking a quarter from each pot in the first hours of the game, to pay for beer for the guys, organic apple juice for myself, frozen pizza, pretzels, tortilla chips and Oreos. The losers were reluctant to leave and grumbled their demand that we deal once more around the table. It's customary at the end of a poker game to give the losers a chance to recoup their losses; the losers, in a frantic effort to make big money in the limited time remaining, always play wildly and lose more—which is probably why the custom caught on in the first place. So we agreed: one more round.

On the last hand of the night, I was holding a ten-seven-six, all clubs. The flop came down ace-trey-nine, one club. I discarded the ten, which gave me long-shot possibilities in both directions; I could make a straight or a flush for high, and, if I got real lucky, the last two cards could make me low. Normally, given my fairly disciplined, by-the-odds style at the poker table, I wouldn't have stayed with such marginal possibilities (even if I made the seven-six low, it could be easily beaten, and the chances of making a straight or flush were poor) but it was the last hand after all, and betting after the flop was tentative, so I let my brat teenager talk me into sticking around: "Come on, man, just one more card, think of the rush if you make that seven-six stand up, their minds will be blown, besides you can always trash the hand after the next card and you'll still be up sixty bucks, but you could jam up the straight and sweep both ways and end the night up a hundred or more. It will be *fun!"*

The next card, fourth street, came up a deuce of clubs, which busted my straight possibilities but kept alive my chances for a flush and a low. At seeing the deuce, Chainsaw said, "All *Right!"*[40] and came out betting the limit. Joe, consistently stony-faced, raised. I called. So did Thrasher. Chainsaw said, "Let's rock and roll," and re-raised. Joe raised him back, and Thrasher and I found ourselves in the middle, reluctantly calling raise after raise because we were in too deep now to do otherwise—the standard rationalization of the poker damned.

One more card to flop: the River card, maker of fortunes and dasher of dreams. It came up a trey of hearts, which busted my flush but made my seven-six low. Not a hand to be proud of, given the low cards on the table (any one of the players could use those same cards for a much better low), but adequate to call. Chainsaw said, "All *Right!"* and came out bet the limit, as usual.

"Fucking River card," Thrasher grumped. "I'm drawing to the nut and the River pairs me, as fucking usual." He tossed his hand in amongst the dead cards.

"We wouldn't be here if there wasn't any River," Chainsaw said, a Zennish sentiment if ever there was one. "That's where the gamble is."

"Fuck the River," Thrasher said.

"Let's see where the gamble is," Joe said. "I raise."

Feeling like an unloved mongrel being led by the pound attendant to the sleep tank, I called reluctantly. The pot

---

40 "All *Right!"* is Chainsaw's version of the traditional poker face. He always acts as though he's ecstatic over whatever cards come up, so that you never know whether they really helped him or not.

was in the neighborhood of three hundred dollars, by far the largest of the game.

The table was quiet now. Even Chainsaw shut up. Joe turned over a pair of aces which, along with the ace on the table, gave him trip aces, a decent high hand but no threat to my low. I had only Chainsaw to worry about.

Joe looked confident that he had the high won, and when Chainsaw slowly turned over his cards, a deuce and a trey, I was so mortified at seeing two low cards that I failed for an instant to realize that his cards were paired. He had a full house of treys and deuces, which beat Joe for high, and I had the only low hand, a lock winner. But in that instant of mortification, Chainsaw's full house didn't register with me. I was so angry at myself for having played the hand like some pitiful compulsive loser who needs to prove how consistently bad his fortune is by putting himself in the most hopeless situations and then giving God the finger when he loses, that I tossed my winning hand into the discards.

Immediately realizing my error, I groveled among the dead cards to retrieve my winning hand. The others watched, amused, and Chainsaw dryly quoted our house rule that once any card touches the discards, it's dead. I knew the rules, but I kept on digging anyway, throwing dead cards in the air until I found my seven and six, which I waved in their faces, shouting maniacally, "See, I did have the lock winner, the biggest pot of the night and I should have dragged half, I dropped a hundred and fifty bucks on that hand, fuck life and everything thereto appertaining . . ."

As Chainsaw raked the whole pot, he commented, "Nice hand, Harmon," and then the kicker: "Some guys have all the luck."

My friends filed out, everyone thanking me for being such a generous host. On the brick walkway Chainsaw turned and said, "I'd stay away from sharp objects tonight, if I were you, Harmon. You probably shouldn't operate any heavy machinery for a while, either." His laughter faded as I shut the front door.

Alone with the dark repressed rage that consumes me whenever I subvert my own good gaming sense with an appallingly dumb move—it takes just one intemperate minute to destroy the work of sober hours—I closed the front door weakly and dragged off in the direction of the back house. The dining room looked more like the snack area at the Lakers' home venue in Inglewood than the elegant, professionally decorated eating area of a well-to-do laundry tycoon's widow. Table and floor were littered with candy wrappers, pizza rinds, beer bottles and cans, sunflower seed husks, discarded Oreo cookies (the first sign that Thrasher is stoned out of control is when he starts scraping the creme filling out of the middle of the Oreo with his teeth while carelessly tossing away the chocolate cookie parts). I ignored the mess. No sense cleaning up one mess and then making another the next day, and then having to clean it, too. I'd do one major cleanup of all the accumulated messes just before Ma got back.

It was pointless to think about sleeping. If I go to bed immediately after losing at cards, I fall asleep just fine, but after an hour or two I drift into a kind of febrile hallucinatory state just below consciousness, in which I'm playing the same disastrous hand over and over, always looking at the same lousy cards, enduring the echoing laughter of the winners, and I eventually wake up soaked in sweat and more exhausted than before I went to sleep. After a bad beat at cards I have to wind down slowly, and so this morning I anticipated a little TV—maybe watch an early-morning exercise program to simulate tiring myself out physically—read some Browning criticism to numb the brain, stuff myself with mini-donuts, and ride the hypoglycemic blood sugar curve from peak excitation into exhaustion and sleep.

I unlocked and opened the door to the studio. Morning was hurling sunlight through the window in sharp javelin-points, and my eyes hurt. I squinted and started toward the window, intending to roll down the rice paper and bamboo blind which I had backed with black plastic sheeting, to maximize the darkness during my sleeping hours. I was in mid-stride, a few steps into the room, when the overpowering smell of natural gas hit me with the same stunning effect as walking face-on into a thick plate-glass window. I stopped, momentarily immobilized, confused more by the incongruity of my living space being filled with deadly fumes than by any toxic effect of the fumes themselves. Shaking myself into sensibility, I backed outside, where I took long gulps of relatively unpolluted air (this *is* L.A., after all, and you take what you can get by way of fresh air), hyperventilating the same way I do when I'm paddling out through shorebreak and I get caught inside by a monster set of waves: The harder and faster you force yourself to breathe, the longer you can hold your breath as you roll under the onrushing wall of churning whitewater. I took a last big lungful of air (actually, it was two last big lungfuls that I took, since I've had neither lung surgically removed yet), held it and ran back inside, throwing open windows and drapes. When I got to the kitchen, I could hear clearly the source of the gas: a loud hiss coming from the little four-burner range next to the sink.

Behind the range, among cobwebs and greasy dust clumps, I could make out two shiny open ends of brass tubing which had, until today, been my stove's gas line. The pipe had obviously not snapped loose on its own, but had been cut neatly, probably with a hacksaw.

They were trying to kill me again.

# ◆ EIGHTEEN ◆

Every week from ages eleven through nineteen I went to Dr. Spence's office for my allergy shot. I spent so much of my adolescence there that Shirley, the registered nurse who administered the shots, became the closest thing I've ever had to a godparent. Her hair was graying when my allergies were first diagnosed, a homogeneous white by the time I discharged myself from Dr. Spence's care, and her sage counseling helped me overcome many of my childhood fears, including that of climbing the ropes in junior high gym class. She told me, "Everyone will warn you, 'Don't look down,' but if you worry about not looking down, you'll look down and then you'll fall. Don't listen to them. While you're going up the rope, *think of a cow*, and don't think of anything else." Fresh out of grammar school, I was already humiliated by a Vitalis-fed acne condition localized at the forehead and by the Bum-Bl-B multi-color striped T-shirts Ma dressed me in; not being able to get up the ropes would have been one disgrace too many. I had seen other boys, fat ones usually, each stalled a few feet off the gray, cotton-batted gymnastics floormat and whopping around like gaffed tuna while the hoots and jeers of the rest of the class set the hangarlike gymnasium to reverberating. I was willing to try anything to avoid that ignominy, even a crackpot suggestion like Shirley's. As it turned out, picturing the sadly vacant brown eyes of a veteran Holstein did distract me enough to allow me to shinny my way up. At the top I touched the metal saucer with a flamboyant clang and then slid down fast, with an exhilarating sense of relief and a satisfying friction-burn on my hands. Shirley's lay psychology turned out to work so well that as a grown-up I still meditate on a cow's face, or Shirley's, when I'm engaged in any perilous activity, from surfing to motocross to foreplay.

Dr. Spence, Shirley's boss, makes a fortune from the thousands of wheezers, snufflers, hawkers, drippers, honkers, and snorters who parade through his office every Thursday—"shot day"—the theory behind the injections being that if you are exposed to the pure protein of an irritant enough times, and in increased concentrations, you will build up an immunity. This theory may work with house dust, cat dander and cheese mold, but unfortunately it doesn't carry over into other areas of human experience, because if it did, I would get used to having my life threatened by enemies to whom I've never even been introduced. Fear of getting murdered seems to work the opposite way. The more times I'm confronted with the pure protein of my own nonexistence, the more worried I get. Right now I was plenty worried.

Someone had tried to gas me in my own house, and the implications were dreadfully clear: Shadowy beings were assailing me, and the fiasco on the freeway wasn't a one-shot *grand-geste* calculated merely to scare me off the trail of *Doctor Syntax*. Still holding what was left of my breath, and dizzy more from a rising sense of mortal terror than from a lack of oxygen, I went outside, exhaled hard and got my breathing back to normal—or at least to the rapid panting that's normal for any small mammal being hunted down by a pack of baying, bloodspoor-delirious hounds. I had no idea where the studio's main gas valve was, but I poked around outside until I found it, in the closetlike enclosure that held the water heater. I got an adjustable wrench from the toolbox in the garage and wrestled with the valve until it finally budged. Once loosened it turned easily, and the gas was off. I left the door and all the windows open so that the studio could air out, and I went back into the main house.

I reflected. A message was settling out of the chaos like grounds in a cup of joe: I was a worse flop as a detective than I was as a scholar. I had a whole slew of clues, even a prime suspect in Sterne, yet I was no closer to finding my books than I was the day they got stolen, and I was *much* closer to a grotesque and untimely death. Going it alone on a few leads and blind instinct, I was getting nowhere; or if I was getting somewhere (and I must have blundered onto something, or shadowy beings wouldn't be assailing me) I had no idea where it was I had gotten. Even though my experience after the theft at Ernst's had soured me on putting my fate in the hands of blasé authorities, and despite my earlier mistreatment at the hands of the L.A.P.D.,[41] I saw no other alternative. I touch-dialed the 911 emergency number, and related the story of the gas-filled studio to the police dispatcher. She didn't sound impressed but said a car would be around soon.

I sat waiting on the quarry-tiled front porch of the big house. The day was already heating up, and the glare of the sun clawed at my eyes. The air was dry. It was ragweed season, which made my postnasal drip worse than usual. I cleared my throat and coughed some yellow-streaked, tapiocoid phlegm into my hand. I rolled it around in my

[41] Cf. Chapter 19.

fingers listlessly until it became a pea-sized bolus—a gross and indelicate image, I know, but who among us has not fingered her own snot at least once? I examined this rhinologic artifact as though it might, like a murky ball of quartz crystal, unfold truths about the human condition—perhaps how to cheat disease and decay out of their ineluctable due. It didn't. I flicked it into the bushes. A black-and-white rolled up in front of the house, and a cop got out of the car.

He looked the classic cardboard neanderthal bull, narrow eyes under a massive brow ridge, a vulgar, saucefleem complexion, upturned piggy-nose with a big knot of cartilage at the end of it, and airbrake ears. His face, especially the angle of the nose, gave him the appearance of a wise guy. As he mounted the brick steps I imagined what it would be like to carry around a face like that: If your appearance makes people expect you to be an asshole, they treat you like an asshole, and you probably eventually become an asshole. I expected this cop to be an asshole, and today I was too tired, scared and mad to have any sympathy for assholes.

I stood up. He extended his hand and spoke in a voice so gentle, so incongruous with his repulsive appearance, that for a moment I had the impression that he was a medium through which someone else was speaking, like a ventriloquist's dummy or one of those trance-channelers you see on cable TV sometimes. "Mr. Nails?" he said pleasantly. "I'm Sergeant Freitag."

I gave his hand a quick pump and quipped, ". . . and all you want is the facts, right?"

A look of martyred forbearance came over the wise-guy face, and he said, "What can I do for you?"

I said, "Oh, I get it, 'To Protect and to Serve.' How about a pound of protection to go, a little mustard, hold the mayo, on pumpernickel?"

"You did phone the police . . . ?"

"No big thing, just a minor annoyance, it irritates me when someone tries to turn my apartment into a gas chamber."

"Can we take a look?"

"Sure, but don't bother to dust for prints. I'm sure he was wearing gloves again."

Sergeant Freitag looked puzzled at this allusion to a former crime of which he could have no knowledge, but he had obviously dealt with hysterical citizens before—even brilliantly sarcastic ones like me. He made an "after-you" gesture with his arm, and I led him around back by way of the hedge path.

When we reached the studio, I said, "I opened all the windows to air the place out, but believe me, the gas was thick in there when I walked in." I led him into the kitchen. "Here's where the line was cut."

"What time did you get home?"

"I guess about six-thirty this morning. Late poker game. Look, is that really important? Don't you want to look for footprints, so you can waste our time making plaster casts or something?"

"It was already light outside when you came in?"

"Yes . . . and from that I think we can deduce that the sun had risen. Are you considering the sun as one of our prime suspects?"

He looked thoughtful and dodged my shots with dispassionate grace, like an aikido master sidestepping an enraged sot. "No, just a hunch. Which light do you turn on when you come in at night?"

"I hit the wall switch, here, right by the door."

"Which light does it turn on?"

I shrugged and motioned to the art-deco lamp. He crouched and fingered some shards of broken glass in the rug, by the base of the lamp. I hadn't noticed them before.

He peered under the lampshade and said, "Look at this."

I looked. The light bulb was broken. I said, "So . . . ?"

"Whoever broke in wasn't trying to gas you, Mr. Nails. It's an old con's trick. You figure out which lamp your victim will turn on when he comes home at night. You break the bulb in the lamp, exposing the filament. You fill the room with gas. When the victim hits the light switch, *boom*, the gas in the room goes up, and so does the victim."

"Boom," I parroted torpidly.

"That last poker hand may have saved your life, Mr. Nails. An hour sooner, before the sun came up, you probably would have turned on the light first thing . . . which might have been your last thing as well. If there was as much gas as you say in your house, odds are you'd be on your back in the morgue right now."

# ♠  NINETEEN  ♠

A stretch of Sunset Boulevard, just as you get into Beverly Hills, used to be called "Dead Man's Curve" because fatal wrecks happened there all the time. Before they installed the raised center divider, and without the steep velodrome cant it has today, the Curve was a lode of gory still photos, the kind they showed us in high school driver's ed, in an attempt to scare us wild teens into driving safely. Some behavioral hack probably got a federal grant to develop the crude aversive technique, but it had a flaw. We loved the photos. A pretty deb impaled and hung out, like wet wash, on a telephone pole spike; Mom and Dad and Skipper and Babs in what was once a sedan, a scene that more closely resembled a melting chocolate sundae than a family on an outing: We would have paid good money to see this stuff. We never associated the dead meat in the pictures with ourselves.

My father broke the law at the Curve, on a clear, wind-blown fall Sunday, ten years before my high school driver's ed class. We were on our way back from my weekly pony ride by the big Owl Rexall in West Hollywood. I was eating Lik-M-Aid in the back seat, pouring the powder onto the saliva-sticky back of my hand and licking it off slowly, absorbed in the simple joy of its sweet-sour grainy roughness. I wasn't paying attention to Pop's driving. I was barely grown enough to see out the window.

Pop must not have been paying attention, either. He said, "Godfrey Daniel, what now?" when we heard the siren behind us. We pulled off Sunset and onto a side street overhung with trees. Leaves brushed past my window.

A tense silence in the car. The officer's heavy bootfalls outside the car got louder and then stopped. Pop rolled down his window. The cop said, "Can I see your license, sir?"

While he fumbled in his coat, Pop asked, "What did I do, Officer?"

"You crossed the double double line, sir."

I was barely old enough to read my own name, let alone study the motor vehicle code, but it was clear my father had broken someone's rule. Pop had always been the summit of authority figures, and I never considered that someone might hold a rank superior to his. This sudden role reversal hinted at a world without absolutes, where power currents can change direction capriciously, like dry leaves in a santana. The new perspective was unacceptable to me. A kernel-sized "No!" took root in my solar plexus, grew in intensity and pitch as it reached my larynx, blossomed into a ululating drop-drill wail of deafening volume by the time the policeman handed Pop's wallet back to him.

The cop craned his neck around the window-post and winked reassuringly at me, which caused me to go into convulsions and make hideous choking noises. I spilled my Lik-M-Aid on the seat cover.

Undaunted, the cop said, "Wait a second." He dug his hand into a trouser pocket, then reached out and dropped a quarter onto the upholstery beside me. From my vantage point deep in tantrum, the coin seemed somehow out of place, like a tiny silvery cruiser from another galaxy. Its incongruity worked to cut me off in mid-mewl; after all, twenty-five cents can buy you a rapturous afternoon with two Scrooge comics and money left over for a righteous Lik-M-Aid bender. I pocketed the cash.

The cop tore the citation from his tablet and gave it to Pop, who was smiling now, no doubt relieved that he wouldn't have to drive me to the Kaiser clinic to have my voice-box cauterized. As Pop started the Buick's engine, the policeman gave me these final words of advice: "Keep an eye on that father of yours. If he crosses the double double line again, you give me a call. You're on the Department payroll now."

Cheap but effective PR. For two bits the L.A.P.D. had bought themselves a supporter for life . . . or at least until my college days. And even in those progressive, loving early seventies, when everyone wanted to Off The Pigs, I remained a loyal ally of L.A.'s Finest—that is, until the night two redneck patrolmen pulled me out of Thrasher's old Austin America with the multicolored shelf-paper flowers pasted on the door panel, tore apart the interior of my roommate's car looking for drugs, and when they found none, nary a roach nor a seed nor a stem, pushed me hard across the hood, my feet spread-eagled on the asphalt, and said, "What's this?" They had uncovered the small ratchet wrench Thrasher and I used to tighten the Austin's fan belt, which was always slipping.

I started to answer, but one of them said, "Shut up, you little longhair fuck. We found this under the front seat and damn if we're not going to have to cuff you and take you in for grand theft auto and driving with a concealed weapon."

The unprovoked cruelty of my former brothers in crime prevention, along with an instantaneous vision of the holding area at the Garden Heights jail—the reverberating concrete austerity, the appalling acrid stench of vomit and urine in the drunk-tank drains and filthy unshaven churls giggling sadistically as they turned me out—gave rise to an unpremeditated response in me. A kernel-sized "No!" took root as it had years earlier, only on this occasion, by the time it blossomed in my larynx, I was already in convulsions and making hideous choking noises. The incongruity of a full-blown fit of weeping hysteria in a physically mature man daunted the deputies. I must have appeared close to a massive stroke which they'd have to explain to their captain at the station, "Gee whiz, sir, we were just havin' a little fun with the hippie, heh-heh, we never thought he'd go and *die* on us . . ."

They let me up, saying, "Go on, get out of here, you fuckin' little fairy crybaby," and gunned off into the early morning darkness. I sat in the borrowed car and shook, and I shook all the way home.

The socket wrench incident undermined my early reinforcement with the quarter and left me with some new and ugly preconceptions about cops, which still weighed heavily when I met Sergeant Freitag after my bedroom almost blew up. It didn't help that his face was in perpetual grimace, as though he smelled fresh vomitus wherever he went. I fully expected him to whip out his riot stick without warning and start clubbing me across the back of my neck while he accused me of trying to gas myself so that my mother would look incompetent as a child-raiser. But when Sergeant Freitag turned out to be courteous, attentive, soft-spoken, direct and intelligent, my initial attitude toward him changed, as did the way I perceived him physically. Over the course of our initial meeting, his grossly heavy eyebrows took on a fierce and determined set, his upturned nose a noble Saxon pride, his red complexion a ruddy glow. You couldn't help but like the guy, or at least feel sorry for his face.

Sergeant Freitag said, "You'd better start from the beginning. I need as much information as you can give me if we're going to find out who did this. Do you know anyone who would want to kill you . . . or give you a good scare?"

"Can I sit down?" I asked. "This could take a long time."

"Certainly, sit."

I collapsed into a chair by the dining table and shoved aside the pile of books and papers that had been sitting there, untouched, for weeks. Sergeant Freitag commented, "Student?"

"Perpetually," I said wearily. I briefed him on grad school and my problems with my dissertation.

"You're fortunate," he said, "and I don't just mean by avoiding the gas explosion. To have a job where you get paid for reading . . ." he picked up a volume of Browning from the table and held it in front of him, "real literature, like 'The Ring and the Book,' that's a life very few . . ."

"You know Browning?" I broke in, forever amazed at the way life reveals porkers to be poets, but more often vice versa.

"The Victorians are my specialty—or were. I was an English major once, too, and I was planning on going to grad school, but Uncle Sam kind of interrupted my plans."

They nabbed him in '67, he said, and he came back from Southeast Asia three years later with limbs intact but a fractured soul. "I was in what they called 'pacification,' which meant I'd kind of tag along with medics and do what I could to help. I guess they figured since I had been in college before I got drafted, that's pretty close to being a doctor."

"There's a certain logic there."

"Yes indeed, the army is well known for its lucid reasoning. It's called, 'Do it my way, grunt.' We used to ride around in this armored personnel carrier, tearing up paddies and irrigation systems that probably took generations to build with hand labor, and then we'd go and mop up after some major operation—a euphemism for bombing villages with no thought to the lives that might be wasted in the process. I personally never fired a round, never dropped a bomb, but I saw enough suffering to last me several lifetimes, and that kind of experience can't help but have a lasting effect on you. After my discharge I knocked around, tried school for a while, but English didn't get it anymore; it seemed like beauty and truth got burned out of me in those villages and fields. I needed a job, and the Department was recruiting. Overseas I developed skills that kept me alive and relatively sane—composure in the face of chaos, an ability to submit to authority figures without respecting them or taking them seriously, physical stamina, a thick skin and an acute sense of justice—but none of these was marketable or even appreciated back home. Police work was the first thing that demanded some of the same qualities as the service, with one exception: On the streets right and wrong are much clearer than they were in the jungle."

I used to harbor a surpassing contempt for those who had had neither the moral fiber nor the courage to resist our little illegal police action in Vietnam by whatever means necessary—emigrating to Canada or joining the Quakers, going underground or to jail, starving or doing so much acid and crank that one appeared at one's induction physical as a dangerous psychotic unsuitable for the courtly complacencies of the military. But time—along with the compelling firsthand horror stories of returned vets who had been pressed unwillingly or inveigled unwittingly into the war at the urging of over-thirty parents, hawkish politicians, American Legionnaires and media which at best told a highly selective version of the whole story—moderated my rigidly antipathetic stance. Besides, the truth is that I got lucky: Because of my age I missed the government's early, wholesale pooling of young blood by a few years and eventually escaped serving entirely by no other virtue than the number 323—my position in the draft lottery. Freitag, one of the less fortunate many, clearly had not gone over with the intention of killing babies or sacking villages and was genuinely appalled by the senseless violence of which he was forced to become a part; his experience seemed to have sickened and scarred—and also strengthened—him in ways I could scarcely imagine. I therefore extended to Freitag a gesture of empathic fellowship, kidding, "Malaria is probably much rarer in L.A., too."

"True," he said. "Being on the force hasn't been a bad job, but even though my love for literature has gradually regenerated itself, like a fractured limb, I don't have much time for it . . . a real waste. Back when I was in school I even had a topic I wanted to pursue: how the Victorian poets revise the whole idea of truth, a constant reminder that throughout history the poet has been the source of truth, and not history itself. It's like . . ." He stopped and looked around the room, and his eyes lit on my ceramic drinking mug, a cheapie Japanese import decorated with a print in which blue fishes were dissolving into diamond-shaped negative space while diamonds of white negative spaces were evolving into fishes. "It's like . . . do you know Escher?"

"Sure, I'm familiar with his work." I had a blacklight poster of some lizards in a castle when I was younger.

"Browning here," he said, raising one of my library books above his head in the manner of a demolition worker hefting a sledgehammer, "does to the whole notion of truth and authority what an artist like Escher does with fishes." His eyes focused, unblinking, on a point in space somewhere between his face and mine. "The author becomes the truth, and the truth becomes its creator. They are inseparable. You can see the same thing happening all through nineteenth-century letters, and not just in poetry . . ."

Sergeant Freitag was talking nonsense, but it was legitimate academic nonsense, the same pure-land critical speculation with which I had been trying to approach George Eliot for months, and failing. He had seen in Browning the very inseparable melding of aesthetic self-consciousness and art that I was trying to point out in Eliot, and he was extemporizing with a passionate clarity that had long since been wrung out of me, in meetings with the members of my dissertation committee, each of whom had a different philosophical slant. Sergeant Freitag may have lived through firefights in Vietnam, but he had not yet been used as a battleground in departmental holy wars, trampled and scorched by factional scholarly crusaders, and so he yearned for nothing more than to pursue the very life I have come to detest.

I observed, "Strange situation. Fraught with ironies. You want to do research more than detective work, and I'm doing detective work to avoid literary research."

"You're doing a damn poor job of it, too, if you don't mind my saying. At least Browning won't get me killed."

"Give him time," I said. I wondered for a moment if Freitag's Vietnam rap was a subtle psychological technique he used routinely to distract crime victims from their hysteria, in the same way that a good parent might use an Aesop's fable to soothe a child awakened by nightmare. Whether a conscious ploy on his part or not, it worked: My extremities had stopped their violent trembling, and I was able to carry on a conversation without having continually to oppose a surging tidal bore of bile and gastric juice in my gorge. "Look," I said, " I'll make you a deal. You help me out of this mess I'm in, and I'll help you get into grad school. I'm a powerful man in academic circles."

"I can imagine," he commented skeptically. He reflected for a moment. "I don't know, it's been five years since I got

back, maybe I'm ready for a career change now. We'll see . . .
but first, let's get your life saved."

"Admirable *imprimis!*" I exclaimed, showing off the delightful inflated vocabulary that grad school imparts. "I
know I'm not going to be able to sleep at all tonight, knowing they might come back."

"First of all, I wouldn't worry about this place getting
hit again. It's extremely unlikely that they'd try anything
here, because they'll assume we have the place under
surveillance."

"Surveillance?" I said, liking the sound of the word. It
had a certain Francophonic austerity, connoting anti-fascist
underground workers with a romantic commitment to
righteousness, or gendarmes with crisp uniforms and no-
nonsense attitudes. "You're really going to do that for me?" I
was feeling better about the cops all the time, almost ready
to put a "Support your local . . ." on the bumper of the family Volvo.

"No. Unfortunately, we don't have the manpower for
that."

"Oh," I said with disappointment infusing my voice.
Scratch the bumper sticker. "So what happens in the 'extremely unlikely' event they do come back, what do I do
then? Check out that window, the frame is all bent. Anyone could stick a hand in there. There's no latch left. My
phone's right next to the window, so if some murderer was
right outside he'd be able to hear me call."

"Common sense," Freitag said. "Just dial nine-one-one
and then whisper into the phone."

"I'm scared they're not going to be outside, they're
going to be inside already."

"You might stack up some Coke bottles or something
like that by the window. They'd have to make so much
noise getting in, over the stereo and everything, they'd
wake you up."

"Terrific. Coke bottles. Is this the latest advance in crime prevention technology?"

"No, but with a place as small as yours, a couple piles of bottles usually work better than those electronic setups people pay thousands of bucks for. Criminals can disable an alarm system with one snip of a wire, if they're pros. And your criminals are definitely pros."

"You have a way of putting a guy at ease, Sarge. I guess I'd better start drinking Coke."

"It's the real thing," said Sergeant Freitag.

# ♥ TWENTY ♥

Beyond his ticky-tack soda-pop security measures, Sergeant Freitag had little to offer in the way of immediate plans. There wasn't much to go on, he admitted, with the information and evidence we had so far. He said that I should continue my conversations with Lissa in order that I might find out more about the Sterne-Syntax connection, and then, when we had gathered as much information as possible, we should take the offensive. "It's like with snipers in the jungle. If you sit around waiting for them to come out into the open, eventually they'll pick you off when you're relaxed and off your guard. So you have to figure out their movement patterns, and then flush them out before they get you first."

"I thought you never shot at anybody."

"I didn't, but I hung out with plenty of people who did. They would have been dead otherwise."

Besieged as I was by murderous absences on whom I was impotent to vent my fury, the prospect of going on the attack appealed to my sense of *soddisfazione* if not my sense of propriety. Medical research has found vengeance to be the best prevention against malignant intestinal polyps—

which, Liz tells me, are just concentrations of repressed rage—and becoming aggressive was certainly better than waiting around for someone to terminate my marvelous existence. Besides, Pineapple Hold-'em teaches this lesson: After careful, disciplined preparation, when you combine ruthlessness with blithe abandon, you turn the odds in your favor. I needed some favorable odds in a hurry; I'd be dead otherwise, too.

Sergeant Freitag said I should be in touch in a few days and, after I thanked him, left. I went back into the big house, locked the windows, bolted the doors and fell asleep on the living room sectional, with half-formed images of myself, Mafioso-style wolfgun resting in the crook of an elbow, holding hooded assailants at bay and blasting their knees to Spam if they so much as twitched. I slept fitfully the rest of the morning and all afternoon.

I woke up feeling less than well-rested. I nuked a frozen burrito for dinner, washed it down with orange juice, then drove to Ernst's, to talk to Lissa. A cold fog was rolling in, thick as attic insulation. My headlights illuminated a few feet of asphalt in front of the Volvo. Ahead, the beams diffused into a milky glow. I was struck by the insular mobility of that singular twentieth-century artifact, the automobile, a cavity of engine-warmed hospitality and bucket-seated civilization easing along through what in ancient times would have been perceived as hostile, impenetrable, Grendelish mists. I came to a stop at the light at Twenty-sixth and San Vicente, by the Brentwood Country Mart, where I used to buy *Mad* magazines as a teen. At the edge of the cloud bank, a few miles from the ocean, the fog was breaking up, exposing occasional patches of clear night. Even though the low grayish clouds were blowing by fast, custom made my mind see them as stationary, and behind them the moon looked for a moment as if it were running out to sea. Thus distracting myself with mind games and optical illusions, I made it to Echo Park without once thinking myself into a panic over the ugly truth: In the short time since I had last talked with Lissa, the stakes of the game had been jacked up profoundly. If there had been any doubt that my life was on the line, now there was none.

The front door opened as far as the chain would allow. A slice of Lissa's face appeared in the opening. Music, only by the very loosest definition of the word, was coming from the back of the house. It was a draggy funk-fusion number, seemingly performed by a congress of eunuchs whose shrieking penetrated to the marrow and resonated there sickeningly,

> Takin' it to the streets,
> Takin' it to the streeeeeets.

Still peering through the crack between door and frame Lissa said, "Harmon." She sounded surprised and not over-joyed to see me.

I cried out with a forced breeziness, "I'm home, dear. Throw your arms around the best thing to come into your life since the Lesbian poets."

She didn't fling the door open and embrace me, but she did after some hesitation unlatch the chain. Passing through the narrows between Lissa and the doorjamb, I jerked my face toward hers in an awkward attempt at a kiss, which she dodged by turning her face deftly away, leaving me to suck hair. Alert to the subtleties of human interaction, I commented, "You seem a little aloof." Under-state the obvious, expose the implicit.

"Oh no, everything's fine," she assured me. In the back-ground an amplified bass continued to pound out the monotonous, rhumbaesque beat, and above the slow fender-thumping and sausage-sizzling of studio-reprocessed drums Lissa said, "Ernst's in back, resting."

"Knowing Ernst's intellect and taste I would have guessed Debussy, not the Doobies or whoever does that lame tune," I said.

"Me too. But you know what they say about taste."

"I make it a point never to listen to them."

"Who?"

"See, you *are* out of it."

"I'm just a little distracted. I'm in the middle of some research."

"Good. For a minute I was afraid you'd just used me for sex and then dumped me."

"We never had sex, Harmon."

"Are you sure? I guess I'm a little distracted, too."

"I'm sure."

"How far have we gotten?"

"We sat on the floor together."

"And . . . ?"

"And that's all. We decided to wait. Listen, Harmon, I'm kind of busy right now. Can I help you with something?"

A fine fare-thee-well: First Jeannie Kraepelien splits for San Jose; then my father ups and dies on me; then Brenny leaves, taking custody of my little cuties Enzo and Rashid; next she refuses to let me visit the kittens or take them to the beach; then my mother splits for Tucson, leaving me to heat my TV dinners for myself; and now this unexpected coldness from Lissa. No wonder Liz says I have unresolved feelings of abandonment. I complained, "'Can I help you with something?' What is this, the Campus Casuals department at Bullocks?" I seized Lissa by the shoulders and mock-shook her. "You're holding back, shweetheart," I said, trying to do Bogie but failing because of my adenoids, "and I want to know why. Don't make me get rough with you."

Unexpectedly, Lissa broke. She wept quietly, running her hands back through her hair, as though stroking a frightened child. Since I had come to cheer Lissa, not dismay her, I started to apologize abjectly, but she interrupted, "I know you wouldn't threaten me, Harmon. But it's been pretty tense around here lately, and no one's feeling particularly safe."

Recalling viscerally the horrors and degradations of the original break-in, aborted rape, and theft of *Doctor Syntax*, I asked, "They didn't come back, did they?"

"No, but somebody has been doing . . . we've been getting messages."

"Messages?" I imagined cryptic warnings burned into exposed ceiling joists by nameless, faceless preternatural wraiths, or omens channeled through toasters and other small appliances.

"Phone calls. Threatening ones."

"Oh, phone calls," I said in a tone of lightsome dismissal. "Probably just pranks, completely random," I conjectured. "I used to make them all the time, for fun. Once I called a meat packing house and had them ship a side of beef to a teacher I didn't like."

"These didn't sound like junior-high pranks."

"Neither was the beef. I did it last year. I wonder what old RearWind did with all that flank steak."

"Harmon, this is no joke. The last one went something like, 'We put a good scare into that punk Nails. Next time he won't be so lucky.' What did he mean by 'good scare'?"

With some reluctance I told her about the gas-filled house, the broken light bulb and the possibility that, but for an all-night poker game, my mortal remains could be part of the studio's wallpaper right now. "But it was strictly an amateur job," I concluded. "I'm still in the way, just as much as ever." I tried to sound chirpy for Lissa's sake, but to tell the truth, all this talk of lethal admonitions brought my former dread back up into my mouth, with a taste like vinegar and green chili.

"My stepfather may be a lot of things, but he's not an

amateur. If he's involved in this, if you've somehow stepped on the toes of Laurence Sterne and the Combist League, that cavalier attitude is going to get you hurt." She paused. "They've even threatened Ernst. The man on the phone said if I didn't stay away from you and forget about *Doctor Syntax*, they'd . . ." She stepped back from me, interposing a volume of negative space that seemed somehow inflated, as though an institutional-sized mound of particularly yeasty dough had risen up between us. "Harmon, you can't come around here anymore," Lissa said. "Not until all this is settled."

An unfamiliar sensation washed over me, a wave of something like the selflessness parents describe when they talk about protecting their kids. Even my own mild-mannered father once told me, "I'd fight a buzzsaw bare-handed before I'd let anyone hurt you." At the time I thought he was just grandstanding for my affection, but now that Lissa was in danger I understood. This is love, I marveled. It must be, for me to forgo swooning at the prospect of an early grave, or for me to abstain from pouting at being sent away. My uncharacteristic maturity dazed me. I heard myself agree with Lissa, in a measured, resonant, reassuring grown-up's voice, "You're right. Until I get Sterne busted and out of commission, I don't want to put you and Ernst in jeopardy."

Lissa looked relieved, and some of the old warmth returned to her regard.

"There's this cop," I said, still sounding uncommonly adult. "His name is Freitag and he knows what's going on. I'll ask him to look in on you. He's a good man, even if he does like Browning. You can trust him." She nodded.

I stopped on the threshold. "But before I go," I said, "I need to know a few things. Like what the fuck is a Combist League?"

# ♣ TWENTY-ONE ♣

We stood on the porch, the front door open, the bug-repellent porch light haloing Lissa in golden light while at the same time keeping moths off us. Lissa leaned against the doorframe and, exhaling forcibly, puffed out her lips with her breath. "The Combist League," she said and then stopped as though gathering energy for some task that required superhuman strength, just as that poor sod in mythology—the one who had to keep pushing a boulder up a hill for all eternity—must have done before he put his shoulder to it. "It's kind of complicated," she began. "The Combists are something between a satanic cult and the Jane Austen Society, but closer to a cult."

"That's reassuring," I said. "Last year I took a whole quarter of Jane Austen, and if I learned anything in that class it's that if you spend too much time with them, Austen enthusiasts will sparkle you to death with their conversation. I'll take my chances with devil-worshipers any day."

"You wouldn't be so flippant if you knew anything about the Combist League," Lissa said ominously.

"I don't know anything about them because you still haven't told me anything about them," I responded in a confrontational though by no means hostile tone. "All I know so far is that they don't read Jane Austen, which doesn't tell me much. Nobody reads Jane Austen unless they have to."

With lips still pursed Lissa exhaled again and more sharply, so that I was reminded for a moment of the sound orcas make when they clear out their breathing apparatus upon surfacing.[42] "The Combist League," Lissa fragmentized for a second time, still searching for a firm handhold on the obviously precipitous and crumbly face of the topic. She tilted her head back, resting it against the painted wood of the doorframe, and exhaled yet again, this time with more of a weary sigh than a cetaceous blowhole-blast. "Have you heard of Laurence Sterne?" she asked.

I gave her a puzzled look. "Weren't we just talking about Sterne?"

"Not my stepfather. The writer."

"Oh, *that* Laurence Sterne. Sure, like I said, every English undergrad has to take a novel survey class, and *Tristram Shandy*'s always included in the list of required books. I forget most of what it was about but it was pretty funny, which in itself is rare for old novels; most of them are like four-hundred-page soap operas. I remember there was a blank page in there somewhere, which broke up to monotony, and some pictures, and—oh, yeah—I think a

---

[42] I've observed this phenomenon close-up, by the way, and not from the bleachers at OceanWorld, either. I was minding my own business, waiting for waves at Brockton Point in Santa Carnera, when a school of killer whales, each the size of a full-grown Caddy, surfaced not ten yards from where I was sitting in the water. This gave me an adrenaline-charged start such as I'd never known. As I'm sure you've heard already, killer whales have been unjustly named and are as harmless to people as house cats unless you hit them on the snout with a baseball bat, which only an idiot or a bush-leaguer with a death wish would do, but their dorsal (Continued on next page.)

window comes down on the hero's dick."

"No wonder you're having trouble with your dissertation. You don't always pick the most . . . relevant details to remember."

"I can't help it. It's like a disease."

"You love it. It makes you feel as though you're different, special. Unique."

Ordinarily I won't let anyone get away with using poop-butt dimestore psychoanalysis on me—even uncannily accurate poop-butt dimestore psychoanalysis as this probably was. I knew, however, that any protest by me would occasion lengthy discussion of my alleged developmental strictures, and I didn't have time for that tonight: I needed to find out what I could about Sterne and the Combists and then report back to Freitag. I therefore reined the impulse to defend myself and waited patiently.

Patience, as it always is, was rewarded. Lissa continued, "Anyway, my stepfather is apparently a descendent of that Laurence Sterne, the one who wrote *Tristram Shandy*. And Sterne the novelist was a close personal friend of William Combe, the author of your *Syntax* books. Sterne the novelist

(Continued from previous page.) fins do look just like those of great white sharks, which have been known to swallow whole surfboards, riders and all, and not just in the movies. So when you're in the water and you espy twenty or so gray-black fins heading in your direction, all cutting through the water like scythes in Death's own hand, there's not much time to explore the morphological differences between sharks and orcas; you yell, "Shark!" and everyone hauls ass out of there. Thus did I shout, and—along with the four or five other surfers in the water with me—I paddled for shore with the kind of dedication that wins Olympic swimmers gold medals. We all stood, bare feet on wet sand, and watched silently as the school proceeded downcurrent with a gliding deliberation, a bearing that suggested they couldn't be less concerned with anything so petty as our chilled and dripping humanity.

used to rave about Combe, his brilliance, the 'divine gift' of his wit."

I put my finger down my throat and made guttural heaving sounds. Lissa said, "You're right, Sterne's praise for *Doctor Syntax* was probably motivated more by his friendship with Combe than by any literary merit in the writing itself. Some biographical critics have even suggested Sterne and Combe were . . . more than friends."

"*Quelle scandale*," I said.

"It's probably not true, but . . . whatever. The idea of Combe as a divinely inspired genius got handed down through generations of Sterne's descendents until it reached one real loony—my stepfather's grandmother, Lady Commody. She transformed Combe into a kind of pseudo-God."

My head lolled to one side, mouth open, eyes bulged out as though I had thirty-gauge hemp around my neck and the trapdoor just dropped. In response to my zany antics Lissa said, "It's not so unbelievable, really: When poor people are deranged, they get stuck in asylums, but rich crazies are tolerated as amusing, or eccentric. Lady C. carried the term to new heights. She adopted *Doctor Syntax* as her Bible and saw in it a kind of holy trinity, with Syntax as the father, Johnny Quae Genus as the foundling son, and Betty Broom the laundress as the holy mother."

"JQGENUS," I exclaimed, making another keen investigative connection.

"What?"

"The license plate on the silver El Camino that tried to run me off the road."

"You didn't tell me about any license plate."

"I didn't tell you about my stamp collection, either, did I, or the pet turtle I had when I was ten. His name was Finger. Finger Nails, get it? Because of his claws. My parents made me return him to the animal shelter because they thought I was mistreating him."

"Were you?"

"All I did was melt a candle on his back and then light it so I could follow him around at night. But first I had to drill a little hole for the candle." Actually I'd never do anything as inhumane as drilling a hole in a tortoise, but fictions are often more interesting than facts,[43] and it made me sound as though I were somehow different, special. Unique.

"It's an apt image. Having a conversation with you is kind of like following tortoises in the dark."

"Oh, and I suppose you don't redefine the term 'loose association.' So who's this Genus?"

"Didn't you read your *Doctor Syntax* like I told you?"

"Er, no, ma'am . . . you see, there was this little south swell pumping from a hurricane in Baja, and the tide was just right, and I just happened to have my board in the car . . ."

"Brat," she said. "If you did your homework, you'd know that Johnny Quae Genus was the son of Dr. Syntax—not his real son, but an adopted orphan, a foundling. Betty Broom the laundress was Genus's real mother. Lady C. called her secret Combe society the Order of the Hump, because Betty Broom was a hunchback."

"Foundlings, humps," I repeated numbly. "I still can't buy that anyone, even the most bonkers, could believe the *Syntax* poems are inspired by God. Have you read *The English Dance of Death?*"

"Of course I have. My stepfather raised me on Combe the way most kids get nursery rhymes and psalms. The writing makes me embarrassed for the English language. But as far as believing goes . . . don't you have anything irrational that you believe in, something so embarrassing that you've never told anyone?"

---

[43] . . . which is why I'm telling you this story, I suppose, instead of discussing authorial self-awareness in nineteenth-century letters as I'm supposed to be doing.

"I do, actually," I allowed.

"Well . . . ?"

"Distances are getting shorter."

"I'm not sure I want to hear this."

"You know how Olympic athletes are always breaking records: running faster, jumping higher and farther. It seems to me human beings can't be evolving that fast. In fact, given all the technology we have to take the place of physical work, we're probably going backward, physically. So the only explanation for all these broken records is that we're subconsciously altering our own weights and measures to satisfy our collective desire for ego-aggrandizement as a species. I'd estimate that a foot today is really only nine inches. Give or take an inch."

She couldn't resist fixing her eyes on the crotch of my trousers and speculating, "And seven inches is actually only three? Give or take an inch?"

"I'm serious."

"You're serious."

"How else would you explain all the broken records?"

"I wouldn't explain it because I wouldn't think about it; if I did, I'd start worrying about *my* mental balance. Anyway, we're talking about Lady Commody's insanity here, not yours. Her legacy to my stepfather was this Combist League, along with a few fanatical followers and a lot of money—an unstable combination. Unfortunately, my stepfather isn't harmlessly bizarre as she was; there's no limit to his ruthlessness and cruelty. He saw in the Combist League an opportunity to wield power in a way that few people can, especially people who act within moral or legal bounds. He kept some of the trappings of the Order of the Hump but added his own ground rules. They're very simple and compelling: Just as Quae Genus had to sin before he was saved, so do we all. Each of us has to sink to the depths of depravity before we can be reborn into a state of grace. It's that Blakean innocence-experience-innocence thing taken to criminal extremes."

"A convenient paradox," I observed. "The more evil you do, the more holy you become."

"That's it in a nutshell. Before my stepfather settled here, the Combist League had a practically nonexistent enrollment—just a few street people willing to believe anything in exchange for a handout—but when he got to southern California he was delighted to find that the League really took off. All of a sudden he had more recruits than he knew what to do with."

Having worked in a local "alternative" bookstore[44] and watched occultist fads, cults, and religions blow in and out like spring storms, I knew what she was talking about. "Compared to astral travel, pyramid power, UFO abductions, and trance-channeling, I guess the Order of the Hump would be welcomed by New-Age junkies as reasonable. Conservative and scientific even," I conjectured.

"Exactly. All Sterne had to do was put some ads in the paper, give some talks, feed people the motto, 'Sin to be saved,' and they ate it up. Of course when people found out what was really going on, most of them dropped out, but that was part of Sterne's plan: The more sociopathic ones—the ones Sterne really wanted—found a home and stayed. So now he's got a core group who obey him unquestioningly, like he's some kind of führer. That's the mentality you're going to be dealing with if you don't give up chasing your *Doctor Syntax*."

If Lissa was telling the truth, and I no longer had any reason to believe she wasn't, then the organization she was describing might have been directly or indirectly responsible for two serious attempts to terminate my precious self, not to mention Ernst's blindness, my missing heirloom, and the

44 Cf. Chapter 24.

suspensory, which I had finally healed enough to discard. Nevertheless, the idea of a paraliterary cult that enshrined some of the world's worst poetry was preposterous—so preposterous that only a fool or a habitual reader of fiction would be able to suspend disbelief so efficiently as to take it seriously. I therefore made light of her warning. "No problem," I said. "Beyond good spelling I believe in nothing unquestioningly. And in the end, nothing wins. Ask any physicist or Buddhist, or a poker player who can run a good bluff."

We were both shivering from the cold now, and I had the information I needed. It was time to go. I reached out to embrace Lissa, but she backed away, saying, "Don't, Harmon. Let's keep it clean and painless." Behind her, I saw Ernst appear at the far end of the hall, striding purposefully in bedroom slippers, a magazine under his arm.

I suppose it should have struck me as odd, a blind man with a magazine, but I dismissed it as one of those all-too-human quirks. We all have them. I, for instance, invoke the memory of Newton Minou, my former striped tabby (long defunct since her run-in with a diesel street-sweeper), if I'm overcome by a burst of manic joy during a Laker telecast.[45] There's no logical reason for my calling my cat's name; she never truly appreciated televised sports. Nonetheless, I always squeal "Neeeewtn!" at certain epiphanic

---

[45] Relative to my preoccupation with pro basketball, Liz spun the following parable: The Mayas (the Incas? Details, details . . . ) invented basketball. They had a hard ball made of dried sap, and a hoop made of dried vine. The chief of one clan would play the chief of another clan. To these superstitious folk, the ball represented the earth, and the hoop represented infinity; if you put the ball through the hoop, you brought your clan closer to immortality. The two clan chiefs played to a certain number. Whoever won got to kill the loser, disembowel him, skin him, and wear the loser's skin over his own body for three days.

(Note continues on next page.)

moments, as when Kareem makes a soaring rockabye double-clutch reverse slamajama in the face of a player from a particularly hated opposing squad, like Boston.

I stood, struggling to fight off the harrowing intuition that I was leaving her for good. Irrational, absurd. I'd be back, and everything would be all right. The rock beat thumped on spiritlessly,

> *Takin' it to the streets,*
> *Takin' it to the streeeets.*

Loud as the music was, Ernst must not have heard us talking, because he disappeared into the bathroom.

I turned and went.

After Liz told me this story she sat quietly. From her hourly rate I calculated quickly that the story, plus her quiet sitting, had cost me twelve dollars. I said, "Good story, Liz. Wearing the skin of the loser gives new meaning to the expression 'one on one.' But what does it have to do with me?"

"That question," she said, "is your main problem, and perhaps the problem of your whole generation."

# ◆ TWENTY-TWO ◆

After being put on hold and transferred a few times, I reached Sergeant Freitag at the county jail in Garden Heights. He said he was interviewing inmates as leads in an armed robbery he was investigating. "I should be through by noon. I'll have a free hour before I have to go out on a case. Meet me here at the jail."

I used to drive through Garden Heights to get to the legal draw-poker clubs in Gardena, and it's neither high nor verdant. 103rd Boulevard runs the whole level length of South Central L.A., from Redondo Beach where they turn the city's sewage into drinking water, past Gardena where the putty-faces congregate to push poker chips around tables and blow cigar smoke, to the tragic urban decay of Compton, Watts, and Willowbrook. At the Heights, between Gardena and Compton, 103rd runs through hurricane-fenced expanses of tarry dirt littered with otherworldly gas-storage spheres, twisted gray pipes, and a multitude of dormant oil-well pumps that look like the remains of an infestation by gigantic locusts. South, at the base of Beacon Hill, refinery smokestacks issue forth wisps of steam that marble the dirty air briefly and are then subsumed by it.

The correctional facility—the jail and honor farm—shares a tract of government-owned land with the county dump. As I parked and got out of my car, the smoke from incinerated refuse made my sinuses swell up and my eyes sting. Lured far from the ocean by the promise of an easy feed, gray-smudged seagulls massed and screeched over mountains of bulldozed garbage.

Sergeant Freitag met me in the courtyard in front of the jail. He made an expansive sweep of his arm. "I know it's not much, but I call it hell."

What struck me was how surprisingly little like hell this part of the jail was. Between two immaculate brick sidewalks, rose bushes were pruned to a uniform domed shape, and wherever a branch had been cut off, there was a neat daub of black tree-surgeon's tar. The blooms were profuse and radiant. "Hell," I said. "This place is nicer than some front yards I've seen in Beverly Hills."

"The honor farm guys keep it up. See those bricks? They have to get down on their hands and knees and scour the grouted spaces with a toothbrush and Ajax. Somehow I have trouble appreciating a place that's tended by forced labor." It occurred to me that anything you might call labor is by its nature forced, whether you're a single mom keeping the kiddies in Swanson chicken pies by soldering microcomputer parts for minimum wage, or you're a Hollywood producer supporting a two-hundred-dollar-a-day nose by pandering to the popular taste, or you're a graduate teaching assistant, as I am, force-feeding free verse to a generation of bookkeepers. But I kept my mouth shut. Nobody likes a guy who's always critical.

At the glass-enclosed reception desk I signed in and got a plastic-coated visitor card to clip on my shirt. I followed Sergeant Freitag down a hallway of offices filled with uniformed men and women hunched over clattering typewriters and adding machines, to a solid metal door with a round brass key-fitting and an iron handle. Sergeant Freitag pressed a button on an intercom by the door and said, "Three-six-eight." The intercom buzzed, the latch on the door snapped loudly, and he pulled the door open. We walked through, and the door slammed shut behind us.

We were in another hallway with still more offices, but these were empty, and already there was an oppressive change, as though inside the building a cold front had dropped the barometric pressure suddenly. I shivered. At the end of this hall was another metal door, also shut. On the other side, said Sergeant Freitag, were the "tanks," rows of multi-occupancy suites which housed the inmates.

"What do they call them?" I asked.

"Call what?"

"The multi-occupancy suites that house the inmates."

"Tanks."

"You're welcome," I said waggishly. Jejeune, but it always catches them off guard. It kills them. Sergeant Freitag looked at me as if I should be locked down in solitary. I said, "Just trying to lighten the mood. This place makes me nervous."

"You get used to it," he reassured me.

"I don't think I want to."

He motioned to a room at the end of the hall, on the left.

"We won't be disturbed here. It's an interview room: cops investigating cases, psychiatrists writing up reports, lawyers, priests."

"How do inmates get out here from the tanks?" I asked.

"From the what?"

"Don't start with me," I said. Freitag caught on fast.

"You give a note to one of the deputies at Inmate Records, that window where you signed in and got your badge. A guard takes the note to the inmate and brings him here. Inmates call the procedure 'flying a kite,' I guess because the note disappears into thin air for a while. Sometimes it diasppears permanently, like a kite with a snapped string."

"Lively convict metaphor."

"Indeed," he said.

The interview room, like the rest of the jail, was painted the color of last weekend's guacamole dip. There was a cheap braided throw-rug over the concrete floor, a metal table with two metal chairs in the middle of the rug, no windows, flickering overhead lighting. We sat down.

"I hate fluorescent light," I said. "Do you know that if a fluorescent lamp flashes at the same speed as your brainwaves, it can throw you into a *grand-mal* seizure?"

"Then it's lucky for us the med-tech's office is next door," he said. "They have plenty of epilepsy medicine. The inmates fake seizures and save up their meds to get high."

"Sounds like my kind of evening . . . Jesus, what's that?" I was distracted by shouting and laughter coming from across the hall.

"The property room."

"It sounds like some serious partying."

"Property's where the new admissions come after they're booked. They sign over their clothes and valuables, take a shower, get their uniform. Fumaroli's the deputy in charge. He's notorious for being abusive to every inmate who comes through."

Deputy Fumaroli's voice echoed through the hall, so that unless you shouted, as Sergeant Freitag did, you couldn't hear anything else. "Jeez, Rick," Fumaroli said to his assistant, "look at the nightstick on that big nigger. Hey, Amos, you ought to have a permit to carry that thing around in your pants." He laughed at his witticism and then started singing, *"Strangers in my pants,"* and farting at the end of every bar. Rick laughed. "Here, Amos, drink this, it's your vitamins."

A high-pitched voice whined, "Doesn't taste like no vitamins."

"Don't drink that, you dumbshit. He believed me. That's shampoo, dumbshit, to kill the crabs. He really drank it. What a dumbfuck." Rick laughed. "Here, take another capful, and use it on your dick this time." Fumaroli started singing and farting again.

"I can't believe this," I said. "Are all the guards sadistic redneck bigots?"

"Are all the professors in the English department pompous asses?"

"Yes."

"That was supposed to be a rhetorical question, to which the correct answer was supposed to be 'no.'"

"Sorry, but I can't lie, not even to an officer of the law," I lied.

"Well, most of the bulls are OK, but unfortunately Fumaroli is the first one inmates meet."

"Sets a nice tone for their stay."

"It doesn't get much better, either." He got up and shut the door. "Listen, it's really swell having you drop by the country club for a visit, Harmon, but we've only got an hour."

"Right." I repeated what Lissa told me, about how Sterne periodically holds Combist League meetings in which he presents his lame demonic theories. "He doesn't care how many people get offended and walk out. He recruits from the ones who stick around."

"Hmm, bizarre concept, literary gangsters," Sergeant Freitag mused. "At this point there's not much I can do legally, Harmon. We need concrete evidence before I can go in there with a warrant."

"So what do we do?"

"We have a couple of choices. We could just sit and wait for them to come after you again and then try to catch them in the act. Or we can go on the offense."

"Like your army buddies and the snipers."

"Right."

"Why do I get the feeling this is going to involve more 'me' than 'we.'"

"Because you're a sharp guy, a regular Einstein. Officially, my hands are pretty much tied; I can't even offer you an official recommendation. But off the record, if I were you I'd find a way to infiltrate, you know, get in with the Combists."

"Of course you would. You're a battle-crazed vet with delayed-stress syndrome and a serious death wish. What am I supposed to do once I get in there?"

"Play it by ear. Take a little tape recorder and tape conversations. Look for your stolen *Doctor Syntax*. Find evidence of other crimes. That way you can get the police involved. Of course that's only what *I'd* do. What you do is up to you."

"Oh good, I can view this as an opportunity for personal growth. Liz says I need to practice taking responsibility for my own actions."

"Who's Liz?"

"My shrink, sometimes."

"Ah," he said. I might have been overly sensitive, but his tone seemed a tad patronizing to me.

"What does 'Ah' mean?" I demanded.

"Nothing, just 'Ah.'"

"There's no such thing as just 'Ah.' You meant something by saying 'Ah.'"

"I certainly wasn't implying anything critical by saying 'Ah.' We've all done our time on the couch at one time or another."

"So you admit you have, too."

"It's nothing to be ashamed about, for godsakes. These are the seventies."

"Does that mean yes you have?"

"Yes, it means yes I have."

"Ah," I said.

"But that was a long time ago."

"Asshole."

"No thanks, I've already got one," he said in equally infantile repayment for my "tanks" crack.

"Funny," I said. "You kill me, Freitag." I picked up the dangling thread of our conversation, "Anyway, I agree with you that anything, even going to their meetings, would be better than waiting around for the Combists to come and kill me. But the problem is, they know what I look like. They'd recognize me as soon as I walked in."

"Have you ever done any acting?"

"I played Cabeza de Vaca in a Cub Scout Explorer skit. I had one line: 'So thees is the Nuevo World.' Should I try to pass myself off as a conquistador?"

"You want to get them arrested, not slay them with mirth."

"My cousin Bradford was an actor. Maybe he could help me come up with a disguise."

"Much better idea. Just keep it simple. It's amazing how little you have to change your appearance to throw people off. And keep me posted."

"Okie doke," I said, trying to sound casual. In reality the prospect of going on the offense mortified me. My skin felt too tight for my ribcage. I had trouble taking in air.

"Oh . . . listen," I said between shallow breaths. "I told Lissa you'd come around to make sure she and Ernst are safe. I'd really appreciate it . . ."

"I can do that. But, Harmon . . . remember: You're just there to look around, gather information, find clues. Don't do anything crazy."

I croaked: "Hey, this is Harmon Nails you're talking to, not some green kid. Would I do anything crazy?"

"Ask Liz," he said.

# PART FOUR

♣  ♦  ♠  ♥

# MASTERS OF ILLUSION

# ♠ TWENTY-THREE ♠

Bradford lifted the hem of a hanging garment. "This place brings back some memories," he said. "Did you know I played Lady Macbeth one time, when the lead got sick?"

"Save your confessions for temple, Dame Woodlawn. I need a convincing persona of my own, and I need it now."

We were poking around the dressing area of Bradford's former repertory company in Venice. Originally a warehouse, the building had been divided into two separate walled sections. The section closest to the street had been converted to a kind of amphitheater, with a semicircular plywood stage, shake-shingled in front, and surrounding seats. The rear half of the building hadn't been much altered. It had high brick walls smoothed out by decades of enamel in various pastel hues, exposed plumbing and electrical conduit, and heavy wooden rafters ornamented here and there with long-vacant birds' nests. Props and sets from previous productions were massed in loose organization, like piles of raked leaves that the wind keeps messing up. I recognized the cardboard rhinoceros heads and one huge dummy rhino from the Ionesco play Brad had been in, among other pieces incongruously heaped together: a ship's wheel, papier-maché trees, drawing room furniture, a worn-out western saddle, toy guns, a rowboat.

Costumes, including the Lady Macbeth getup Brad was currently fingering nostalgically—a shapeless crimson gown of a roughspun silky fabric—hung from long racks assembled out of galvanized plumbing pipe. Against the building's rear wall, behind some head-high bamboo screening, ran a long workbench built of two-by-fours laid and lag-bolted across sawhorses. There were a few mirrors for applying makeup, and some folding chairs. I straddled one of the chairs backward, bronco-buster-style, with the metal back-support against my belly.

Picking up a plastic pot of rouge and brandishing a small sable brush, Bradford said, "So what kind of look did you you have in mind?"

"What do I look like, Vidal Sassoon? That's what you're for. Any actor who could pass for Lady Macbeth without shaving his beard must know some swell disguise secrets."

"I did have to shave, and . . . hey, that's perfect, you're a genius."

"I know, a regular Einstein."

"It's true, you are: Shaving's a great idea. Whacking your mustache will make all the difference."

I seized Bradford by the wrist. "No one touches the 'stache. I've had it since I could shave. It's part of . . . it's like hair growing out of my soul."

"That's disgusting." He wrenched his arm free. "That's also the point of disguising yourself. To hide your most distinctive features and substitute new ones."

"Couldn't we just put some greasepaint or latex or something over my upper lip, like they use for fake bald heads on TV?"

Brad rummaged in an antique wooden orange crate and

pulled out a barber's electric clipper. He said, "Close your eyes. This will only take a second."

The clipper snapped on and hummed. As Brad passed it across my lip, it made a business sound, like freshly cut redwood trunks being forced across a bandsaw. Two passes, and Brad said, "Done. That wasn't so hard, was it? Here, take a look." He handed a round mirror to me. The face in it was lopsided. It reminded me of police composites of serial murderers, grainy blowups of faces whose right and left halves didn't match up. My upper lip was a waxy, embalmed-corpse white, like those albino ivies that grow in the dark, under houses.

"I look like a pervert," I moaned. "Like I've been pressing my face up against windowpanes watching people undress."

"Good, your appearance finally matches your personality."

"Not amusing."

"Look on the bright side. You'll fit right in at the Combist League, if they're as weird as you say."

"I guess that's something. What else can you do to humiliate me?"

"How about glasses?" He brought out a pair of thick black plastic frames from a shoebox. "Try these on."

I looked in the mirror. "Gee, I could carry my Strat to the meeting and go as Buddy Holly." I was of course referring to my vintage mid-fifties Fender Stratocaster, the most soulful electric solid-body guitar ever made and the axe I used to play in bands around town before the English department wrung every last ounce of creative joy out of me.

"Now you're getting the showbiz spirit," said my cousin the ex-ham. "See, dressing up is fun. I think we can find some buck teeth around here somewhere."

"We're not doing a remake of Rocky Horror, Brad. My life is on the line here."

"OK, forget the guitar but keep the glasses. They're a nice touch."

"How about my hair?"

He feathered a hank of my hair through his fingers. "I don't know. Maybe a little Vitalis, to give you just a hint of the two-bit down-and-out hood." He squeezed some clear oil onto my hands. "Run this through your hair, and then comb it straight back. That's it." As I combed, I imagined the ghosts of my adolescent pimples being stirred to life by the brilliantine. My scalp tingled. Brad looked pleased. He said, "Now, to complete the effect all you have to do is not shave for a couple of days."

"Two days nothing. I'm like Nixon. Five hours after shaving I look like a skid-row bum."

"What a man. You're my hero."

"I know. It's a hard standard for you to live up to. Don't even try." I inspected myself in the mirror. We had created a physical persona that would doubtless scare little kids and make upright citizens blench with revulsion. While I was understandably disheartened to realize that such a slight amount of pruning and tweaking could reveal a brutish Harmon who must have been lurking just below the surface all along, I was also satisfied that I could walk amongst acquaintances without their recognizing me. I said, "Now I need a personality, a role to play."

"Who's the most repulsive person you know?"

Tough question: I knew so many repulsive people. I let my mind wander. It passed briefly and ungratefully over my mother, onto Martin Wolf, past Brenny and Chainsaw and my Uncle Frankie in New York, who picks at his roast beef and then eats the fat, leaving the meat on his plate. Each of them had repulsive qualities, I realized, but each had ample portions of what you might call goodness as well. None was repulsive without mitigation. I shared this insight with Brad.

"Try harder," he said.

I did, and I lit all at once on the sublimely repulsive person I had met—or at least been exposed to, like toxic waste—recently. "Deputy Fumaroli," I said. "He works at the jail. Brains and sensitivity of a cashew."

"Good. Close your eyes and imagine that you're Deputy Fumaroli . . ."

"Do we have to do the Stanislavski thing? It's so embarrassing. It's like when my therapist tells me to relive my dreams: 'Be the big black dog and tell Harmon why you want to bite his ass.'"

"Shut up. You don't have to do anything. Just close your eyes."

"OK."

"Are they shut?"

"Yes?"

"No peeking."

"Peek at this." I grabbed my crotch and jogged it up and down, an obscene Italian gesture of disrespect I learned from my oft-repulsive Uncle Frankie.

"Later. Now imagine Fumaroli in your mind."

I did. It was unpleasant.

"Let yourself experience his experience: his past, his family, his anger, his secret little pleasures . . ."

I opened my eyes and shuddered, as though waking suddenly from a night terror. "I can't do it. It's too horrible."

"All right, skip his secret pleasures. Just try to get into his negativity."

I cheated. I plugged into my own negativity, the repressed loathing I usually allow to surface only when I'm having trouble dropping off to sleep and I soothe myself by imagining ladder faculty screaming and falling bloodied, like duckpins, before my car. I took that feeling and overlaid it with Fumaroli's unique conversational style.

"Suck my dick," I said.

"What?"

"You heard me, you little jewboy fuck." I tried to fart like Fumaroli but came up empty. I swallowed some air and belched instead, and then I laughed, a deep goony laugh.

"How's that?" I asked, reverting to my own adenoidal timbre.

"You had me fooled. A little bit more and I would have gone for your throat."

"Perfect. That's how Fumaroli affects everybody. Now all we need is a name for the new me."

"How about something to go along with your new personality. Something tough and hard, like Spike."

Brenny's parents had a huge dog named Spike, an ursine Newfie who used to charge down the hallway of their condo in Sherman Oaks and knock the wind out of me. I hated that dog and didn't want to be reminded of him. I countered, "How about something completely out of character, to confuse them. Something gentle, sensitive, artistic . . . painterly." I ran a quick memory scan over old masters I knew and hit on a guy very much like myself, a genius whose own sensitivity undid him in the end.

"Lippo," I said.

"The birthday clown on TV?"

"Not Chucko. Lippo."

"Oh . . . Limpo," he said, obviously not making the literary connection.

"I said an artist, not a lame Marx brother. Lippo, as in Fra. Didn't you ever read your Browning?"

He tried covering up his shame at his own ignorance by exaggerating it. "My little sister was a Brownie, but I never read any of her manuals. I did go to her promotion ceremony, though. I think they call it 'flying up.' Very moving, even my father cried."

"You're pathetic, not an ounce of culture."

"I know, and I just feel sick about it."

"Just tell me what you think about Lippo."

He tried it out. "Lippo. Lippo. Nope, it doesn't fit."

I complained petulantly, "It's my disguise, and I want it. I want Lippo."

"Sure, Lippo, whatever the artist wants. Just don't cry or throw your finger paints."

"And then a last name to inspire fear. Maybe something Teutonic, to bring to mind vicious goose-stepping shock troops."

We sat silently, thinking. You may have noticed this already, but it's hard to free-associate Prussian names when you have to. Brad was better at it than I was. Every few seconds he'd come up with one, and I'd dismiss it.

"Biesner." He strung out the first syllable, so that it sounded like 'Beeeeeznair.'

"Nah," I said, "It reminds me of my motorcycle."

"Wussmann."

"I don't want to crack up when I introduce myself."

"Rheingold."

"It's a beer."

"Schmeling."

"A boxer."

"Schtupfer."

"Nothing dirty."

"Ludendorf."

"Nice rhythm. Reminds me of a city where they make cough drops for the Panzer divisions. You're on the right track, but 'Lippo Ludendorf' is too . . . alliterative, it's too cute. I like the 'dorf' part, though. A lot."

"How about Urmandorff? The Rams have an offensive tackle named Urmandorff. Real mean sonofabitch, too. He once cut a Pontiac in half with a pair of tin snips."

"Why?"

"I don't know. Maybe the battery died and he got frustrated. Steroids have funny side effects sometimes."

I tried it on. "Lippo Urmandorff. Please allow me to introduce myself, my name is Lippo Urmandorff, and you can suck my dick. I like it. I'll take it." As I spoke, a wave of peristalsis moved in my large bowel. A miracle, His will be done. I farted violently, without effort.

"Whew, I'm impressed," Brad said. "I think you're ready."

♥  TWENTY-FOUR  ♥

You'd have to agree that the *Los Angeles Free Journal* has sunk sadly in quality—that is, unless you're a fetishist, narcissist, pedophile, gallophile, voyeur, frotteur, coprophage, compulsive masturbator, or any combination of the above, in which case you no doubt applaud the editorial direction it's taken.

The newspaper was conceived in '66 as an asexual organ of the political left, a scholarly journal with uncompromising, well-researched attacks on Vietnam escalation, urban police brutality, media brainwashing. In its first incarnation, the *Free Journal* admitted no advertising, a noble experiment, which soon went the way of most noble experiments, like the rear-engine Corvair and Social Security: It was a flop.

The paper was sold in less than a year. The new management's concerns were more practical, if less politically pure, than the founders'. They adopted a less strident rhetorical tone, ran a few feature articles on topics of countercultural interest, mainly psychedelics and Carnaby Street fashion, and they decided to run ads—nothing tastelessly mercenary, mostly soft-sell blurbs for environmental groups, organic diners, psychic aura readings, herbal laxatives. They also decided to experiment with a classified section at the end of the paper.

In the beginning the Personals listings were tame and sweet:

> CANDY. Your roomates and best friends in the Dharma wish you a groovy Birthday and Love.

Et cetera. But not long thereafter the content and tone of the Classies changed. Throw the sexual revolution and the Hollywood flair for the garish into the Cuisinart, and you get a pretty reeky puree. By the late sixties the *Freege*'s Personals section had gained coast-to-coast notoriety as an open forum for devotees of off-center sex, with come-ons like,

> WHITE male, presently incarcerated and getting out in a week. Happy, and clean. I like sunsets, window-shopping and electrode pain. Seeking guys to boldly go where a few Goodmen have gone before, no holes bard, and bi-gals into creative restraints and chocolate waterfalls. No weirdos need apply, please. Weight not important. Must provide references.

It was in this atmosphere of murky erotic promise that I began working for the *Freege*. As the paper's circulation had grown, the *Freege* had expanded into merchandising, as any shamelessly capitalistic venture will do. They had opened two bookstores, a main branch in Hollywood and a spinoff in Westwood Village. There I began my brief literary career, not as a writer—the demands of writing gave me reflux esophagitis even then—but as a stock clerk and cashier. I sought the inglorious position and accepted it reluctantly, only because Ma insisted. She said an eighteen-year-old should develop a sense of responsibility. Even though I reminded her that I took out the trash every Sunday evening, she said it wasn't enough. "You're spoiled," she said.

I argued, and correctly I thought, "I wouldn't be spoiled if you hadn't spoiled me."

"It just so happens I'm reading a book," my mother announced, "and Doctor M. Dudley June, M.D., says you are what you choose to make yourself."

"Psychology is like fireworks, Ma. It should only be handled by trained professionals. Mothers shouldn't be allowed to read those kinds of books."

"Dr. M. Dudley June says you could be a mensch if you wanted to."

"I'm sure he didn't put it quite that way," I said. "Besides, his trip is just classic European existentialism chewed up and then regurgitated in a form of psychobabble that's palatable for the supermarket set. *Reader's Digest* meets Sartre and Camus."

"Burns and Allen, it doesn't make one iota of difference to me." Slow death by nagging. With one dated phrase my mother will plant me like a dahlia bulb some day. My right eyelid started fibrillating, so that it looked to me as though a monstrous fly was hovering, its wings beating frantically, in front of my face. I held the insubordinate eyelid down tightly with two fingers and at the same time tried desperately to rally. "My point is that . . ."

"No point. My son comes home every day from school, he eats three bowls of Sugar Pops, not a word to his mother. Then he says, 'I'm going in my room to study,' and sleeps or who knows what else until I call him for dinner."

"Doesn't he . . . don't I set the table every night?"

"I have a saint for a son, he sets the table. Look at your cousin Bradford, he'll make something of himself in the community one day, he's following in his father's shoes, going into the office after school and learning the business."

"Ma, you hate insurance work. You said Uncle Ed was turning Braddy into an undercover operative for the Gerald Ford Youth Bund, or something like that."

"At least Bradford's not giving his mother heartache."

"Aunt Doreen's dead."

"So kill me, too."

We replayed this conversation, with minor variations, for weeks. In that time the nervous tic developed into a painful neuritis toward the rear of my right eye socket, where the optic nerve tunnels its way toward the brain. This painful malady gave me double vision and convinced me I was coming down with multiple sclerosis. It was either accept part-time employment or resign myself to becoming the invalid Ma always predicted I'd become.

Ma beamed when she heard I was going to be working around books, as though she imagined the collective brilliance of the literary masters would somehow reach me through the books' jackets while I was pushing my dustmop across the linoleum. What Ma didn't know was that the *Freege* in Westwood was a "bookstore" only by the loosest definition of the word. It did have a few books, mostly arcana describing conversations between houseplants and their masters, compendia of actual after-death experiences by allegedly normal citizens, tales of travel to extraterrestrial holiday spots. The bulk of the merchandise, though, was drug-oriented. Hung high on the walls of the store were hundreds of psychedelic posters for sale, each with a letter and a number stapled to the bottom, so that we salespeople could find the corresponding rolled-up and cardboard-tubed poster under the display counter. My Escher fish print, a relatively unpopular item, was E-7, and I paid nothing for it: the usual employee's discount if you don't tell the boss you're taking it home. The biggest sellers, the classic Day-Glo yellow "War Is Not Healthy . . ."

flower litho and the blacklight Hendrix close-up with paisley headband, were W-1 and H-3 respectively.

The cash register, which I operated when I wasn't reshelving books or taking inventory or sweeping, sat atop the counter that ran half the length of the store. The glass-topped wooden case contained the fruit of inventors' feverish attempts to cash in on the unprecedented vogu-ishness of drugs. It held water pipes, some of research-lab austerity and others of multicolored Plexiglas fancy, with tubes twisted into graceful, evocative shapes and bowls like rare fungi. There were cigarette rolling papers in a thou-sand exotic flavors, from banana to carob, cigarette rolling devices machined and assembled with a precision that would rival the finest Swiss watches. There were coke spoons made of silver and gold, coke grinders that resem-bled pepper mills, brass coke scales for precisely weighing portions for sale, coke vials of sensuous hand-rubbed teak. All this stuff might eventually have swayed me in the di-rection of heavyweight doperhood, but luckily for my mucus membranes and my immune system, the *Freege* ex-ploded one morning.

I came to work at 10 A.M. as usual, only to find what was once a storefront—a metal and glass facade which had been wholly unremarkable in its intactness—being boarded up. A few gawkers stood around pointing and making jokes, while several long-haired workers, some on the sidewalk and some balancing on low scaffolds, were nailing up lengths of grayed, paint-stained pine planking and redwood lath. I looked around, wondering if I hadn't missed a turn and happened onto the wrong street. I hadn't. It was the same neighborhood, with the same businesses, all seemingly unaffected by the sudden demise of one of their number. Facing the *Freege* across Galen Av-enue, the Westwood Commerce Bank stood as it had since the early fifties in staunch immovability, with the low center of gravity and expansive squatness that money sometimes effectuates in buildings as well as people; to the north was the ParkRite lot, its kiosk as yet unopened for the day, the heavy, painted chain still across its entrance; and just to the south, on the corner of Galen and Braxley, there still stood the Wanton Weiner,[46] a quick-serve eatery where all the employees of the *Freege* used to get their CornDogs and foamy Orange Frappers for lunch. Thus assured I was in the right place, I turned my attention to the *Freege*. Through gaps between the boards that had been put up at eye level, I could make out piles of charred paperbacks, incinerated furnishings, splintered glass. A blackened poster of Albert Einstein lay beside the glass paraphernalia case, which had miraculously survived the blast, its only visible injury being one long hairline crack that ran its entire width. Taking in the violently deconstructed gestalt, I reasoned with astonishing clarity that there would be no reshelving for Harmon Nails ever again, nor pushing of brooms, nor petty pilfering of merch. I walked slowly toward the Wanton Weiner and an unplanned CornDog brunch. Above, the sky was a very pale blue. The morning breeze was very cool and felt very good.

Nobody ever found out who trashed the bookstore, or why, but the explosion, besides liberating me from the rigors of regular employment, also jarred loose any vestige of respectability the *Freege* might have had. Shortly after the bombing, the *Free Journal* abandoned all pretense of social involvement and devoted itself exclusively to hardcore sex. The paper's only saving grace had been a certain self-deprecatory sense of humor about itself; now it was scowlingly pornographic, unreservedly abusive, cruelly demeaning, and as a result more financially successful

[46] Although the Semitic misspelling was probably unintentional, in this mainly Jewish part of town it was appropriate.

than it ever had been. Advertising generated so much revenue that management stopped bothering to sell it for a quarter. Today you can pick up the *Freege* for free on any busy corner in the city, next to other sleazy rags like *Singles at Play* and the *Wall Street Journal*.

I found Sterne's notice in the *Freege* on page five, just below an ad for ribbed condoms. It was an eye-catcher. Two columns wide and bordered in black, it screamed in blocky boldface,

SEX! RELIGION! DRUGS!
You've Tried Them All
And You're Still Unsatisfied!
The
COMBIST LEAGUE
Has the Answers!

It gave a date, an address on Westwood Boulevard, and a time, 8 P.M.

To prepare myself for the meeting I dressed myself in the Lippo costume that Brad and I had chosen carefully: a shiny gray sharkskin suit as wrinkled as a well-used hanky and a size too small, and a brown Perma-Prest polyester shirt whose gullwing collar turned up and over the coat's lapels, its points almost reaching to the coat's shoulders. I unbuttoned the shirt to the solar plexus, revealing a particularly noxious piece of Salvation Army costume jewelry that hung from a chromium-plated chain and winked suggestively from within deep bramble-patch tufts of my own Mediterranean chest hair. Below the pants' high-water cuffs was a pair of vibrant saffron acrylic socks which, having lost their elasticity, sagged down and bagged out of a pair of black navy-surplus oxfords, scuffed and stained so that it looked as though I had missed the toilet badly while taking a leak—suggesting, Brad and I hoped, that scar tissue from some horrible wasting venereal infection had all but sealed over Lippo's penile meatus, causing urine to shoot wildly in no predictable direction. On my shoulder I carried a beat-up canvas ammo-holder overflowing with dirty clothes, as if I had seen neither home nor laundromat in months.

I shambled onto the 83B Wilshire bus and sat down with my back to the window. The grayish plastic upholstery was covered in graffitti. Next to my left thigh the seat proclaimed Manny's love for Gina in black indelible marking pen. By my right thigh Manny suggested by what means I might sodomize myself.

I was nervous about my confrontation with Sterne. Undigested Raspberry Pop-Tarts, the remains of my hasty dinner a few hours eariler, were working their way past my hiatal hernia and back into my throat, which felt raw, acidic. I re-swallowed the Pop-Tarts and pooched out my belly, hoping to keep the food down. The Pop-Tarts started their burning climb anew.

A heavyset woman in a long blue cloth coat, support hose and heavy black shoes got on the bus and sat down next to me, smothering Manny and his message of love. The woman's perfume was overwhelming, like sitting inside Ma's clothes closet with the door closed. I slid open the window behind my head. Grimy air blew in. I got a little souvenir of Los Angeles in my eye. I squeezed my eyelids tightly and tried in vain to recall precisely why I was on my way to infiltrate the lair of a dangerous paranoid psychopath. Something to do with a book, a girl, snipers in Vietnam . . .

To capitalize on my dark mood I practiced my Lippo Urmandorff act. I opened up my copy of the *Freege*. A banner headline across the top of the paper screamed, "WHERE TO FIND IT IN HOLLYWOOD," and below the headline was a sepia-toned gravure of a hooker on her hands and knees, her tongue out to the camera and an opaque rectangle of glossy black printer's ink modestly obscuring the ends of her dangling tits. I rustled the paper loudly and grunted as I turned pages. The woman in the blue cloth coat got up from her seat next to me and moved across the aisle of the bus, to a seat facing me.

Inspired by her reaction, I began moving my hand back and forth rhythmically behind the screen of the open newspaper while making suffering animal sounds to the beat. In reality I had my hand in my pocket and was rubbing my Benzedrex nasal inhaler on my thigh, but it created the illusion that I was stimulating myself. The woman in the blue cloth coat got up and said something indignant but inaudible over the diesel whine, the crashing gearbox and the jarring fulminations of traffic. She moved once again, this time to the back of the bus.

I watched her recede down the aisle of the bus, bobbing and lurching on her thick black heels. I felt vulgar, seamy, a perfect cad. The feeling cheered me somewhat. The disguise was working.

♣  TWENTY-FIVE  ♣

Westwood Boulevard near its intersection with Wilshire is bounded by some of the city's most expensive commercial real estate, on which stands a double row of skyscrapers, obelisks of glinting stainless steel and obsidian-dark or Mylar-reflective glass built to bend like palm trees in a storm when the next quake hits, as geologists predict it surely will, and disastrously. If you get off the 83B bus at Westwood and walk a couple of blocks south on Westwood, the character of the community changes dramatically. You get a glimpse of the business district before the high-rise boom, when hopeful entrepreneurs, many of them Depression refugees from the midwest or immigrants not long off the boat or under the barbed wire, tested the tepid waters of the promised land with small capital ventures. The ethnic makeup has changed, but the multinational flavor of the businesses remains. Today on Westwood near Pico you will find Thai and Vietnamese restaurants, Pakistani import bazaars, al fresco sushi bars, falafel and taco and burrito stands, chili-burger joints, and a kosher deli or two interspersed among old, multifamily apartment houses, all waiting to be leveled once the commercial reconstruction wildfire jumps Wilshire.

The address on Sterne's ad in the *Freege* led me to a wooden walk-up that seemed more architecturally appropriate for a residential block of turn-of-the-century San Francisco than for mid-seventies L.A. Here, even in this older and more heterogeneous part of Westwood, the structure looked strange, baroque, occult even, from the ornately carved railings flanking the front steps to the peaked dormers which looked out over city traffic three stories below. The exterior walls were shingled and layered over with a fresh coat of flat white gesso, while the rococo detailing of window trim, door frame, banister posts, rain gutters, and roof spires was painted a cold steel blue. A company of crows massed on the steep slated roof, pacing lethargically and watching the seekers of a better way mount the steps and enter.

The front door was open. I walked into the anteroom. People were milling around, talking in hushed tones, some of them taking their places at a ponderous oaky table, the kind that knights with names like Hrothgar and Hwaetflath used to sit at and swill mead and eat sheep's brains from the skull, with their fingers. There was no other furniture in the room, just the long wooden table, high-backed wooden chairs, hardwood floor and a black wrought-iron chandelier suspended over the table. I pulled out a chair and sat honing the finer points of the Urmandorff persona, picking my teeth with little, sharply folded pieces of *Freege* which I flicked onto the floor when they got soggy. No one seemed interested in seeking out Lippo Urmandorff to engage in lively religious discourse. The seats around me remained empty. Beyond the lecture hall, past a stairway to the upper stories and through a double doorway, I could see a sitting room with some antique furniture and a stone hearth.

In my Lippo costume I had expected to find myself inconspicuous among a rough assemblage of debased

*Freege* devotees, freaks dressed in baggy olive drabs, puffy-eyed balding men in garish polyester jumpsuits. Instead, aside from me and a thin bearded guy in ripped jeans, a dirty gray hooded sweatshirt and black high-top sneakers, the congregation that filled the hall looked abnormally sober and clean-cut. They spoke to each other confidentially, and I could only make out snatches of conversation: ". . . yes, but Unitarianism allows for a greater diversity of . . ."; ". . . after I told him my mantra, my meditation no longer had the same . . ."; ". . . as a tax shelter, convertible debentures aren't out of the ballpark with . . ." Sterne must have advertised in the straight papers as well as in the *Freege*, I figured.

A couple sat down next to me. They were wearing slim, tasteful gold wedding bands. The groom had short blond hair neatly trimmed and brushed back, clear blue eyes, a manly underbite, and an elongated dimple by his mouth, which gave his face the perpetual hint of a self-satisfied smile. He was wearing a summer suit of a correct linen fabric. His bride looked equally Mormonic, with straight, shoulder-length hair even blonder than hubby's and a simple blue cotton shift that came to mid-calf. They sat with their hands folded on the table and waited, both half-smiling without a hint of impatience. Their composure had all the vacuity of cows grazing, and it irritated me. I started rapping my fingernails on the table, to the rhythm of the awful pop number I had heard at Ernst's and a thousand times since, on car radios passing, in news program lead-ins, in elevators, at the supermarket,

Taprap rap rap tap rap
Taprap rap rap tap raaaaap.

My drumming was just starting to make the groom a little nervous—his jaw muscles under the great trench of a dimple were starting to pulse to the Euro beat—when our host came down the stairs, followed by a huge man, no doubt his bodyguard. Instantaneously I recognized the bodyguard and made a solid association: This massive, pink-faced lumbering devotee was the same bleached-blond thug who had tried to shoot me from the speeding El Camino, the very Robert Sweeney, or Sid Dickey, or Bobby Sweet who had stood by while his partner near-violated Lissa and assaulted me. I was definitely on the right track. The realization made me feel light-headed, dizzy, as though I had experienced a spontaneous onset of infundibulitis, which rendered my senses of balance temporarily inoperative.

I regained my equilibrium by first thinking of a cow—it works every time, I guarantee you—and then focusing my attention on Laurence Sterne. Until now I had imagined Sterne to be tall, hawkish, predatory, but as with so many of our great psychopaths throughout history, he was physically less than imposing. Pretty Boy Floyd had been on the butt-ugly side of plain, Billy the Kid looked like my Aunt Doreen before the tuck job, and the heavy-lidded Son of Sid serial murderer (who in newspaper photos seemed perpetually to be grinning like Henny Youngman at some private one-liner) could be mistaken for my wacky cousin Martin Wolf, son of Sadie. Likewise, Sterne turned out to be little and doughy, with thick, wavy black hair combed straight back, a sallow, jowly face. He was wearing a black suit, portly extra-short, and glasses with black plastic rims just like the ones Brad had given me to wear as part of my disguise, only Sterne's were tinted slightly. As Sterne reached the landing, I had the feeling I had seen him somewhere before. I tried to place him, but I could get no further than Kissinger: He looked like Dr. K. on his way to a costume party dressed as a fifties Beat poet. I puzzled. Was there something more corporeal to this wraith of a memory, or was it just another meaningless hallucinogenic flashback, triggered by my having recognized Sweeney, or Dickey, or Sweet? More likely the latter.

Sterne walked toward the seated assembly the way a tennis ball rolls when it's wet on one side, a lurching, tipsy gait which pitched his roundness awkwardly onto one stubby leg, then the other. He yawed his way to the head of the table, set his black briefcase down, and popped it open. He remained standing. The bodyguard stood close by.

Sterne didn't sound like Kissinger. "Welcome, earnest seekers," he said in a resonant, well-modulated TV weatherman's delivery, as though he were practicing his diction lessons. "I am truly gladdened that you decided to take a chance and widen your perspectives on life." We earnest postulants rustled and settled in our chairs expectantly. I took out a stiff red bandanna and blew my nose in it.

Sterne cranked up his speech. Even though he was working without notes, the lecture had an overly rehearsed quality, as though he had given it a thousand times and the meaning of the words had worn off gradually, like detail from Etruscan statuary.

"Like you, I was not always a devotee of Mr. William Combe. My parents were Catholic. I was raised Catholic. I attended confirmation, catechism, parochial schools, Mass on Sundays. But something about it never seemed quite right, did not ring true to what I knew in my soul to be the truth, even at a very young age. I knew that my grandparents had embraced another belief, and I wanted to learn more about this belief, in order that I might make my own choices concerning my beliefs. But my parents wouldn't tell me anything about it, other than that we mustn't talk about those things, ever. That of course made me all the more interested—as all small children will be when they are told they must not do something, ha ha."

I have an unusually short attention span even for lectures

that interest me, but I was losing Sterne faster than I used to lose Dr. Brunkard when he would fawn over Jane Austen's delicate humor, her common sense, her light and bright dialogue, her keen social insight, her gigantic swollen clitoris. I found myself drifting, thinking about Lissa, the pale white nape of her neck, the soft copper-colored hairs that curled gracefully behind her ears, the smooth, unmottled expanse of cool flesh between her shoulder blades. Daydreaming, when its penalty is no more tragic than a lowered course grade, is acceptable, even welcome diversion, but now my continued breathing depended on my paying attention to Sterne. I shook myself back to the present, as when you're just about to fall asleep on the freeway and some little kernel of self-preservation grabs you just before you veer head-on into a concrete overpass abutment. The choice is clear. Fight the drowsiness and pay attention, or die. I forced myself to follow Sterne.

"I obeyed my parents' dictates, not so much out of duty as because I had no choice in the matter. However, when I was in my early teens," he droned on, "I was sought out by an old woman who had been close friends with my grandmother. She did not try to sell *Doctor Syntax* to me as a way of life. Rather, she offered me a course of study in which I could use the *Syntax* books as a basis, to read and answer whatever questions I had. I began reading, and I discovered what Mr. Combe had to say on certain subjects."

Sterne summarized the Combists' version of the scriptural prophecies, the Betty Broom-Syntax-Genus trinity, and so on. His discussion was reserved, academic, safe. No one seemed alarmed. Some even looked as sleepy as I felt. Sterne paused and closed his eyes, as though gathering his energies or consulting some private dark muse. He looked up at the ceiling, like a building inspector checking for structural flaws. I did, too. It was made of plaster, now cracked and crazed in several places. Probably damage from an earthquake many years earlier, or from a succession of raging parties on the second floor. There was a brownish water stain radiating concentrically outward from one corner of the ceiling. I studied it. Detectives have to attune themselves to meaningless detail, and an overflowed toilet upstairs might turn out to be a case-breaking clue, the one that puts Sterne behind bars for good.

As I pursued the criminal implications of spilled sewage, Sterne took a deep breath and continued. "What I've been considering of late is the whole idea of good and evil. Why, if there is a God, there's so much pain and sickness and starvation. And why, if—as the satanists say—the devil has the upper hand on this planet, there are so many people with good intentions. No one has any satisfactory answers. Listen to this."

From the briefcase he took up a small leatherbound volume of *Doctor Syntax*. It looked exactly like one of my own stolen books. He opened the book to a dog-eared page near the beginning and read:

> *The more I hear, the more I see,*
> *The more you deal in mystery.*
> *This Mistress, sure, of which you tell,*
> *Is an INCOMPREHENSIBLE.*

He clapped shut the book. "Incomprehensible!" he shouted. "Religions, philosophies provide no answers. At least none that satisfies me. Does any one of you have any answers?"

Sterne pointed accusingly at a tall man at the far end of the table. "Do you?" The tall man shook his head sadly.

"Do you?" He pointed at the guy in the sweatshirt, who during Sterne's discourse had been sneezing intermittently, as though allergic to pious drivel. He wiped his nose on his sweatshirt sleeve, a Lippo-like gesture which made me feel a certain spiritual bond with him, and said, "Nope, that's why I'm here."

Sterne pointed at me. "Do you?" he challenged. I felt the same involuntary hot rush of shame that I felt in the fifth grade, when Mrs. Walker called on me to read out loud from *At Home With the Horners,* and I was astonishing my peers with the fluid ease of my delivery until I came to the word "brazier." Even though I was Spelling and Vocabulary monitor in class, "brazier" was a new one to me. I hesitated, then took a stab at it. It came out "brassiere," and the children broke into shrill peals of sadistic laughter. I flushed in ear-burning embarrassment and mumbled something they couldn't hear and which I've blocked from my memory to this day. But I wasn't little Harmie Nails now. I was Lippo Urmandorff, fully grown lout, self-confident in his manliness and stupidity. Entering the consciousness of the bull Fumaroli as my cousin Braddy had instructed me, I said, too loudly for polite conversation, "Who the fuck cares why. It just is. The world beats us down, and it owes us. What we wanna know is how to get what's coming to us." I hawked up some phlegm violently, for end punctuation. I always knew my postnasal drip would pay off, if I gave it long enough. I swallowed the oyster with revolting gusto.

A few of the earnest seekers looked at each other and shifted uneasily in their seats. Some coughed. Sterne fixed on me curiously. "Well put, my friend. Syntax doesn't try to guess why the world is the way it is. He leaves that up to the religious fanatics, to the evangelists and the devil-worshipers. All Syntax says is: Look, there is goodness and there is pain. Organized religions, like Catholicism, say evil in the world is the result of man's breaking away from God's guidance and direction. Eve ate the apple, and it was all downhill from there. We should avoid temptation, they say. Buddha,"—he pronounced the name in the same way that Uncle Frankie in New York pronounces "butter," without the "r"—"goes them one better. He says life is suffering, and you have to accept it. Fine. That's certainly more efficacious than attempting to be chaste when it's so abundantly clear that we were not meant to be. Mr. Combe takes this concept to its logical conclusion. He says that merely accepting suffering isn't enough, because it puts one in a passive position. If one is passive, one gets taken advantage of—'beaten down,' as our friend here says. Each of you must embrace suffering and evil, even promote suffering and evil, in order to realize your full potential as a human being."

The tall man slid his chair back quietly and tiptoed out the front door. Sterne ignored him. He was on a roll. "The son of Dr. Syntax, Johnny Quae Genus, let himself experience all the degradations possible on this earth. He gambled, he assisted a corrupt surgeon in fleecing poor sick patients, he consorted with a Jewish money-lender, he engaged in riotous drinking and fornication . . . and in the end, because he lowered himself to all this, he was reunited with his father. Mr. William Combe says this is the lot of each of us. Only if we allow ourselves to sin openly and wholeheartedly, will we," he quoted from memory this time,

> *Enjoy that calm and tranquil state*
> *That does on Independence wait,*
> *Nor spurns the low, nor courts the great.*

People were exiting steadily now. "This," Sterne concluded, lowering the volume of his voice for rhetorical impact, "is our message. Encourage misfortune, sink to the depths of depravity, and be reborn into a state of all-acceptance, as did the child Genus."

The groom with manly dimples was the last to go. As his wife padded out before him, he turned and dispatched a glare of righteous disapproval in Sterne's direction.

Sterne didn't notice. His gaze was fixed on me and the guy with allergies. He opened his fat arms wide and said, "Welcome, seekers."

I was in with Sterne.

# ◆ TWENTY-SIX ◆

The den was full of antique furniture that would have been costly if it had been original, only everything was fake, from the import-bazaar travesty of a Persian rug to the blue rayon Ming tapestries, to the wholesale-outlet sham Edwardian divan covered in a nubbly machine-stitched embroidery that depicted some faceless peacoated anthropoids mounting up happily for a hunt. In the whole room, the only authentic period piece was a blond cabinet of the aerodynamic Danish style popular in the late fifties, around the same time as tailfins on cars. This particular movable enclosed a pair of small stereo speakers, a turntable-receiver combo, and records. Given the pretentiously dated decor of the room, I expected nothing but cut-rate chamber standards in the record stack, but Sterne apparently preferred slick, overproduced trash-pop, like the Bee Gees and the Doobies. The radio was on, its dial set at a station whose program director shared Sterne's pedestrian tastes, and in this strange, hostile house I was comforted by the familiar inanity of the tune coming through softly: ". . . the streeeets . . ."

The rest of the furniture—a coffee table covered by a

chunk of frosty beveled glass, a couple of pine end tables stained dark to simulate mahogany, an oak-veneer hutch—was cluttered with quaint knicknacks that any real antiquarian would reject as junk: a cast-iron jockey enameled carelessly, so that his eyeballs appeared to be melting down his cheeks, his jowls down his runny silks; a tin replica of a turn-of-the-century locomotive; a brass elephant with a truncated trunk; a blond cricket bat, chipped and splitting; a chaos of china vases, plates, cups, silver baby spoons. The fireplace was walled in solidly, with no flue. On both sides of its stone facade, plywood bookcases covered the wall from floor to ceiling. Old volumes, leatherbound, gilt-embossed and clearly for show, were lined up carefully on the shelves, so that no offending spine broke the plane formed by the books' massed butts. His own big butt to the books, Sterne sank his plumpness into an overstuffed Chippendale copy and motioned to me and my allergic friend to sit also. We did, on straight-backed Louis XIV copies. Sterne's large companion placed himself behind us, out of our field of vision.

Under the bright reading lamp by his chair, Sterne's flesh had a glossy, slightly bloated quality, like a buffed eggplant or a cat shaved and preserved in formaldehyde for science. Sterne's hair was even shinier than his skin, and of too dark and uniform a color to match his eyebrows. An amateurish dye job: I wondered why a man of Sterne's wealth would go the Clairol route when he could obviously afford a hairdresser. Pride or embarrassment, or both, I projected. Behind the smoky lenses Sterne's eyes had a yellowish cast.

Sterne turned to the allergic guy. He cleared his throat and announced, "I am Laurence Sterne," although he had already introduced himself to the entire meeting an hour earlier, "and this is my associate, Mr. Bobby Swedenborg." Impressive new alias for Sweeney, I thought.

My allergic friend said, "I'm Rick Masters."

"Any relation?" Sterne asked, chuckling at his own ability to make witty associations in a snap.

"Relation to who?" Rick Masters asked blankly.

"I allude of course to the distaff member of the famous sex research team, to whose research I've added extensively on my own. At some future point in time I plan to come out with a report that will push into the background the famous team of Masters and . . ."

"Bators," I put in, adopting the style of facile sexual wordplay which, for Deputy Fumaroli and others of his kind, often passed as wit.

"Please," Sterne admonished me, "I'm conversing with Mr. Masters for the moment. I would prefer that you reserve your comments for the moment." I was about to comment on his overuse of the phrase "for the moment," but I could feel a slight stirring of cool air behind me, which meant that some part of the large person's body was moving close to my neck. I held my peace . . . for the moment.

Sterne turned back to Rick Masters, who was wheezing quietly. This Rick fellow seemed frail, shy—not at all the type to go in for Sterne-style terrorism. Under my Lippo Urmandorff masque the too-human Harmon Nails felt a twinge of . . . what? Pity? Protectiveness? Lippo shoved the feeling aside. Still addressing Masters, Sterne said, "And so, my friend with the illustrious surname, what brings you to *Doctor Syntax?"*

Rick Masters spoke quietly. His respiratory condition gave his voice the uneven timbre of a teenage boy caught in that temporal limbo between Little League shrill and valedictory bass. He said, "I've been doing a lot of, kind of seeking around on my own, like you say, for answers."

"And you found none that made sense."

"When I was in jail back in the Midwest, you know, I done some serious reading." He stopped talking, as though satisfied that he had explained his position clearly and exhaustively.

Sterne prodded him, with a hint of impatience at Rick's reticence. "And . . . ?" he asked.

"And they all seem sort of like bullshit, like you said."

"And so . . . ?"

"So I'm just seeking around."

"Mr. Masters, I gather that you are a man of few words." Brilliant inference by the genial Dr. Sterne, a coup of rationality, a victory of the human mind's classificatory powers over random stimuli in their usual tumultuous disarray. What a weenis, I thought. "I admire a quality of reserve in a fellow seeker," he went on. "From your terse comments, it seems that you have been toying with different belief systems and finding none of them satisfactory."

"Not toying," Rick said. "I take it serious."

"I'm sure you do, my friend."

During this fascinating interchange, I sat quietly, enervated from keeping my fear at bay and from low blood sugar. If I don't eat a protein-containing snack, some space-age "cheese food" or a Soya-Krunch Bar at least every hour, I get bad hypoglycemia, in which I become shocky and even more resentful than usual. My head felt hollow, my eyes as though packed tight in their sockets with shredded cardboard. I hadn't had a bite since the Pop-Tarts. Bright electric light was falling on my knee, and caught in the incandescent beam was a small spider, a leggy speck picking its way carefully along the wrinkled gray fabric of my trousers. In the dark twilight of my soul I resented the invasion of my personal space by this presumptuous creature, so much so that I considered crushing it between my fingers, slowly, to teach it and all life-forms in the room a lesson.

I looked up at Sterne and Rick, who were talking about something. "At any rate, Mr. Rick Masters," Sterne was saying, "I welcome you to our small but dedicated band of Combists. I hope you will not object to staying here over-night for a few days. We find that immersing oneself in Combe study is far and away the best method by which to assimilate his teachings. After the initial indoctrination pe-riod, our followers are free to lodge wherever they like, pro-vided they attend regular bi-weekly training sessions. Does that arrangement sound acceptable to you, Mr. Masters?"

Rick nodded his head. "OK," he said slowly, as though under hypnosis. I watched my spider pick its way down the side of my leg and disappear from view. Sterne looked at me. He cleared his throat.

"I am Laurence Sterne," he said.

As long as I was doing my Urmandorff number, I seemed to have the shakes under control, and being on the edge of a hypoglycemic coma added an edge to my offen-siveness. I said, "You told us your name already. Twice." I pointed at the empty anteroom. "I guess no one was im-pressed the first time."

He nodded and smiled confidently. "We do not expect that our message will appeal to everyone, Mr . . . ?"

I said, "Urmandorff's the name," and then added, "but my friends call me Lips." For some reason, hoods always have plural nicknames like Fats and Sticks, and for some reason, probably the same obscure reason, the etymology of the names is always Anglo-Saxon rather than Latinate. Otherwise, hoods would have names like "Hemiptera" Moran and "Tibiae" Diamond and "Errata" Braciuoli. I wondered how that particular convention got started, whether all the hoods called a summit meeting, a kind of nomenclatural Apalachin, to standardize the nicknaming rules, or whether the nicknaming occurred all at once, independently and by chance, like the discovery of radio-activity in the same year by researchers working indepen-dently on two different continents.

Sterne broke into my linguistic musings, "And why do they call you Lips?"

"That's what *she* said last night, and I showed her." Leering and flicking my tongue lewdly, I leaned over and punched Sterne hard in the thigh with my fist. Better Sterne's fat leg than an innocent little spider. Sterne's flesh caved in, like a yeasty bread dough.

He winced. Sweeney moved into my field of vision. He didn't look happy. Perhaps I had pushed the Urmandorff routine too far.

Sterne regained his composure smoothly and halted the bodyguard's advance with an offhand gesture. "I fully comprehend your sexual allusion. And as a Combist I approve wholeheartedly of your exploits."

I threw up a cloud of dated hipster and B-movie crook argot. "I reckoned you'd dig where I was coming from. That's why I decided to hang out when the rest of the rats flew the ship after your lecture." I pronounced it "lecher." "What I dig the most is the part about fuck to get saved."

"That isn't quite how I phrased it, but your interpretation of my message is entirely accurate, Mr. Urmandorff."

"You don't hear so good, do you, Sternie? I said my friends call me Lips."

"Of course, Mr . . . Lips. And my followers call me Doctor Sterne, as I received the licensate in theology prior to my arrival in this country."

"Oh, excuse me, *Doctor* Sternie." I exaggerated the "Doctor" for satiric effect. "You like giving the little girlies their physicals, eh, Sternie? Do you use the rubber pinkie cheater, or you like the barehand technique?" I leaned over to punch him again, but this time Sweeney, with surprising nimbleness for a man of his bulk, grabbed me tightly with one hand, like a plumber closing down a pipe-wrench. My wrist was the pipe.

"Ow," I whined.

"I'm sorry, did Mr. Swedenborg hurt you?" Sterne said pleasantly. "I assure you, he meant no harm. If he had meant to inflict injury, you would be on the floor at this very moment, writhing in agony." Poor Rick shifted uneasily in his Louis XIV copy. "How about a nice glass of chilled white wine to calm your nerves? I'm certain we could all do with some refreshment at the present moment."

As I may have mentioned previously, I don't hold my alcohol well. Two thimblesful of beer and I'm ataxic, stupid, completely out of control. The acidity in a single glass of wine gives me a bleeding esophageal ulcer and a week of burning urination. I bluffed, "No, thanks, I only drink the hard stuff."

"An excellent idea. Bobby, a Pernod for each of the three of us. We'll drink, to cement our fledgling association with one another."

"Nah, I'm still full from dinner," I protested desperately.

Sweeney didn't seem to hear me, because he poured some liquor into three large snifters, and carried them over to us on a tarnished silver tray.

"To William Combe," Sterne said, raising his glass. "May he guide to us a life of self-realization, impeccable health, enduring fame, and wealth beyond our wildest dreams." Not much to ask from a two-bit greeting-card versifier, long dead and turned to bandini. We raised our glasses. My excuses exhausted, I resigned myself to a sip.

The brandy tasted just like the cherry cough syrup my mom used to give me whenever I came down with the croup. The memory was pleasant, familiar, relaxing, so much so that I took another swallow. "Good shit," I commented, buoyed by an absence of the horrible distending gut-ache that usually visits me when I drink. I took a third big gulp confidently.

Sterne started orating again. "Gentlemen, regard this snifter. It is made of Austrian lead crystal, the purest and strongest in the world. Items of this quality will belong to you as well, if you commit yourselves to the ambitious programs of the Combist League." I observed Sterne clinically, from over the tops of my glasses, while tilting my head downward and taking birdlike nips at my drink. With nothing in my digestive tract to absorb the brandy, the alcohol was already starting to work on my nervous system. My limbs, previously frozen with apprehension, were thawing. My belly felt warm, my tongue absent. I nodded my head involuntarily, rhythmically, autistically, as I watched. Sterne announced, "I am told that as jarring an activity as hammering nails is entirely feasible with these snifters; they will not shatter upon impact as will crystal of lower quality."

I was momentarily taken aback by what sounded like my name coming from Sterne —the very same words my Nonno had uttered when asked his name by the clerk at Ellis Island—but in spite of the amber-hued alcoholic haze that was massing about me, I managed to recall where I was and who I was pretending to be, and thus to refrain from answering. Sterne tapped the rim of the glass with a fingernail. It chimed softly, with astonishing clarity, like a little silver egg falling through the clear ether and breaking on those little bones inside my ear.

I tried to talk, but the liquor had already clouded my sensorium to the point that I could only manage to mumble, "Pow nail jew say?" Rick Masters' eyes widened. Sterne remained outwardly placid. Sweeney took a step in my direction, expecting trouble.

"Less giddit a try." I chugged down the last of the drink and, grasping my snifter by its splayed base, brought it down hard against the arm of my chair. The glass shattered into an expanding universe of tiny glittering fragments which fell on the mantel, and the hearth, and the sham Persian rug, and all of us.

"Rainen inna house," I observed.

"Perhaps we should retire now," Sterne suggested with forced calmness. He lifted himself with some effort from the seat. There was a deep crater in the cushion, where his rump had been.

"Doughn wan sleep havn gootime," I objected strenuously.

"I think we could all use a little rest now, Mr. Urmandorff. It's been a most enlightening evening. Mr. Swedenborg will show you to your quarters."

Sweeney grabbed me under the armpits and hefted me up.

"Nawww," I complained, and struggled to free myself from his grip.

He hauled me, flopping like a beached seaskate, in the direction of the staircase. As I was dragging across the floor, heels digging into the rug and bunching it up like ripple candy, my muzzy alcoholic awareness took in the elephant statue on the coffee table. In spite of its recently broken trunk, I recognized it, like an old acquaintance emerging from darkness into misty street light. It flashed me back, and in a moment of dreamy compressed time I relived the break-in at Ernst's, the shotgun humiliation of Lissa, a frantic search by a faceless gunman, books into a bag, a brass elephant lifted also, intense pain from a sharp blow to my sweet soft nards.

"Doughn doot! Not my bawwwlz," I moaned, and I got sick all over the hardwood floor.

# ♠ TWENTY-SEVEN ♠

I've always had to get up at least three times a night to pass water, and the older I get, the more water it seems I have to pass.

The first time I slept over at Braddy's I was shocked to discover, after fending off his gay sorties, that he had an unbroken sleep. Between my insomnia at being in a strange bedroom and my hyperuria, I was awake most of the night, and I never saw Braddy get up once. That was the first inkling I had that I was different from other guys. I asked my dad about it, and he told me, "It's simple, Harmie. When our bodies tell us to micturate, we micturate. Some people micturate more, some people micturate less. Bradford is one of those people who do it less, you are one of the people who do it more, and there is no point in getting angry about it." To a child who had not yet seen the extent to which the universe metes out its blessings unevenly, the inequity suggested by my father's advice— that I should put up with more aggravation than Braddy did—was unacceptable. After all, I got better grades than Braddy got in school; should that fact alone not entitle me to sleep as well as Braddy? Unfortunately not, was my father's message, and piss-bitter experience was backing him up. Disappointments come fast and cheap when you're a kid, and they only get more expensive with time. Eventually I learned acceptance, along with the invaluable skill of relieving myself in a TreeTop apple juice jar while simultaneously standing up and semi-sleeping. You might give this technique a try if you have the same problem, and if you do I offer the following advice: Rinse out the jar in the morning and use a new jar every week or so, because bacteria seem to like it in there.

I woke before sunrise with that familiar urgency in my bladder, but I was in Sterne's house, not Braddy's, with a strange allergic roommate named Rick in the next bed and no TreeTop jar nearby. I stumbled out of bed to find a toilet or at least an empty vase I could use. My head throbbed from my recent drunkenness, and a wash of vertigo forced me to sit on the edge of the bed until it passed. My ears buzzing, I got up and groped my way toward the window, which, despite its being curtained, admitted some ambient city light dimly. Rick Masters was sleeping soundly, wheezing on each intake of breath and snoring as he exhaled. "Annhhh, zzooop," he said. I found the bathroom, turned on the light, did my business, turned off the light, and groped my way back to bed.

I lay down and closed my eyes, but each time I drifted toward sleep, a vivid image of the elephant with the broken trunk jarred me back to wakefulness. I stared up into the dark. I was here to get clues, and the elephant was the crucial link between the theft of my inheritance and Sterne. If Ernst could identify the brass knicknack as his, and if I swore that I found it at Sterne's, that might be all the evidence necessary to persuade some judge to issue a search warrant. Then Freitag and his buddies in blue would have the right to trash Sterne's house. I'd retrieve my books, and along with them the scrap of paper that would enable me to finish my dissertation, and Sterne would do some serious time.

I got up again and went to the door. I turned the knob slowly until the latch clicked. Easing the door open a crack, I peeked through. The hall was lit by a cut-glass fixture overhead. The two other bedroom doors at either end of the hall, Sterne's and Sweeney's I supposed, were shut. No sound. I opened the door slowly. It creaked on its hinges, just as in old comedy horror flicks when they want to heighten the hilarity by building suspense. Any more hilarity and my tender, hungover stomach would go into dry heaves on the spot, alerting Sterne and ending all my days. I opened the door fast, so that the pitch of its creaking rose beyond human audibility, into the doggie-whistle range. In my bare feet I tiptoed downstairs.

There was enough street light entering through the windows that I didn't need to turn on any light in the den. My vomitus, along with the shards of the snifter I'd broken, was gone: evidence of Sterne's passion for total order and of his authority over Sweeney, who must have been assigned the cleanup chore. The room was just as I remembered it before the brandy bullied me into semi-consciousness. The elephant was still on the coffee table. I saw no other incriminating evidence in the room, no bloodstained knives, no cache of plastic explosives, no vials of poison or blinding acid.

Disappointed, I reached for the elephant, and as I did, I heard a thumping sound from the ceiling above me. Out of sheer reflex I dove behind the fake Chippendale, a great headfirst slide into second base which embedded a stray fragment of Austrian crystal in the heel of my right hand. I lay perfectly still. Someone was walking above me, but I couldn't tell what room the sound was coming from. It could be Rick, or . . . not. I stayed motionless behind the chair. The walking stopped. I heard water running through the house's old plumbing, more walking, and then the house was quiet again. I grabbed the elephant and flew upstairs. Back in the bedroom I jammed the elephant into my army surplus rucksack, among my underwear. I jumped into bed, my heart beating erratically or my spastic esophagus constricting wildly, I couldn't tell which, and it didn't matter.

With my eyes closed I lay quietly, breathing in circles. I have a rule about my insomnia. If I can't have sleep, at least I can give my body a good rest, and so I lie quietly and practice the Tibetan yogic breathing I learned from a pamphlet I borrowed permanently from the *Freege* store before it exploded. Provocatively titled something like *Lung of Fire, Bowel of Applesauce*, the pamphlet was a brief but stirring paean to the benefits of fruitarianism and correct respiration. The "medical expert" who authored it (I think he was a chiropractor, actually) stated that if one gave up all "mucoid-producing comestibles"—red meat, dairy products, fish, poultry, eggs, anything sporting legs or produced by something sporting legs—he would bask in the radiant glow of perfect health. The book made this extravagant promise: If you eat nothing but fruit, "your sweat will smell like orange blossoms, and your bowel movement will have the sweet aroma and velvety-smooth consistency of apple butter." It sounded like grandiose quackery to me, but why not, I thought. If fruitarianism doesn't help me sleep, at least it'll cut down on Ma's applesauce bill at the market, since I'll be manufacturing my own. Following the advice in the "Lung of Fire" section, I learned to take a breath in through the nostrils, to follow it down the back of the spine, into the crotch, up through the belly and the esophagus and out the mouth. I learned to imagine each of my breaths as luminous entitities, colored brightly like different Christmas tree bulbs. I also learned that yogic circular breathing does indeed make you fall asleep, chiefly because it's so boring. Whatever works, says Liz.

My breath was a stunning cobalt blue butterfly on my coccyx when I heard Rick Masters stir. He made a grunting sound, only it was more a high-pitched croup, like that of a congested child. He rustled his covers, and I heard his bare feet make contact with the wooden floor. I happened to be lying with my head turned to the right, so that Rick was within my field of vision. Light from the street filtered through the gauzy sleeveless undershirt he was wearing, and in silhouette I saw the outline of his torso: narrow hips, a narrower waist, a curvature of breast that appeared not the least bit masculine, with a nipple that stood out like the almond morsel on one of Nonna Nails' cookies she used to send parcel post from New York every year during the holidays. I caught just the briefest glimpse of this confusing profile, and then Rick disappeared into the bathroom. I heard Rick put down the toilet seat, and then the sound of human micturation—not the pointed, pure-toned and melodic plainsong of a manly stream, but a gushing polyphony rich with supertones. I knew that music. I had heard it enough times when I was married, while waiting impatiently for Brenny to come to bed. Like my ex-wife, Rick Masters was a woman.[47]

Rick, or Regina, or whatever the hell her name might be, came back to bed without flushing the toilet. Not knowing that I rarely sleep anyway, she probably didn't want to risk making noise and waking me. When she returned from the bathroom, my head was turned discreetly away from her, and I made apneic sounds of imitation of her own, "Annhhh, oorrrp," only deeper. She rustled the covers, and after a few minutes began snoring in unison with me. I resumed my Tibetan breathing and meditated on the implications of Rick's sex change.

[47] I wanted to say "unlike," but that would be cruel, and only half true.

Facts. Rick was a woman pretending to be a man and sharing a room with me. I was an asthenic uptown *scugnizz'* pretending to be a sleaze (and, somewhat worrisomely, having no trouble playing the role) in order to get the goods on Sterne. Sterne was a marginally imaginative grifter with suburban tastes and a Continental front, the slick facade of which he kept intact with the help of Sweeney. Sweeney was exactly what he seemed: thick-necked and obedient as a trained sea lion but not half as bright. I understood the motives of all parties but Rick. Why was she pretending to be a man? Was she a lesbian transvestite going to droll lengths to fit into the world of men generally, and the world of the Combist League more specifically? Doubtful: Not even the most steroid-bent butch would set the soft, poppin-fresh homunculus Sterne up as the embodiment of rough manly virtues. Was Rick a beautiful, sinewy model who had somehow latched onto me as the object of lusty obsession,[48] had thrown her dignity to the wind in order to tail me here, and was hotly awaiting the right moment to leap into my bed and take me, shy and unsuspecting, in the full flower of my youth-

[48] I've noticed—and probably you have, too—that my footnotes seem to be getting shorter and scarcer as this story unfolds. They are, it appears, a dwindling resource, the vermiform vestige of intellectual apparatus that is no longer operational in me. If there ever was any reason to persist in the token attempt to make this thing look scholarly, I can no longer see it. While this is one more bit of bad news for the future of my dissertation—which I now realize has about as much chance of ever being finished as you or I have of participating in the colonization of Pluto—it's good news for my digestive and urinary systems, which have been systematically ravaged by stress, and it's good news for you, the reader, because I can at last devote myself earnestly to the most interesting subject of all . . . me, and my gripping tale of deceit and redemption. I figure I'll turn this improbable narrative in to my committee and then have fun watching them agonize over what to do with it, and with me. Cf. Epilogue.

ful virility? I hoped the latter was the case, but it seemed unlikely that my luck would suddenly change after all these years. What seemed most likely was that she was working for Sterne in some capacity, perhaps as a shill whom he used to spy on prospective inductees into the Combist fold. Her assignment was to keep the new guy, me, always in her sight, play stupid, and report my every movement to her pudgy boss.

It infuriated me that I was being scrutinized, tested, examined, observed like a laboratory chimp. What had happened to simple trust and decency in the world? What end could possibly justify one person's dressing down and spying on another? What filthy species of vermin would stoop so low? My kind, that's what. I could play this game, too, only better. I would watch my step, act the perfect Fumaroli, make no wrong moves while Rick was around, frustrate the disreputable slut totally while getting the goods that would nail her and her boss.

Yet, despite my indignation at her invasion of my privacy, I couldn't repress a certain rampant eroticism at being in the same room with a lithely curvy woman who didn't know I knew she was such. Teenage fantasy made real, I suppose, hard evidence of a psychosexual development arrested at age thirteen or so. I tried practicing Lung of Fire to distract myself, but my Tibetan exhalations colored the area of my hips mauve and raised a hummock in Sterne's stamp-catalog patchwork-print quilt, like a gabbro column extruding, forcing itself into soft, yielding shale. I forgot all about my circular breath, gave in to the auto-tectonic geology of the moment and jetted into sleep at last, with a smile on.

♥ TWENTY-EIGHT ♥

The room was bright with midmorning light, and my eyes felt as though they were posted shut with mucilage. Two blurred human shapes stood by my bed and loomed above me. My eyes came unglued and focused after a moment, first on Sterne, whose shortness prevented him from looming in the true sense of the word, and then on Sweeney, who had no trouble looming, with loom to spare. Sweeney had a pair of my grimy choners in his hands. Handling my soiled laundry would make anybody scowl, and Sweeney was scowling and looming at the same time, probably a severe test for a man of Sweeney's questionable evolution; I knew several anthropologists who could make a career out of studying a guy like him.

The rest of my underwear was dispersed randomly over the bed. Sterne had the elephant in his hands, while the falsely bearded Rick sat expressionless on the edge of her bed, fully dressed now, both feet on the floor, knees apart macho-style.

Sterne said, "Good morning, Mr. Nails. I trust you are feeling improved over your condition of the evening previous. Perhaps your early morning constitutional invigorated you."

I tried to get up, but Sweeney pushed me back down effortlessly, as though rebuffing an affectionate kitty. Sterne reprimanded me. "When people walk into quicksand, they are advised not to struggle, as beating the viscous admixture of sand and water with their arms and legs only draws them down more quickly. Mr. Nails, you are in quicksand, and I suggest you lie quietly."

I struggled up once more, only to get one of Sweeney's rumproast hands in my solar plexus. I lay back, breathing in shallow pants, cornered and scared. "You know my name," I remarked.

"I admire your powers of observation. An appreciation of the subtleties is essential in an aspiring critic of British letters, especially the critic of an artist so insightful and elegant as George Eliot, don't you agree?"

"You figured out my name and you know what I do," I blurted.

"Indeed, we know many things about you, Mr. Harmon Nails. We have been observing you for some time." I shot a withering glance at Rick Masters, girl spy. She stared straight ahead, blankly. Sterne said, "Let me introduce my associate. He was introduced to you as Bobby Swedenborg, but that is only a stage name, like your own clever and amusing *nom de plume*, Urmanndorff. His real name is Robert Sweeney. You have met him before, on more than one occasion in fact."

"I know. I recognized him. The robbery at Ernst's, the freeway. I missed him when he visited my house and forgot to turn off the gas. I can't wait to hear what my mother has to say when she gets her utilities bill next month."

"Do you not find him entertaining, Mr. Sweeney?" Sweeney nodded and remained stony-faced. "You see, in the parlance of your former persona, you crack him up. Mr. Sweeney agrees that you are a richly comical young man, and that your disguise was most whimsical. Nevertheless, when you arrived at our little gathering last night, he knew you at once."

I fired a stinging accusation, "He knew me from the time his partner hit me in the balls. They almost raped Lissa."

"You are wrong, Mr. Nails. Actually, my associate here was only a detached observer of your unfortunate accident, as I was, and he actually *stopped* Mr. Dill, a former associate of ours, from proceeding any further with my stepdaughter. In spite of my warning, Mr. Dill became a trifle too . . . enthusiastic with Lissa. Reluctantly I was forced to have him excused."

"Excused as in how Ford excused Nixon, or *excused* as in excused to the bottom of the Zaca Reservoir?"

"Exactly," he responded ambiguously. So much for avenging my wounded manhood. Sterne had taken care of the job for me, probably much better than I ever could, given my unfortunate lack of experience at torture and murder. Dill's cruel Dick Cavett voice forever silenced, and I couldn't dredge up even one iota of satisfaction in it. "A crude fellow, our former Mr. Dill. We will not have dealings with him anymore. You see, Mr. Sweeney does excellent work, thorough and enduring as the pyramids. He has a great deal of professional pride, and, truth to tell, he's more than slightly irritated with you. He attempted repeatedly to deter you from your reckless meddling in our affairs, and yet we find you here. Mr. Sweeney is not accustomed to failure."

"I'm not accustomed to having my personal belongings stolen and my life threatened," I complained in the tone of a kid who's snitching to the teacher about a schoolyard bully.

"A minor inconvenience, Mr. Nails, compared to the trouble you have brought upon yourself at the present moment." He waved the elephant in my face. "Clearly, you have too much concrete information concerning certain of our activities. That is most unfortunate, as is the fact that you will never have the opportunity see your lovely mother when she returns from her sojourn in the Arizona desert."

"Leave my lovely mother out of this. I'm not scared by your threats," I said, my stomach muscles constricting fiercely, the cramps forcing bile up into my mouth, my bladder control leaving me. "How do you know where Ma went, anyway?"

"My stepdaughter informed me of your mother's pending departure."

"Bullshit. Lissa would never volunteer any information to you."

"Crudely expressed, but nontheless true. Miss Sterne would never volunteer information knowingly to her stepfather, the evil Laurence Sterne, but she would to her own beloved father, Ernst Gablonzer. Or to the man whom she believes to be her father." Obviously enjoying himself, Sterne pulled from his coat pocket what looked like a gutted prairie dog which, in what might be interpreted as a momentary rapture of rodent love, he pressed to his face. It adhered and shaped itself to his chin, a lumpish goatee. Removing his glasses, he lifted the cheap wig flamboyantly from his scalp, and his alternative identity began to emerge like a projected image coming into focus on a screen. Sterne opened his coat and removed a thick flak jacket or bulletproof vest which had, it became apparent, accounted for a goodish percentage of his formerly ample girth; while he was still not what you'd call scant or sylph-like, he was by no means the grain-fed porkloaf he had pretended to be, either.

Sterne gave me a bloodsome smirk. "You fill rrrecock-nise me now, fill you not?" he said, putting on the familiar

silly Austro-Oxbridge accent, and at once the picture became sharp. Standing before me was Ernst Gablonzer, a
man I had recently come to admire as one of the few truly
good people I had met in my life, and to love almost as
much as my own father—the same man, with some cos-
metic revisions, who not five minutes earlier had threatened to kill me, and who clearly had no intention of
changing his mind now.

## TWENTY-NINE

Before Sterne, the closest I had ever come to death was Point Zero. It was early morning in the summer of my seventeenth year, and two hurricanes, one in Baja and one just south of Hawaii, were pumping huge southwest swells, twelve to fifteen feet measured conservatively, from the back of the wave. I had driven up with my high school friend Randy Rhea—his parents had sprung for a new Mustang as his graduation present—to this secret spot we had discovered at the mouth of La Tolteca canyon, just north of the L.A. county line. We named our secret spot Point Zero because it sounded scary. You had to climb down a steep, crumbling sandstone cliff and steal across some private beachfront to get there, but there were never crowds. When there was surf, it was worth the climb. When there weren't waves, we played heads-up, nickel-ante poker on the barnacle-encrusted rocks and waited for the tide to change or a swell to come in.

On this morning, it was more than worth the climb. It was Absolute Zero, big and hollow. The sky was mottled with high storm clouds, the air tropical, still and languid, the ocean a foamy brown from the seaweed and sand that a powerful shorebreak had churned up and the rip current dragged out. Carried swiftly by the rip, I made it out between huge sets, turned and caught my first wave, a smaller peak, merely bungalow-sized. As my board's speed caught up with the wave's, I looked down its steep face into the gnarly, kelp-entangled trough, and I pulled out; the tide was too low, the barrel was hollowing out too fast. I wheeled my board around to paddle out, but I couldn't. I was caught inside a procession of larger and larger waves which pounded me relentlessly as I tried to make it out beyond the surf line, to get my breath. With each successive pounding I got carried farther down the coast and away from the point and my friend. It was too big to ride now, the huge lines closing out all the way from the point to the beach, and Rhea, sitting safely past the reef, was waiting for a break in the sets so that he could paddle in.

I was alone. I rolled under and scratched over wave after wave, each bigger than the next. I barely made it over the top of one huge wave, this one the size of a two-story townhouse, already cresting and feathering as I reached and punched though its summit. The wind showered me with salt spray, which blinded me for a moment. I squinted and shook my head to get the water and hair out of my eyes, and I looked out to the horizon. It wasn't there. Instead, I was facing a towering, silent monster, a molten Great Wall about to collapse its full mass on me.

Too tired even to attempt to hold onto my board, I ditched it and dove to the bottom. The wave broke like a sonic boom over my head, and, while I was in deep enough water not to be caught and dashed senseless in its turbulence, it held me under until I had no choice but to claw my way up for breath. I knew that fighting up through the hissing, aerated whitewater would take everything out of me, and that I'd have no strength left to swim in to shore. Comprehending my utter helplessness—my engulfment by natural forces infinitely more powerful than my picayune self—should have terrified me, but as I rose tumbling and clawing there was no panic; instead I experienced a kind of emotional fermata, a strange relaxation of tempo, an unexpected calm at having lost any pretension to immortality, even an absurd gaiety in the face of this pointless recreational death. Tiny air bubbles, rising like carbonation in a fine aged root beer, sparkled in the aqueous light with random bursts of brilliance like fireworks on the eve of some saint's birthday, and I was surrounded by a glowing nimbus of sunlit foam. I glided up effortlessly the last few fathoms, and when I broke the surface my board was lying in the water next to me, unaffected as a snoozing pet. It must have gotten caught by the wave, flipped straight up and settled on the still whitewater after the wave had passed. I straddle-sat on the board, laughing at my ridiculous deliverance by chance—the longest shot ever, like winning at gammon by rolling boxcars five times in a row—and rivulets of salt water ran down my face, some from my wet hair, some from my eyes. The big set past, I paddled feebly toward shore, got picked up by a small inside wave which had already broken and spent its violence, and I managed to belly onto the sand, where I rolled over on my back. Behind my closed lids the sunlight colored my world a vibrant rose. The heat hurt my eyes, and it felt good.

Now, wedged between Sterne and Sweeney, in the back seat of an AMC Pacer that had the appearance of a plexi-bubbled family runabout from some futuristic TV cartoon, I was recreating that feeling of blithe, hyperconscious abandon I had when I was underwater at Zero. They were going to kill me over bad eighteenth-century poetry, there was no custom-built semibanana surfstick going to descend providentially and deliver me, and I watched with detached curiosity as unfamiliar valley scenery flashed by, a Carpet World, some filling stations out of business and boarded up, a vacant lot overgrown with sourgrass all emerald and lemon, empty storefronts with "Space for Lease" signs on unwashed windows, a body and fender shop, the neighborhood bar on the corner, closed until dusk. Van Nuys: You might find the same blighted beauty in Modesto or Gilroy, or enjoy an even purer nothingness underground while nudging up pansies. I smiled from time to time, a tourist observing myself rooted tuberously between a serene little fop, the undersized feet at the ends of his stubby legs not quite reaching the carpeted floor of the car (if the feet and legs are any indication of penile dimension, and many women insist they are, there was no telling how larval Sterne's wand might be) and a hulking sloth-man with a revolver in his paw. All because of some craftless pentameter. It was priceless, if you didn't think about it.

Rick was driving, following instructions as Sweeney grunted them to her.

"Hung a luft," he said in his lazy Hermosa Beach gyro accent.

"OK. Straight now?" asked Rick, making her soprano sound as husky as she could. I knew Rick wasn't a guy, Sterne and Sweeney knew she wasn't a guy, but Sterne and Sweeney didn't know I knew she wasn't a guy, and Rick didn't know I knew she wasn't a guy, so Rick had to keep up the act all the same, just in case they needed her to spy on me at some point in the future. I liked that. The old illusion versus reality theme. Once when I was teaching a poetry class I wrote a surreal poem called "Rods 'n' Cones" under the pseudonym Elie Aperto and had it published in the college literary mag, *Speculum*. The magazine's editors will accept anything incomprehensible, figuring it must be deep. Sadistically, I had the class write a formal explication/analysis of the poem, purposely neglecting to inform the class that it was my poem, so that they would be brutally objective in their judgment of it. A few days later I mentioned to Chainsaw at a poker game that my class was expecting Elie Aperto to come and answer questions; did he want to come and play the effete literato to my class.

"Why?" he asked.

"I want to give them a firsthand demonstration of the old illusion versus reality theme. It's the only way they can really get it," I said. "You'll do it," I added confidently, "because the class is mostly women. College women."

Chainsaw wanted to know if there were any sexy girls in the class, and I fed him the usual fabrication: The pheromones were so thick in the small room, the running shorts so brief, the tank tops so sheer, that the few men in the class were reduced to crawling on all fours and howling and humping air. He said, "I'll be there." There was never any doubt.

I informed my class that a crazy pal of mine was going to pretend he was a poet, and that they should pretend they didn't know he was an impostor and ask him the most inane questions they could think up, to demonstrate the old illusion versus reality theme to him. Chainsaw arrived dressed in a rumpled herringbone sportcoat and cords, so stoned that his eyes were mere happy slits behind his wire-rimmed glasses, and my class outdid themselves with questions that were even dumber than their usual ones. Chainsaw was having a great time, making grandiose pronouncements on the nature of the creative process while leering at Sally Rideanour, an ample brunette who always wore the sheerest tank tops of all and the briefest running shorts, and who always sat in the front row, her legs crossed and a pink wad of Bazooka in her mouth.

When I finally announced to Chainsaw that the class was putting him on, that they knew all along he was a hoax, he was confused. He looked around at the class for some support, but they were all in hysterics at the specta- cle. He looked to Sally Rideanour, who blew a bubble with pert nonchalance and uncrossed her bare legs, which dis- turbed him even more. At a loss for words, Chainsaw punched up my arm, bringing a red welt. The class roared their approval: How often, after all, do you get to see one of your profs attacked physically in the front of the class- room? Not often enough, for my money.

"Don't get mad," I said to Chainsaw. "It's just a little theater of cruelty to illustrate a point: the old illusion ver- sus reality theme. It's the best theme there is." Having made my point, I bowed deeply to Chainsaw, like a magi- cian who's just performed a particularly rad trick, then to the class, and I swept out an open window. Luckily we were on the first floor.

So here I was again, still dramatizing the old illusion versus reality theme, except this time with Rick in the role of Chainsaw, Sterne in the role of airhead underclassman, and myself in the role of—what?—how about a fly banging willfully against the glass of the window, or any other in- sect whose lifespan might be measured in ticks on a time- piece. "Ngh," said Sweeney to Rick, and she straightened out the wheel.

Because I was feeling so irrationally buoyant—and, more importantly, to gain a handhold on the twining con- volvulus of the Sterne psyche so that I might discover some vital bud of information that would enable me to effect an escape—I tried to engage Sterne in conversation. I tried several openings: "How's the family?" "Stolen any good books lately?" "Nice day if it don't rain." None worked.

I resorted to flattery. "Awesome disguise. With the wig and beard you had me completely fooled."

"Of course I did, Mr. Nails."

"No, really, I thought I recognized you, but I said nah. But I should have known, when the fake antiques started arranging themselves around you and the books started fixing breakfast."

"I beg your pardon?"

"Never mind. What really amazes me is that you fooled Lissa."

"It's not at all amazing if one considers that my stepdaughter probably would not have recognized me, even had I appeared before her with no disguise whatsoever. You must understand, I parted company with Miss Sterne and her mother when my stepdaughter was still quite young, and unless she had seen recent photographs of me . . . but of course I could not take that chance. Hence the disguise, which admittedly was, as you say, awe-inspiring."

"And Ernst—did you excuse him like you excused Dill?"

"By no means. Mr. Gablonzer is an extremely valuable man. We have kept him, at considerable expense I might add, in the depository of my textbook firm, where he pursues his scholarship uninterrupted. That is the reason for which I had him abducted in the first place, and that is where we are taking you now, if you have no objection."

"I do have." Sweeney jammed the muzzle of the gun in my ribs. It tickled. "Why take me there to kill me? Why not get it over with right here?" I demanded, rather intemperately I realize in retrospect. But you must understand: Sterne and Sweeney were abridging my basic freedoms, my human right not to spend time in textbook depositories if I so chose, and there's nothing more infuriating than having your freedoms abridged, especially where textbooks are concerned.

Sterne paused thoughtfully, as though considering a business offer. "I never attend Mr. Sweeney's eliminations, just as I never supervise the slaughter of cattle whose steaks I consume. Besides, I have no intention of killing you, Mr. Nails."

"You don't?" I was starting to feel giddy, as I did when

my board landed next to me. Sterne put the damper on my mood.

"Oh, no, I have no intention of harming you at all," he said. "I intend to put you to work."

# ♦ THIRTY ♦

Kennedy's assassination gave the textbook depository a sinister association it will never shake, an implication of unseen diabolical superpowers preying on vulnerable little men with telescopic gunsights and seducing them—the weak little men, I mean, not their gunsights—with intimations of dark fame. Textbook warehouses mean madness and violent death to the millions who caught every repeat of those shaky home flicks, like junior's birthday preserved in super-eight only instead it was a president's head going nova in gleaming skull fragments and brain stuff. We suffered the ceaseless video panning across that grassy knoll, because we all wanted reasons, and if you stare at something hard enough and long enough maybe sense will emerge, like strep colonizing in lab agar. In the case of JFK's murder it never did, and it never has. Nevertheless we memorized every sharp-edged shelf and dusty packing crate of the sniper's vantage point, we saw the warehouse from every angle inside and out, so that the book depository now resides in the collective dreamscape as a stark tower in which man proves his suggestibility, his willingness to do evil for vague motives, his boundless, squinting, self-righteous compulsivity, and as a shadow upon grassy fields where love proves itself as easily and permanently dispatched as an electronic tone beamed into dead space.

I articulated this poignant observation to my captors, hoping for some speculative intercourse on the subject. Sweeney said, "It's jest a fuckin wurrhouse," which effectively stifled any intercourse. Rick seemed more interested but dubious. She studied me quizzically. Sterne was still climbing. I could hear him panting, petite shoesteps ringing out in the hollow stairwell. When he reached the top of the stairs he bent at the waist like an orchestra conductor after a particularly volatile final movement, put his hands on his knees and, catching his breath, said, "Welcome to your new home, Mr. Nails. I trust you find the surroundings agreeable."

"Peachy. Books are my friends."

"As are they mine. I sensed all along that we were kindred spirits."

"Please, you'll give me a fistula. Are all these yours?"

"Actually, most of these books are in transit. You see, in addition to my activities as a collector of rare books, I deal wholesale in public school texts. I began this enterprise as a showcase of honest endeavor behind which I could conduct my more covert dealings. Besides solidifying my good name in the community, the business has turned out to be not a paltry source of income. Additionally, it puts me in touch with other book enthusiasts, who often have information concerning rare first editions and such. The connections can be most rewarding. Come, I'll show you." Sweeney pushed me roughly in the small of the back.

This level of Sterne's warehouse was divided into a number of walled-off areas. They led me to a room filled with what appeared to be authentic old tomes, including whole shelves full of original Combes. Rick came, too.

"So why such a big deal over my *Syntax* copies? You have millions of them."

"To be accurate, hundreds. In fact, I have most of the works of Mr. Combe that are extant. There is an old adage in business, one which I learned early in my career and which I have followed scrupulously ever since: If one controls every single unit of a given commodity, then one can command whatever price he decides to fix for that item. Toward that end I have endeavored to collect all of Combe's works, along with the original editions of a number of other authors. Most of these volumes are relatively inexpensive reprints, but the first editions which you see here," he motioned toward several shelves jammed with antiquated, leatherbound volumes from the *Syntax* series, "are considerably scarcer. Their price has risen dramatically every year since I have cornered the market on *Doctor Syntax*. Your inheritance, however, is exceptional, Mr. Nails, and when you brought it to me for appraisal, I knew at once that I had to possess it."

"They all look the same to me."

"In that assumption you could not be more erroneous." Sterne disappeared from the room for a moment. He returned with my books. I could tell they were mine. There was the corner of a piece of newsprint sticking out of one. Impulsively I lunged at it. "My books," I said. "Gimme."

Sweeney blocked my way by gingerly shifting the vast biomass of his hip, like Dawkins setting an illegal back pick. I ricocheted off his meaty rump and into some cartons, which fell down. Sterne corrected me, "They *were* your books, Mr. Nails, and if you had relinquished their ownership more gracefully, you wouldn't be in this inglorious position now. The reason I wanted this particular set of *Syntax* books so badly was this." He let one of the volumes fall open to no particular page and pointed to some handwritten notes in the margin. He riffled carefully through the fragile old pages. There were notes on almost every page. "This set of *Doctor Syntax* is unique, Mr. Nails, because it contains annotations by my ancestor and namesake, Laurence Sterne, and a handwritten inscription to Sterne by his friend, the author, William Combe. There is no other volume like it in the world. Therefore it is priceless on the open market, and of considerable interest, personal as well as financial, to me. Your bringing your inheritance to me was a miracle, a godsend if you will."

"We're all Combists here. Let's call it a gift from the child Genus. A Johnnysend if you will."

"Very good, a Johnnysend, ha ha ha ha, I stand corrected. I had heard of the existence of such an annotated *Syntax*, but it was out of circulation for many years, apparently in the care of your grandfather. When you brought your inheritance to me, I had no choice but to arrange the little farce of a robbery, in which you were unfortunately injured. My involvement in the case would never have come to light, had you not interfered."

"Sorry," I said. "Let's pretend it never happened. Let bygones be, and all like that."

"I'm afraid it's far too late for bygones now, Mr. Nails. We have covered our tracks thoroughly, and you are the only unresolved issue. But I have a resolution which I believe will be mutually beneficial to both of us. You are going to join Mr. Gablonzer in the very comfortable and very secure study we constructed for him, so that he would be at ease to pursue his classical scholarship. You are going to live, and as repayment for my kind consideration in sparing your life, you are going to make me famous."

"I? At what?"

"Why, at literary criticism, of course."

# ♠ THIRTY-ONE ♠

The fourth and top floor of the warehouse was barred from entrance and egress by a thick metal trapdoor which lay horizontally across the head of the stairwell. Holding the trapdoor shut was a steel rod which ran through a series of iron rings welded to the bottom of the door, and which abutted at one end in a hole bored raggedly into the bare concrete wall of the building. From the looks of the door, it would be impossible for an elderly man like Ernst to lift it, even without the steel rod. But Sterne was a cautious, thorough man, and he didn't like to take chances. You had to admire him for that. He was also out of his mind.

As Sweeney worked the steel rod out of its fittings with one hand, the shotgun in the other, Sterne explained the nature of my prospective employment. "All I've ever wanted," he explained in a candid tone, as though this were an encounter session and he had some material about a juvenile impropriety to share with the group, "is to make my name as a man of letters, to follow in the footsteps of my illustrious forebear Laurence Sterne, as a famous novelist or critic. It was noted many times that I had verbal promise when I was prepping, but as I grew older I came to the tragic realization that I am tragically flawed. I simply do not have the patience to write."

"Hey. Me neither."

"Perhaps, but our lives are not comparable, Mr. Nails, because you have mongrel bloodlines, while I descend directly from the pure stock of literary legend. Whenever I meet someone, I tell him my name is Laurence Sterne, and he inevitably quips, 'Oh, you're the man who wrote *Tristram Shandy*. What have you written lately?'"

It occurred to me that few people, if anybody, would make that obscure authorial connection, but I wasn't about to accuse Sterne of paranoid delusional ideation, since Sweeney had his hands on a steel rod he'd probably enjoy working into a tight Windsor around my neck. Sweeney had worked the bar loose from the trapdoor and was presented with an intellectual dilemma. He had a shotgun in one hand, a rod in the other, and he needed both hands free in order to push the trapdoor up and open. He stood with a perplexed look on his face and turned several uncertain circles, the rod and gun describing an elliptical orbit around his largeness. It was pathetic low comedy, like watching an unusually pea-brained Irish setter with a can tied to its tail. At length, and with admirable ingenuity, Sweeney set down the rod. He passed the gun to Rick, who apparently had never touched a firearm before. She took it in both hands and held it out at arms' length, as though it were a fishing pole and she was preparing to cast over a pier railing. She aimed the shotgun unsteadily in my direction, although it was actually pointing at a point in space which had most recently been materially occupied by the metal rod as it revolved around Sweeney. Sterne was still blathering.

"You must understand that people continue to have extremely high expectations of me," he complained. "I am expected constantly to produce literature or literary analysis of the highest quality. Sometimes I imagine I am beset by a horde of ghostly ancestral presences, terrible Harpies who descend on me, tear at my flesh, harry me mercilessly for my verbal output."

"I should introduce them to my mother. They'd get along great. Do you think your ghostly ancestors play canasta?"

While we were chatting, Sweeney put a shoulder into his task and pushed open the trapdoor. We ascended the last few stairs into a room that reminded me of the interview cell at county jail, only higher and darker. It had but one small window, high up near the ceiling and smeared with greasy dust that cast a deathly yellowish pall on everything in the room: stacks of wooden packing crates and cardboard cartons, a few wooden chairs, a half-size refrigerator with a plastic pitcher of water on top, some paper cups and paper plates, a wooden library table covered with books, and a boxy, old-fashioned dictaphone, behind which sat the real Ernst. He looked inanimate, like a wax replica of the more robust Sterne-Ernst I had known, or like those sallow, eyeless eels that marine biologists have recently discovered living at the bottom of the ocean, moving about slowly in the dark and under extreme pressure. Ernst cocked an ear attentively as we entered his remote world.

Sterne said, "Dr. Gablonzer, I'd like to present Mr. Nails, about whom we have told you much already. Mr. Nails has graciously consented to join our happy operation."

"I will enjoy your company, Mr. Nails," Ernst said quietly, in a distinctly Oxford accent with not a trace of Sterne's silly Boris Karloff overlay, "although I regret your loss of freedom. If it's any consolation, I empathize."

"Thanks, I appreciate it." I said. "But I'm not staying." To this bit of bluster Ernst responded with the wan smile of a duty nurse dispensing real solicitude to a terminal patient.

Sterne was feeling peppy, enthusiastic. "Of course you will stay, Mr. Nails," he effused. "I'm certain you and Dr. Gablonzer will become fast friends. Ernst is our resident scholar. Shortly after his arrival in this city I abducted him, as his presence was a reproach to me."

"You mean you actually felt some pangs of conscience over having Ernst blinded?"

"Oh no, that is not what I mean at all," he said, and rather sharply I thought, as though offended by my implication that he might actually harbor some shred of decency within his sociopath's corrupted soul. "What reproached me was the fact that Dr. Gablonzer had literary success, while I had none. I brought him here and installed myself in his home, so that I might have a taste of the critic's life. It has been most illuminating. I have had the best of both worlds. As Laurence Sterne, spiritual head of the Combist League, I have gained a certain reputation for myself, and I have access to eager recruits more than ready to help me with my more . . . sensitive enterprises."

"Recruits like Rick here," I said. Rick's face reddened, and she looked away, which gratified me. The best theme there is.

"Precisely. But kidnaping Dr. Gablonzer has added a new dimension to my life. It has allowed me to experience the respect which the world accords the scholar. We supply him with books in braille or on audiotape, and he dictates his articles into this recording device. I re-dictate his articles in my own voice and then pass them on to Miss Sterne to transcribe. I submit the articles for publication, and not one of them has yet been rejected, even by the most prestigious journals in the field. Dr. Gablonzer has a sterling reputation, you see, and I have managed to wear the mantle of that reputation as my own. In fact, I have so thoroughly assumed the character of Ernst Gablonzer that I have had numerous lively discussions with his friend, Dr. Zacky, along with several other of his colleagues, concerning my research into the Lesbian poets."

"Ernst's research," I reminded him.

"You are correct. And therein lies my problem . . . to which you, Mr. Nails, are my solution. The scholar's life has been everything I have dreamed. But I must continually play the role of Ernst Gablonzer, in order to cover my impersonation of him and to keep myself out of the federal correctional system. Playing the role of the eminent Dr. Gablonzer has been but an appetizer, a piquant antipasto to the main course, in which I have brilliant work published in *my* name, so that people will bestow upon me the respect my heritage demands. Dr. Gablonzer simply does not have time to create masterpieces for me as well as do his own work. I have tried any number of means—some of them painful—to persuade him to increase his output, but . . . as you can see for yourself, prolonged confinement has depleted his energies somewhat. You will change all that. With the addition of the brilliant Harmon Nails to our authorial stable—with Dr. Gablonzer covering the classics and you, Mr. Nails, writing criticism in my name—we will make the name of Laurence Sterne once again shine like a bright jewel with works of great importance. You will bring me enduring fame as a scholar of eighteenth- and nineteenth-century letters."

"People can't get off on fame that comes from someone else's work," I argued naively.

Sterne reinvented the classroom in order to correct me. "People cannot? The phenomenon you describe is common practice," he lectured, "and I know for a fact that many professors do just that, without suffering any qualms of conscience. For his last article on Renaissance pagan symbolism, for instance, Dr. Zacky instructed each of his graduate assistants to research and compose a section, which the eminent professor then revised in his own words. He merely compiled the sections and thus added yet another title to his list of publications. This is considered perfectly acceptable practice in academic circles, and what I propose to do with you is no different. Besides, a very wise man once said, 'The world beats us down, and all we want to do is get what is coming to us.' Worldwide recognition is no less than my due."

Desperately I countered, "The police know where I am. My mother will hire people to find me. My cousin is a world-famous investigator. I have people who love me very much. They won't give up until they find me . . ."

"Oh, I have no doubt that your so-called loved ones will nose about my Westwood headquarters for a time, but my legitimate business owns several warehouses, and this one I own under an assumed name. We obscure our tracks carefully and visit this location rarely, primarily to replenish Dr. Gablonzer's supply of nourishment, to drop off or pick up a load of literary antiquities we have acquired by less than legitimate means, and to pick up Dr. Gablonzer's latest dictation. No one knows of the existence of this warehouse, except for my closest circle of associates and I."

Abjectly frustrated by my own inability to reason Sterne out of his demented plan, and recently made aware that Sterne's failings as a writer constituted his area of greatest vulnerability, I hit him below the belt, at sentence level: I criticized his grammar. "'My closest associates and *me,'* not 'I,'" I said. "Object of the preposition 'for.' Any bonehead freshman knows that."

Sterne was not wounded, at least not outwardly. "Ah, a fine critical mind *and* a sound sense of mechanics as well," he said. "You will suit our purposes perfectly, Mr. Nails. Your loved ones will search weeks, perhaps months, and then they will resume their lives, no doubt greatly saddened by the loss of someone so engaging as yourself.

Your mother will mourn you, and you will miss her terribly, I'm certain. But be consoled: All the while you'll be doing valuable research for me, fourteen hours a day, seven days a week."

♥    THIRTY-TWO    ♥

$D$eath is one thing. I could perhaps deal with the prospect of infinite nothingness, but not forty years of research and *then* infinite nothingness. Criticism: An hour in the fifth floor stacks of the humanities library almost drives me insane. I feel as though I'm drowning in a whirlpool of periphrastic abstractions, I'm fluttering like a bat without sonar through a haze of cirrate diction, being crushed to toothpaste under the awful G-forces of bibliographies and footnotes. There was no way in hell I could last a day as a critical slave for Sterne. I lost control, began screaming obscenities at the top of my lungs, and in a paroxysm of horrified loathing, I charged Sterne.

Sweeney stepped nonchalantly in to block my headlong flap, and I pummeled his chest with my tiny fists, not a pretty sight. Sterne said, "This will not do, Mr. Nails. A display of this ilk is not seemly in an employee. It is bad for worker morale. I'm going to have to request that Mr. Sweeney relax you."

"Relax as in how Ford relaxed Nixon by letting him off the hook, or relax as in how Sweeney relaxes you by giving you blowjobs under the table at Combist League meetings?"

"Neither," he said coldly. "I mean relax, as in relax your musculature by beating you senseless, Mr. Nails." Sweeney all but salivated—or perhaps he really did salivate, since, now that I think back on it, I do recall some dime-sized puddles appearing on the concrete floor just before Sweeney stepped forward and delivered a short jab to the soft area just below the base of my sternum. Unlike the blow to my groin by Sweeney's deceased colleague, Dill—that blow was chastening but beyond pain—this shot hurt bad and incapacitated my diaphragm temporarily, so that I had the panicky impression that I had suffered massive respiratory arrest and would suffocate within seconds. I curled up involuntarily in a tight ball like an armadillo under duress, so tight that Sweeney had to use his beefy arms to pry me open in order to deliver the next blow, at the impact of which I curled up again. Sterne said, "It is either unendurable agony or literary criticism, Mr. Nails. Make your choice."

"They're both the same," I gasped. "Why do you think they call it the Anguish Department?"

"An assertion born of ignorance. You have no idea how unendurable anguish can be." Sweeney punched me in the kidney, which made me go rigid. I was getting the idea. "Give in to the inevitable, Mr. Nails. Be my ghost-critic, and your agony will end."

"I won't," I grunted. Sweeney kicked. "Fuck you," I exploded. Sweeney punched, this time to the cheekbone. I swung wildly at him, a haymaker and a big mistake, because he landed a surgical counterpunch flush on my nose. Blood started running freely, down my upper lip and into my mouth. I could taste it, warm and sweet as an In-Out Burger, rare, hold the onions. I was reeling away from Sweeney, who caught me down low with a rabbit punch that brought me to my knees. He was circling me, cocking his leg for a soccer-style kick to the groin, when I heard a voice say, "Stop."

Through my pain it sounded thin, hollow, distant, as though it came from inside a garbage can somewhere across the street. In fact, it had come from just a few feet away. Rick had swung the shotgun in Sweeney's direction, and she was pointing it at him. She was trembling wildly, and the gun was inscribing quick little arcs in the space between Rick and Sweeney. Sterne said, "Ah, our newest recruit appears to be squeamish at the sight of blood. This will not do in a colleague." Sweeney left off playing with me and approached Rick, who said unconvincingly, "Don't. I'll use this."

Sweeney was smiling now, which distorted his features horribly, unnaturally; unused to smiling as it was, his face buckled at odd stress points, so that he resembled a prize-winning cabbage with teeth and eyebrows. Sweeney hefted a huge packing crate over his head and moved menacingly at Rick, who backed up. Sweeney kept on coming, gaining momentum as he approached. Rick kept retreating until she bumped up against the concrete wall. Sweeney was charging fast now, chin out, no longer smiling, and Rick fired twice. Fragments like turkey meat burst forth . . . not from Sweeney's body, which Rick had missed altogether, but from the wooden crate beside him.

The force of the first blast hitting the crate sent a shock wave of debris into Sweeney, which jarred him from his headlong course, and the similar effect of a second shot set him to reeling unsteadily as he tried to establish a center of support under the bulk of the crate. He veered left, then right, and collided finally into a tall stack of wooden boxes, nearly ceiling high, which bent like a palm tree in high wind, then toppled. Sweeney bellowed as the wall of wooden crates collapsed on him. He went down hard to the floor, crates continuing to impact his body like a shower of meteors on a muscle-bound moonscape. The topmost crate broke open on impact with his collarbone, spilling contraband books over the now-inert Sweeney. I crawled over and picked one of the books out of the pile. The great beast Sweeney had been felled by Alexander Pope. You live by tedious, moralizing eighteenth-century poetry, you die by it.

Sweeney wasn't dead, just dazed. He poked his head out of the pile of books and looked around stupidly, like a bear coming out of hibernation. In a high-pitched quaver Sterne admonished Rick, "There is no possible excuse for your traitorous cowardice, Mr. Masters. I am terribly disappointed in you, for the moment. It is not, however, too late for you to redeem yourself in my eyes. If Mr. Nails is unwilling to work for me, he must be excused. His reticence has already seriously damaged Dr. Gablonzer's morale. Therefore you have another chance to prove your allegiance to me, Mr. Masters. You have the firearm. *Take care of Harmon Nails."*

Rick swung the shotgun at me. I cringed, expecting the sudden white-hot flash to explode inside my head and that was all I ever felt, but it didn't come. Instead, Rick said, "Take this, would you, Harmon? Guns make me nervous."

I looked up. She was proffering the gun to me. I took it and pointed it at Sweeney, who settled back down into his pile of literary rubble.

"Can I take this to mean you're not working for Sterne anymore?" I asked Rick doubtfully.

♣    THIRTY-THREE    ♣

I never was. I'm a journalism student at UCLA, undercover like you. I had a term paper to write, and I came up with the bright idea of infiltrating a cult and doing an exposé on it for the *Daily Bruin*. Sterne's ad in the *Free Journal* looked like a natural. But I never thought I'd end up using a gun, or rescuing a kidnaped scholar. I'm a pacifist.

"Not a bad shot for a pacifist . . . and a girl," I said, my entire face throbbing from the indelicate makeover Sweeney had recently performed on it. Normal breath was returning, and, while it was clear that I would walk with a pronounced stoop for several days, my physique seemed otherwise to be in working order.

"You know!" she cried in surprise.

"All along," I said, throwing truth to the winds. "I figured you were a spy for Sterne."

"What gave me away?"

"Something in the way you walk, perhaps, or how you cross your legs. Real men like me have a way of sensing these things. That's why Sterne never figured it out. Right, Sternie?"

He growled.

"Don't feel bad, dude. Look on the bright side, think of all the time you'll have to produce your *own* brilliant scholarship. Forty or fifty years at least."

"Grrr," he said.

"No, really, I'm sure the library at San Quentin is well stocked with minor eighteenth-century poets for you to read. Maybe you can even start a prison chapter of the Combe society. Get the cons to appreciate *culchah*, when they're not taking turns probing the profundity of your rectum."

Sterne started baying, emitting a low, mournful feral wail, the kind young beagles make when their masters are away at work. "Aoh Aoh Aoh Aoh," he said, choking off each syllable with abrupt glottal stops, in a rhythm very much like the deadly disco music to which he was so partial.

"Groovy beat," I commented, dabbing at my nose with a wad of old packing material. Good news: no fresh blood. "Sternie got soul, don't you think, Rick?"

"The name is Marianne."

"Masters?"

"No, I made that up, too. It's Evans. Marianne Evans."

"Hey. That's George Eliot's real name."

"She spelled Marianne differently. Two words. And you can stop calling me Rick now."

"It could be the hair and the beard."

She rolled her eyes upward. "Oh. I forgot." She took off her cap, and the hairpiece came along with it. Her own hair was wound tightly and pinned flat against her skull. She removed the pins one by one and then bent over and shook her head from side to side. Her plaits uncoiled gracefully in gentle undulations, chestnut brown with spicy amber highlights at their crests.

"Hey now," I said.

Marianne Evans turned her head to one side and peeled

234 ♣ Doctor Syntax

off the false whiskers. Rubbery glue clung to her face, first stretching out in the same way that mozzarella clings to lasagna noodles, and then snapping back in a way that melted cheese never does. She rubbed her face with her fingertips, and most of the rubber cement pilled up and rolled off. Despite the few remaining pillules of glue left on her cheeks, Marianne was lovely, with fine chiselings of jawline, cheeks made rosy by rubbing, and all defined more sharply by contrast with the shabby men's clothes she was wearing, to the effect that her face appeared a cameo against them, ivory-clear and rare. I was awed by the transformation and recalled greedily the body I had espied in the darkened upstairs bedroom. "I knew you weren't a guy, but I had no idea," I said with a certain constriction of vocal cord.

"Now you'll stop calling me Rick?"

"I'm used to it."

"Remember, I saved your life."

"Right, and I really appreciate how you let Sweeney kick the shit out of me before you decided to move."

"I was scared, all right?"

"Not me," I bragged. Marianne looked at me penetratingly, suggestively, with eyes the chalk blue of wild ceanothus, whose kinky blooms smell on first sniff like spurts of semen. Really, they do; check it out if you're skeptical. "Well," I admitted, "perhaps I can admit to a slight timorousness. However, may I add . . ."

"That's what I like about you, Harmon: Honesty is rarely your first response, but you know what a bad liar you are, so truth is never far behind."

"Terrific. Real journalistic savvy. Can we leave now?"

"After you."

Our party, looking weird to a one, like a convocation of Fellini extras, made ready to quit the warehouse. Sterne and Sweeney, after having been trussed securely by Marianne with baling wire from the dashed Pope crates, lead the way, followed by me, still in my Lippo uniform and the shotgun over my shoulder, bootcamp-style. Marianne helped the blind Ernst down the stairs. His step was springy. He breathed liberation in through the nostrils, savored its sweet liquor, and expelled the dread and hatred of the past weeks forcefully through the mouth, his shoulders and ribcage relaxing visibly with each exhalation. Once reunited with Lissa, his abduction publicized widely, he would no doubt be a celebrity for a while; this he would probably endure as stoically as he endured Sterne, and then he would resume his quiet pursuit of truth and beauty. Ernst was a survivor.

We descended the stairs. On the third floor I saw my lost *Syntax* books lying on the table where Sterne had left them. The original object of this whole ordeal, they now seemed unimportant, an afterthought. Still, I was curious. I picked up the one with the note to myself in it. Marianne stopped me. "Don't touch that," she said sharply. "We have to leave everything just as it is, for evidence."

"I'll leave my books, but I need this." I slipped the folded scrap of newsprint out of the inside cover of *Doctor Syntax*. "I wrote this while in the transport of an intellectual ecstasy. This note will change my life."

"Really? How?"

"It contains my perception of the crucial unifying thread that runs through all George Eliot's novels, an original thematic assertion that will bring my dissertation together and propel me to scholarly superstardom, to a luminous reputation that even Sternie here never dreamed of, and a cushy teaching position in some prestigious eastern school."

"All of that's in there?" she asked doubtfully, indicating the raggy shred of paper.

"That, and probably more," I said in a tone plump with promise.

Now everyone was curious. Sterne even stopped his whimpering long enough to hear the dramatic revelation. Sweeney dropped his mouth open, as though he might catch subtle concepts in the same way that frogs catch flies. Ernst said, "Please read, Harmon. You are torturing us with suspense." Marianne nodded enthusiastically.

I unfolded the paper and read, or tried to. Words, a scrawl that looked like a first grader's penmanship homework, snaked around the margins of a story about the upcoming NBA draft. I read my notes once to myself, shook my head, read them again.

"Well . . . ?" said Marianne.

"I'm not sure . . ." I said.

"Just read," she said.

"OK, but . . . OK, here it is: *'G.E. says—Love, too much. get Out. Poptarts dingdongs Tpaste windx toi.tis.'*"

I crumpled the paper into a wad. Sterne was delighted. "Lasting fame indeed." he said spitefully. "You should have remained in my charge. Hao hao hao hao," he roared.

"What does it mean, Harmon?" said Marianne.

My mind raced with the possible implications of the cryptic note and with the questions it raised, paramount of which was this: Had I been so wasted that I merely imagined producing some of the world's most penetrating critical insights during my quasi-psychedelic raptus? Certainly it was possible, and there was historical precedent as proof. One time Thrasher had a class in Asian history, and he hadn't cracked the book all quarter. Time came, as it inevitably does, for the final exam, and he had an endless procession of dynasties to memorize and only one night in which to do it. He swallowed tab after tab of white crisscross methedrine, stayed up all night, and took a massive dose of crank the next morning, before the test. When he got home, I asked him how he'd done, and he exulted, "Great, the essay question was a fucking joke. I aced it for sure," and collapsed on our beanbag cushion, where he lay inert for a day and a half. However, when he brought the test home at the beginning of the following quarter, it had an enormous red "F" on the front of the bluebook. While Thrasher had written brilliantly and without pause, his writing—all three hours' worth—was concentrated in an inky blob approximately an inch round, a tiny black hole whose gravity had sucked up twelve centuries of Chinese history and rendered it unintelligible, illegible. But that was Thrasher, notorious for his pharmaceutical excesses and for the high prices he routinely paid for them. Could a couple of hits on a Droddy spliff have produced the same effect in me, or was there more subtextual meaning in those few words than appeared on the surface? More to the point, what had excessive love or junk food or toilet tissue to do with George Eliot, my Ph.D. thesis, and my future?

Thus swept up in a tornadic fugue state of confusion, I once again envisioned George Eliot as I had on that night many weeks ago, only now even more vividly—her dark eyes deepened by loss of faith and family, her mouth per-petually pursed as though mocking the sphincteral con-striction of polite Victorian society, her head cocked to one side in that cute way she had, so that her dark hair, parted in the middle and brushed down around her ears and be-hind her neck, perturbed the starchy formal whiteness of her lace collar—and all at once the scales fell from my eyes, as I believe is the expression. George hadn't visited me that day to speak of herself, nothing so uncharacteristically im-modest as that. Rather, she'd come to deliver the Truth about an awful ambiguity whose resolution would shatter the delicate crystalline orderings of my own self-awareness as absolutely as I had shattered Sterne's crystal goblet. "It's not about criticism at all," I told Marianne. "It's about me."

"You!" Sterne squealed. "Lasting fame indeed," he repeated.

Sterne was certifiably insane but most likely correct. Perhaps, as my mother, my graduate advisor, and Liz had insisted, I did have the intellectual apparatus requisite for literary scholarship, but the extraordinary and often dangerous lengths to which I went to avoid schoolwork pointed to one incontrovertible fact: I didn't believe in research, and I had little respect for people who did. It's only the most grievously wounded people who require the hollow recognition that fame brings, and fame in academia is hollower still, a marrowless bone scrabbled after by professors and lecturers and graduate students, pathetic worried creatures who sell their fine and creative intellects for the protection of the university, at best a cold-titted and psychologically abusive mother who, while providing them with health insurance and barely enough cash to make their house payments, neither loves nor nurtures them, and who eventually turns them in upon themselves and ultimately against each other, like those lice I read about once—or maybe it was mites—that devour their brothers and sisters in the womb. No art in that, of course, and little satisfaction. If Art itself was the subject of George Eliot's art,[49] then George had come to remind me that Art presents only those truths whose contraries are also true, and that if your dick is caught in one theoretical windowframe of reference, then you're probably missing the beauty, and surely the humor.

I had undertaken to pursue the intellectual grail because my family prized it above all else. My grandfather, steeped as he was in a Talmudic tradition which viewed scholarship as a singular act of devotion leading one directly to

[49] D. Hein, *To Hear Her Voice: Artifice in George Eliot's Novels* (Dissertation, University of California at Santa Barbara, 1984), p. 79. Hey, I had to include it. It was the only piece of real research I managed to get all the way through, and it didn't even have pictures.

favor in God's jaundiced eye and status in the community, handed this prejudice down to my mother, who didn't love me too much—there can't be too much love, I still believed almost a decade after the Summer of Same—but with too much of the wrong kind of love, a solipsistic clinging by the self to its own idealized image, which in my mother's case was so tangled up with her only child that she used my diplomas unknowingly to paper the holes in her own ego—that is, to gain favor in the critical eye of her long-dead father, my sweet Zaydeh, who once snubbed her for marrying a Gentile, and in the smog-reddened eye of polite L.A. society, if such a thing exists. Ma didn't see, because she couldn't, that schoolwork was not something I loved to do, but rather something I had to force myself to do because it was expected of me; and George Eliot's message, by the example of choices she had made in her own life, was clear on that point. Nobody should make a career out of doing what they don't like or believe in, said George. (Not unless it pays a whole lot more than a T.A.'s salary, adds Harmon.) Discretion, wisdom even, would therefore lie—for this wave-shredding, dirt-riding, blues-picking, poetasting gumshoe at least—in relinquishing the custody of literary antiquities to those who deserve them.

What it all amounted to, when you totted up the pros and cons, was that it wasn't too late. I was still a kid, not yet thirty and in reasonably good shape, and I could go scholarly renown one better. I could get my life together by moving out of the house, by finding a more expansive, more generative, occupation, one worthy of lifelong attention . . . and I might even revive my blasted sexuality in the process. I recalled the moment when providence dropped my surfboard right beside me at Point Zero and saved my life. This time, I understood, the tiny sliver of my salvation had come not from sheer luck—however welcome—but from deep within myself, and in the unlikely image of George, who had never looked lovelier. Liz would be proud, and out of a client, if I could tenderly nurture the seed of my insight into a blossoming of emotional health and maturity.

"What does it mean?" Marianne asked again.

I moved my mouth vainly, like a hooked perch trying vainly to form words that might express his rage and horror at being untimely yanked from the sea, and his astonishment at the surpassing beauty of the world out of water.

Sterne beat me to speech. "It means," he said with a sneer, "that there are a lot of geniuses who find themselves out of work, and Mr. Nails is going to be one of them."

# ◆ THIRTY-FOUR ◆

My first act as a free man in my own house was to fry up a mess of Hoffies and Wonder Bread in Teflon and butter, pour a mess of ketchup over them and scarf. Sated, invigorated by my first substantial meal since who knows when, I felt strong enough to call Ma in Tucson. She asked where had I been and why hadn't I called. I said busy, I'd explain when she got back, and I loved her. I meant it, too. Maybe George Eliot was right: It takes a not-so-casual brush with extremity to make us appreciate what we once took for granted, and Ma's voice never sounded so good.

Unfortunately, Ma had no idea how much extremity I'd brushed up against recently, so she thanked me with sarcastic effusiveness for my attention to her "needs," the ever-lengthening list of which she scrolled out telephonically while I nodded and intoned the random "Mm-hmm" into the mouthpiece. I told her again I loved her, and I still meant it. With Ma, repetition is the sincerest form of flatware: I keep on forking it out, and she eats it up, reluctantly at first, like a zoo elephant warily sniffing out a tendered nut roll, but then always lickerishly. I used to get annoyed at having to make the same loving filial pronouncements over and over again, but this time I was mellow, benevolent even, and pronounced with patient fondness until she got it.

Pleased—not to mention surprised by what must have seemed a dramatic improvement in the attitude and comportment of her formerly bratty boychik—Ma said she'd be home in two days and gave me more than enough information to locate her: the airline and flight number, the projected arrival time, her seat number, aisle non-smoking, the names of the pilot and flight crew and the air traffic controller. I promised I'd be there to meet her at the gate. Without undressing I got into bed and slept half the day and all night. For the first time in a quarter-century I didn't have to use the TreeTop jar.

I got up and called Lissa first thing. Even though my face still ached and I had a dull throb in the lower back where I had caught Sweeney's rabbit punch, I was in high spirits, expecting a tearful exchange of vocables with Lissa, to be followed by a mutual pledge of undying love. In choners and my Walt Whitman T-shirt I stretched out in the breakfast nook of the big house, my bare feet up on the red Formica table and my head on taut red vinyl. I touch-toned, and the faint electronic beeps, which resembled in their timbre the plastic Emenee trumpet I had when I was a kid, heralded a much-anticipated joyous reunion with the poor tragic soul who had been yearning for me miserably during my brief absence. I would re-weave her frayed psyche with assurances of immutable contentment and unnatural sex.

Two rings over the wire, and Sergeant Freitag answered. I wasn't expecting to hear him, and he plainly not me. There was a long impromptu concert of static in dead air and muffled human sounds in the background, and then Freitag said, so heartily that I had to hold the receiver at arm's length, "Harmon. I was going to call you. We need you to come in and file an official complaint. Ms. Evans already did. I just came here to get Ernst's statement, and I'm getting Lissa's now."

"It's swell of you to make house calls, Freitag, and terrific to hear your voice, but can I please talk to Lissa?" I asked impatiently.

"Sure. No problem."

More crackling dead air and mumbles. Lissa got on. She said, and a bit formally I thought, "Harmon, what a lovely surprise. Larry told me all about what you did. Isn't it wonderful, my father is back, you have your books, and Larry and I can't begin to express our gratitude. You must be very proud."

"Larry and I?" I demanded with nascent suspicion.

"Yes. If it hadn't been for you, we never would have met."

My mind contorted itself into cruller-like whorlings, writhing to misinterpret the obvious truth for which Lissa was preparing me none too gently. The best misconstruction my mind could come up with was a tautologically fatuous, "If it hadn't been for me or you, of course you and I would never have met."

"Not we you and I."

"We who then?"

"Larry and me. We're engaged," she fluted.

"We must have a bad connection," I said. "A lot of static on the line. You say you're enraged at Sergeant Freitag?"

"Engaged to him."

"You don't mean . . ."

"Yes, Harmon."

"As in betrothed, with a ring and a smooch, Minute Rice and dog-food cans?"

"Yes, Harmon."

"But I thought. You and me. We had."

"Harmon, I think you're really cute and fun, but you're a little bit too . . . how can I say . . ."

"Witty? Debonair?"

"Puerile I think comes closer."

"Puerile? Frippery! Certainly I possess a boyish sense of wonderment at a world forever revealing its mysteries, but underneath I'm really a mature, evolved being. Besides, I've changed."

"I'm sure you have. But I just can't see myself living with a guy who goes over his body every morning like a road map, to make sure none of his beauty marks has gone malignant overnight."

"You can't be too careful," I responded defensively. "The AMA says the big C is the number two killer right behind heart disease, which is what you're giving me now. I think I'm developing an aneurism."

"Besides, Larry is serious about his literature. He's going to quit the force and go to grad school. You've been reading Browning for six months, and the most you've said about him is that he makes your urethra seep. Larry says Browning can turn himself into truth like fishes turn into lizards in surrealist art. The author becomes the truth . . ."

". . . and the truth becomes the poet," I repeated wearily. "I've heard it before. Larry probably practiced that speech a thousand times while he was in the psych ward at the VA hospital, doing the Thorazine shuffle through the halls and blowing spit bubbles out the corners of his mouth."

"Please don't be bitter."

"No, really, it's OK, Freitag's a great guy. He helped me engineer this whole Sterne business, and I owe him. I guess it's only fitting that I pay the debt with the only woman I've ever truly loved." At least this month, I told myself. "But I thought we had something."

"If it's any consolation, I still feel physically attracted to you, much more than I am to Larry, in fact. Don't ever tell him that. But there's no way we would work out, Harmon.

There are just too many little things . . ."

"Name one," I challenged.

She spent no time. "Your eating habits. You equate frozen food with autonomy. Your idea of gourmet fare is to take a burrito out of its wrapper and microwave it instead of eating it cold. You eat peas and carrots right from the freezer, without bothering to thaw them out, like M&Ms."

"If you cook frozen foods, you run the risk of boiling away all the essential vitamins and nutrients."

"See. Puerile."

"So I can change some more. I promise to steam my succotash from now on," I begged shamelessly.

"I'm sorry, Harmon."

Thrown over for an acne-scarred cop. In a world where puzzling crimes are solved routinely, if sometimes blunderingly, where the loose folds of plot are tucked neatly into hospital-cornered denouement, leave it to relationships to provide the surprise endings.

"This might make you feel better. Larry says this Marianne Evans has a thing for you. When he was taking her deposition, all she kept talking about was Harmon this and Harmon that."

"I'm not that kind of guy. I don't shift my affection casually from one person to another, like *some* people."

"Larry says she's probably more your type, anyway. She's beautiful and sensuous and bright and she knows it, but she has a fragile self-image and she sneezes all the time. Larry says . . ."

"Fuck Larry. I'm sick of hearing about Larry."

"He likes you a lot, you know. He feels terrible about this. He feels like he stole me away from you. It was my choice, completely. He never revealed the slightest interest until I literally threw myself at him."

"Literally? Any fractures?" I quipped, all hope dashed.

"I bent him a little bit, yes."

"I don't want to hear this."

"Will you call Marianne?"

"No. I'm too broken up. I'll never get over you. You're the only woman I'll ever truly love, you capricious, smug, apostatic, untenanted, punic cow."

"Always with the sweet talk, Harmon."

"It just came out," I apologized. "Truly, I hope the two of you will be very happy together," I said, with every iota of selfless goodwill I could sift out of the arid sands of my despondency.

"We already are," she said, measured, relaxed and melodious.

"I'm glad." I imagined my hands inclining, tightening around her neck, the thumbs pressing hard into pulsing carotids, nails popping soft white flesh, bringing eructations and floes of bright blood. "I really am glad for you."

"Thank you, Harmon. I appreciate your setting aside your hurt and anger like this. It's a side of you I haven't seen. I take back puerile."

"Does that mean we're on again."

"Harmon."

"Just kidding. Hey. This is Nails. I always land on my pedipalps. I'll get over it."

"You're a wonderful man."

"I know. So are you."

"Thank you," she said ecstatically, sideslipping my sly jape.

"You are more than welcome, Lissa." And in a voice oozing courtesy: "There'll never be another you in my life."

I called Marianne Evans the same evening. Fay Nails may have raised a private-I despite her earnest libertarian intentions, but she don't raise losers.

♠ THIRTY-FIVE ♠

Hard bed.

In Marianne's apartment. We had had an early dinner to celebrate our vanquishing the forces of nastiness and returned to her place after. Marianne made some tea and said she wanted to watch the news, in case they had anything on about Sterne. I agreed—not so much because of Sterne, of whom I'd had my fill, as because her tubie was on a stand at the foot of the bed, which seemed like a move in the right direction.

"Sorry," she said. "It's a Japanese futon. It looks cushiony but it's really not, so it's kind of a shock when you hit it for the first time. My ex-boyfriend hated it so much he would never sleep here."

"I like a firm mattress," I said reassuringly. I also liked hearing that her boyfriend was an ex. "I sleep on polyfoam and plywood at home because I hate any extraneous motion when I'm trying to sleep. I actually got seasick the one time I tried a waterbed."

Most people, when I relate to them my true-life confrontation with the awesome and universally solvent elements untamed within the waterbed, consider the story apocryphal, a mere pleasantry. But it's no laughing matter to have such a low threshold of motion tolerance when it comes to sleeping apparatus, especially since one finds oneself on so many different beds in one's life unless one's a hermit or a celibate. Since I'm neither—at least not usually and never by choice—such a condition is a drag, and also odd if you think about it, since I never get the least bit queasy when I'm waiting for waves, sometimes for fifteen or twenty minutes at a stretch, in a restive squall-blown windchop. Go and figure. Anyhow, unlike your average well-adjusted sap, Marianne didn't laugh. "Me, too!" she exclaimed. "I don't even like the rocking motion you get with the normal box-spring-mattress setup."

"Way too unstable," I agreed.

"Plus, if you sleep on your side with your ear to the mattress you can hear the springs vibrate like a bunch of tuning forks or something, which is every bit as annoying as the bounciness."

"Amazing," I said.

"What is?"

"I thought I was the only person in the world who gets bugged by box-spring sounds." Actually, I was so moved by the discovery of this shared quirk of bedding that I considered asking Marianne whether she also pissed in an apple juice jar every night. After brief deliberation, however, I thought better of it. After all, we were only just getting acquainted, and those are the kind of intimate oddities, like wine-colored birthmarks and fungus-eroded toenails, that have to be revealed slowly, organically, as prospective lovers drop by degrees their pretensions to perfection.

"Well, so far we're compatible, at least in our taste in beds," she said.

Now I'm as prone to getting excited about future intimacies with well-proportioned female journalists as the next guy, but I still had a definite wariness about words like "compatible" and "commitment," which—due no doubt to the material failure of those very abstractions in my marriage to Brenny—I associated with grief, rage, denial, immobility, buttered toast, and so on. Therefore, even though I liked Marianne well enough thus far in our exordial friendship and was attracted to her well beyond wellness, I dodged her mention of compatibility with the instinctual finesse of a bantam-weight slipping a jab. "Is anything else on besides the news? It's just more stuff about the election, and Ford's voice makes my teeth hurt like when you go to take a shower and there's cleanser all over the bottom of the tub," I said.

"Hm, walking on cleanser never bothers my teeth," she said, and I was glad I hadn't mentioned the juice jar, "but I agree with you about Uncle Gerry's voice. The *Guide*'s on top of the set."

I got up and fetched it. "Time you got?"

"Seven-thirty."

"Seven-thirty." I flipped through the *TV Guide*, always a frustrating task because you get hung up on all those cardboard advertising inserts for cigarettes and painted porcelain dogs. Eventually, though, I found the right page. "Gilligan. Mary Tyler Moore. Oh my God."

"Paper cut?"

"No, there's a Dodger game on. I've been out of touch. Usually I mark them on my calendar."

"Away game? It must be, if it's on TV."

"No, it's at home. Monday Night Baseball."

"Oh, right, Monday night. I thought it was Friday for some reason. All this undercover stuff has really screwed up my sense of time. Who's pitching?"

"Hooton."

"I thought he was on the D.L.," she said. "Last time he pitched—against the Reds I think it was—he pinched a nerve in his neck."

"You hate box-springs and you know about Happy Hooton's nerve," I observed.

"It's all true."

"I could become fond of you."

"Loikwoise, Oi'm shuah," she said, mimicking the nasal timbre of a brain-dead B-movie gun-moll. Marianne was purposely keeping it light. From hard experience with braces of skittish dudes, she must have discovered that a degree of airy distancing—whether real or manufactured—has a palliative effect on the sensitive New Male, thereby keeping him from acting on his impulse to flee like a groundhog from a grass fire when intimacy threatens. By giving him room to move away, you paradoxically give the New Male room to move toward you as well, and sometimes he will. As a sensitive New Male myself (and I hang my head in shame at the admission), I appreciated the soft manipulation. Marianne Evans was a smart woman.

"How come you know so much about baseball, anyway?" I asked, moving imperceptibly nearer.

"I've followed the Dodgers since I was a little kid. Typical tomboy syndrome, you know: Daddy wanted a boy but got a girl, loved me anyway and did lots of boy-type stuff with me, camping, electric trains, bows and arrows, throw the ball around in the backyard. We used to have season tickets. These days I don't see as many games as I'd like, but I still get to ten, maybe twelve a year."

"That's a lot of games," I calculated. "How do you afford it?"

"I don't. My father's best friend is a county supervisor. He gets comps. Season boxes, between third and home, ten rows up. We could go sometime if you want."

"I think I'm in love," I said, maintaining the lightsome tone.

"It's about time," Marianne pronounced with authority, apparently tossing aside her strategy of discretion and restraint in favor of a more genuine aggressiveness. "Why don't we turn off the TV. I think Lasorda can manage without us for a while."

The shift in Marianne's attitude caught me off guard, and I responded with a slight, instinctive drawing in, sort of like an anemone that's been brushed lightly by a kelp frond in a tide pool, except that we weren't underwater, of course. "What if I just turn the volume down? I get edgy without a certain amount of stimulus overload," I said.

"You're weird, Harmon," Marianne responded in a voice at once teasing but also mildly caustic.

I said, "My shrink—my *ex*-shrink—told me I'm not supposed to let other people call me weird, even in jest. I'm me, Harmon Nails, a unique and creative individual."

"OK. You're you."

"Weird."

"Different. Funny."

"Aw heck."

"Here, how does that feel?" One small hurt past, she had begun massaging my neck and shoulders with a strong, chelate grip that penetrated the armoring of my tendons and fasciae and whatnot. As though by some kind of metaconscious inertial guidance, her thumbs homed in on foci of anxiousness and dread that I had suppressed over the past weeks, in order that I might function coolly, efficiently—that is, without befouling my trousers—while I pursued *Doctor Syntax*. Not only was Marianne Evans smart, she had brilliant thumbs. Killer combination. I let my chin fall to my chest as she worked the knotted tissues.

"Really stiff, huh?" I mumbled, it being hard to talk with your chin to your chest.

"Like suspension bridge cables," Marianne remarked. She let off kneading the back of my neck and got serious. "You know, Harmon, the ordeal is over. You can let down now."

Marianne was partially right; I could relax, at least as far as

Sterne was concerned. When I read in the paper that Eugene Withers—the celebrated criminal lawyer whom I'm sure you've heard of in connection with the Little Brown extortion case that was in all the papers—had been retained by Sterne as his defense attorney, I was understandably concerned and immediately phoned my old friend Randy Rhea to pump him for information. Rhea had given up surfing many years before to devote himself to the Absolutest Zero of all—law school—and a subsequent junior partnership with the prestigious and high-powered legal firm of Flumen, Withers and Eyck . . . the very same firm that, it turned out, Sterne had retained to defend him. Rhea couldn't tell me much, client confidentiality and all that, but off the record he said Sterne had been slapped with a contempt citation during his bail hearing, "when he began raving about some orphan kid named John Q. Penis and then stood up and accused the judge of banging a housekeeper named Bessie with a broom handle." After that there was no hope of springing Sterne on bail. The best Withers could be expected to accomplish were reduced sentences on the several counts with which Sterne was charged, with time to be served concurrently instead of consecutively. Withal, Sterne would probably still get twenty-five years on the kidnaping charge alone; after you subtracted good time and parole, he would spend no less than fifteen years behind bars, and that didn't even take into account the murder of Dill, if they could make that one stick. I could therefore allay my hypervigilance with the knowledge that my archenemy would either die of old age in his cell or at worst would return to the streets a withered, broken, harmless old Combist.

Unfortunately the tightness in my neck, not to mention in my brainpan and abdominal sump, was a condition borne less by Sterne than by another, more insidious vector. "No I can't," I kvetched. "My mother's coming back in two days, and I'm dreading it."

"After what you went through with Sterne, I don't see how you could be worried about anyone, least of all your own mother," Marianne said.

"It's just that we're stuck in this toxic way of relating to each other, and I'm afraid once we're under the same roof again we'll fall back into it."

"So why don't you get unstuck?" she asked.

This wasn't at all the kind of question Liz would have asked. Liz would have said, "I see, mm-hmm, a-yes," or, "Can you go with that?" or something equally open-ended and nondirective which would have left me staring off into space, at which she would have said, "What's going on with you right now?" and so on. Marianne's lay response, which bored to the logical heart of the issue, set me back on my heels a bit. "We're talking about twenty-five-odd years of relating to each other in a certain way," I explained. "You don't undo that kind of conditioning overnight, you know?"

"I don't know about that," said Marianne, "but I'll tell you what I do know: If you could track down Sterne, crack this case, free Ernst, and wheedle your way into my apartment and onto my bed all in couple of weeks, you can do anything. Look, your mom is your mom, right?"

"I think so. She never said anything about buying me from Gypsies."

"Good. So with parents, sometimes they get set in their ways, and you have to be the one to initiate a change if you want it."

"Get the ball rolling, so to speak."

"Realize you are the ball, Harmon, and roll where you want to roll."

"Wow, that's deep. So what I hear you saying," I said, restating the obviously absurd, "is that I should be a ball."

"What I'm saying, Lippo,"—she accentuated the idiotic nom-de-pud to mock my obtuseness—"is that maybe it's

254  ♠  Doctor Syntax

time for you to become the adult in the family."

"Oh, I get it. A 'Child is father to the man' sort of thing."

"Right, except in your case the child will be mother to the woman."

"I'm not sure I can get behind that."

"OK, father to the woman then. Whatever. It's either that or a perpetual neckache, and I won't always be around to rub out the kinks."

"You could," I ventured rashly.

"First you get your own place, then we'll see." Smart woman indeed.

"Fine. So I get my own place, and then what? How do I go about doing this fatherly thing? I have limited experience in that area."

"What do fathers do with their daughters?"

"I don't know. According to you they go hiking, they shoot bows and arrows, they have season tickets to the Dodgers. Should I take my mother to a baseball game?" I asked jokingly.

"You could. Sure, why not . . . change your old way of relating to each other. Treat your mother to a game, get her a Blue Wrecking Crew visor, buy her a bag of peanuts and a Kool-A-Coo."

The image of Fay Nails munching away on an ice cream sandwich while filling in a 6-4-3 double play on her scorecard was without precedent in my experience, yet it was not impossible. That such a scene could exist hinted at a universe weighted—if only slightly—toward the good, a happy universe pregnant with the colloidal plasma of possibility, of star-stuff congealed in velvety ether and mystery illumined brightly, of trees blooming in Zion and Dr. J.'s hanging glide shot, of seedless watermelons chilled from the refrigerator and human justice equitably applied, of Velcro shoe-bindings and Albert King's chill guitar riffs, of orgasms shared and transparent Rincon barrels, and mothers carefree under Dodger caps. Marianne's suggestion made me laugh—nay, shook me to the very footings with laughter, the kind of uproarious, unreserved, exquisitely painful laughter that reaches down to the molten core of the soul and purges one of contrarieties and adhesions, leaving me finally to breathe the balmy fragrance of release and all-acceptance.

"That's right," said Marianne with considerable animation, "show her you're a grown man by playing father to the little girl inside her. Everybody wants that once in a while."

"Grown man," I said. I rolled the phrase around in my mouth. It felt funny, like credit dentures.

"I think you know you are, and my intuition is hardly ever wrong. But there's only one way to find out for sure."

"Ooo," I said.

"Yes?"

"Brazen."

"See, I told you. Should I stop?"

"What about the Dodgers?"

"So we miss the Star Spangled Banner."

"How about the ceremonial first ball?"

"I'm willing if you are. Turn over."

"Like this?"

"Very much."

"I guess we may be compatible at that," I allowed, surging against my New Maleness, throwing reticence to the whipping wind, going all in to see that blessed River, the catch that turns marginal possibilities into a lock winner.

"O Harmon."

"O Rick."

"Don't you dare."

"Neeewtn," I said.

# ♥ EPILOGUE ♥

Hello, Mary. Walt Wessex.

"Very well, thank you. Yourself?

"She's very well.

"They're just fine, too.

"Yes. First year of law school this fall.

"They certainly do.

"I don't know where it goes, either, Mary. Listen. Is Karl nearby?

"Thanks, Mary.

"Wonderful talking to you, too.

"You too.

"I will. You too.

"Karl. Walt Wessex. How are you?

"Glad to hear it. All prepared for the new school year, are you.

"Never. But we muddle through anyway, don't we? Ha ha.

"Ha ha. Listen, Karl. The reason I'm calling. I have received Mr. Nails' manuscript.

"Shocked is perhaps too mild. We're in a bit of a quandary here. Bill Pulsinger wants our decision within a fortnight.

"A fortnight.

"Yes, that means two weeks, Karl.

"I don't know. Two weeks from today, I suppose.

"I am aware of that fact.

"Yes. But our young friend insists we consider this effort the final version of his dissertation, and he instructs us to render judgment on it accordingly.

"Yes, he is. Absolutely serious.

"Indeed. However, you must realize it's all we can ever expect to receive from him.

"I know.

"Certainly.

"I agree. But he's finished his course work three times over.

"Yes.

"He does.

"No, and he never will. He told me, 'Anyone with a certain plodding intelligence can produce a doctoral thesis. Libraries are full of them,' he said.

"Not his exact words, no. But a fairly accurate paraphrase, I believe. He insists on turning in this so-called 'creative' effort.

"Absolutely firm.

"Yes, I have read it in its entirety.

"Yes.

"Hardly.

"Of course it isn't. But.

"Granted. The way I see it, we have two choices. We either confer the degree on him, in spite of his. Shortcomings.

"All right. Gross failures. Or the other alternative is.

"That seems rash to me, Karl. The department frowns on violence by tenured faculty on its grad students.

"Yes, Karl. Even with the Vaseline. We must remain decorous.

"Yes.

"Yes, I am aware that he alluded to me as a 'complacent tenured pedant.'

"I recall he said that, too. And 'pompous ass.'

"I had forgotten that. Uncalled-for, that.

"It goes without saying. Any reasonably intelligent person would have a hard time believing his story.

"Preposterous.

"Insurmountable.

"No argument there. And fraught with plot gaps and inconsistencies besides. Clearly it's fantasy.

"But is the ability to suspend our disbelief the issue here?

"I don't know what. It has more to do with. Integrity of intention perhaps.

"Perhaps even suffering.

"His *and* ours. I'm not as young as I once was.

"I wouldn't say nuisance is too strong a word.

"Yes, I'd say that is too strong. Even for Mr. Nails.

"Of course. But.

"I know. Uniform standards. I am his committee chairman, after all.

"Seven years.

"Yes. Seven. This is his eighth.

"No. Not a record. But it is close.

"Certainly, I will confess to feeling a certain fondness for Mr. Nails.

"Sincere but misguided.

"Well put.

"No.

"No, it's never been done before. No one has ever dared submit a fiction as a doctoral thesis. There is precedent, however.

"Yes. It has been done. One of our own non-tenured composition instructors, in fact.

"Dan Lewsite.

"I was surprised, too, when I found out.

"Not a novel. Worse. An opera.

"Correct. Our own Dr. Lewsite wrote an opera, both the libretto and score, as his thesis. And produced it in conjunction with his university's music and drama departments.

"University of California at Fiesta City, I believe.

"That may help explain the oddity of it, but it is nevertheless a precedent.

"No.

"Why on earth not?

"No.

"It boils down to this: Can we in good conscience give Mr. Nails the gate. After all. It comes back to.

"I'm not sure I want that responsibility.

"Certainly not, but I have no doubt he'll make a damn fine teacher. His students' evaluations of his teaching performance are always top-notch.

"Exactly.

"Very well, if you insist on leaving it up to me, I say, 'Congratulations, Doctor Nails.'

"Take a deep breath. Pour yourself a scotch.

"You'll be accustomed to the idea in no time.

"You see. Pour yourself another.

"Oh, absolutely.

"Yes.

"I don't believe that's a strong enough objection to warrant booting him. Dan Lewsite never attends meetings, either.

"No.

"Once, last spring.

"Right. He woke up only when the secretary taking the minutes nudged him.

"Carla.

"Damn fine ones. Lovely long legs, too.

"I wouldn't turn her out. Heh, heh.

"Under her desk. On my hands and knees.

"Karl, you're a scoundrel. Don't let Mary.

"Nor I. Heh, heh.

"No.

"No, I am by no means certain we've arrived at the right decision, but it is a decision I can live with.

"From whom?

"I really don't anticipate any problem. Usually they file without reading beyond the title page.

"Yes, I have as well, I must admit. Would you read three hundred pages on a phenomenological study of time in 'The Fall of Hyperion'?

"Keats.

"Keats. The English poet.

"Yes, that Keats. Ha ha. You see. I rest my case.

"Yes.

"Agreed.

"Yes.

"So. We are in accord, are we not? Mr. Nails finally has his degree. And we have a new colleague.

"Nor do I.

"I am. I will. I think you will, too.

"Have another drink.

"Yes.

"Oh. The inflatable cushion really is quite comfortable. All the difference in the world.

"So do I. Chronically inflamed tissues seem to be a punishment for the sedentary lifestyle we academicians have chosen to lead.

"Indeed it does. Like magic. Why don't I lend it to you for a day?

"Of course not. And if you find you enjoy it, I'll give you the address of the medical supply store where you can purchase your own.

"Yes.

"Say no more. Say no more. What are friends for?

"No.

"Yes.

"No, I believe we've done the right thing by Mr. Nails.

"Albeit unorthodox. Best to Mary.

"Thank you. I will. Good-bye, Karl.

"Good-bye."